8.00

D1412330

NEVER TELL A LIE

ALSO BY HALLIE EPHRON

1001 Books for Every Mood

Writing and Selling Your Mystery Novel

NEVER TELL
A LIE

HALLIE EPHRON

Doubleday Large Print
Home Library Edition

WILLIAM MORROW
An Imprint of HarperCollins *Publishers*

This Large Print Edition, prepared especially for Double-day Large Print Home Library, contains the complete, unabridged text of the original Publisher's Edition.

This book is a work of fiction. The characters, incidents, and dialogue are drawn from the author's imagination and are not to be construed as real. Any resemblance to actual events or persons, living or dead, is entirely coincidental.

NEVER TELL A LIE. Copyright © 2009 by Hallie Ephron Touger. All rights reserved. Printed in the United States of America. No part of this book may be used or reproduced in any manner whatsoever without written permission except in the case of brief quotations embodied in critical articles and reviews. For information address HarperCollins Publishers, 10 East 53rd Street, New York, NY 10022.

ISBN 978-1-60751-535-7

**This Large Print Book carries the
Seal of Approval of N.A.V.H.**

**To my family,
Jerry, Molly, and Naomi**

ACKNOWLEDGMENTS

I am indebted to many people who helped me with this book. For help getting the details right, thank you, Scott Johnson, Lee Lofland, Trooper Edward Stanley, Lieutenant Detective Charles F. Paris, Sergeant Prosecutor Brian P. Cherry, Doug Lyle, M.D., and the Honorable Judge Kenneth Freeman. Thanks to fellow writers Lorraine Bodger, Lora Brody, Jan Brogan, Donald Davidoff, Susan W. Hubbard, Roberta Isleib, Floyd Kemske, Jonathan Ostrowsky, Naomi Rand, Hank Phillippi Ryan, Barbara Shapiro, Sarah Smith, and Jerry Touger. Thanks to the smart and indefatigable Gail Hochman. And special thanks to Katherine Nintzel, Carolyn Marino, Wendy Lee, and the other excellent folks at HarperCollins.

NEVER TELL A LIE

Tuesday, Nov 4

Pregnant Woman Missing from Brush Hills

BRUSH HILLS, MA Police continue to search for clues in the disappearance of Melinda White, 33, who was last seen on Saturday. Authorities yesterday issued a bulletin describing the pregnant woman as "at risk" and a possible victim of foul play.

Ms. White, an administrative assistant with SoBo Realty, attended a yard sale in Brush Hills on Saturday morning and has not been seen since, police said. Her sister, Ruth White, of Naples, Florida, reported her missing on Monday.

"She calls me every day, and when I didn't hear from her, I knew that something was wrong," said Ruth White. She added that the close family was bearing the strain "as well as could be expected."

Brush Hills Police Detective Sergeant Albert Blanchard said authorities have no suspects in custody.

"We're trying to interview everyone that she knew and anyone who saw her on Saturday, but as far as leads to show us what happened—no," Blanchard said.

Anyone with information is asked to call the Brush Hills Police detective division.

1

Saturday, November 1

Rain or shine, that's what Ivy Rose had put in the yard-sale ad. What they'd gotten was a metallic gray sky and gusty winds. But the typical, contrary New England fall weather hadn't discouraged this crowd.

David moved aside the sawhorse that blocked the driveway, and buyers surged in. It seemed to Ivy that their Victorian ark tolerated the invasion the way a great white whale might float to the surface and permit birds to pick parasites off its back.

For three years Ivy had been oblivious to the dusty piles of junk left behind by elderly Paul Vlaskovic, the previous owner, a cadaverous fellow whom David referred to as Vlad. The clutter that filled their attic and basement might as well have existed in a parallel universe. Then, as sudden as a spring thunderstorm, the urge to expel what wasn't theirs had risen up in her until she could no longer stand it. *Out!* David had had the good grace, or maybe it was his instinct for self-preservation, not to blame it on hormones.

Ivy felt the baby's firm kick—no more moth-wing flutter. *Hello there, Sprout.* She rested her palms on her belly, for the moment solid as a rock. With just three weeks to go until she either gave birth or exploded, Ivy was supposed to be having contractions. Braxton Hicks. False labor. The revving of an engine, not quite juiced up enough to turn over.

She and David had reached the obsessing-about-a-name stage, and she wondered how many other soon-to-be parents had tossed around the name Braxton.

Viable, viable, viable. The word whispered itself over and over in her head. She'd married at twenty-four, and then it had taken five years to conceive. Three times she'd miscarried—the last time at twenty weeks, just when she'd thought it was safe to stop holding her breath.

David came up alongside her and put his arm around where she'd once had a waist. A fully pregnant belly was pretty astonishing, right up there with a prizewinning Hubbard squash.

"Hey, Stretch"—the nickname had taken on an entirely new connotation in these final months—"looks like we have ignition. Quite a crowd," he said. She shivered with pleasure as he pushed her hair to one side and nuzzled her neck.

Ivy loved the way David gave off the aroma of rich, loamy soil, the way his thatch of auburn hair seemed to go in twelve directions at once, and most of all the way his smile took over his face and crinkled his eyes. The broken nose he'd gotten playing college football, after surviving unscathed for two years as quarterback in high school, gave his sweet face character.

She was more what people called "interesting-looking"—dark soulful eyes, too long in the nose, and a mouth that was a bit too generous to be considered pretty. Most days she paid little attention to her looks. She rolled out of bed, brushed her teeth, ran a comb through long, thick, chestnut-colored hair, and got on with it.

"They think that because we have this great old house, we have great old stuff," Ivy said.

David twiddled an invisible cigar and Groucho Marxed his eyebrows at a pair of black telephones with rotary dials. "Little do they know . . ."

Ivy waved at a fellow yard-sale junkie, Ralph of the battered black Ford pickup, who was crouched over a box of electrical fixtures. Beside him, amid the tumult, stood Corinne Bindel, their elderly next-door neighbor, her bouffant too platinum and puffy to be real. Her arms were folded across the front of her brown tweed coat. The pained expression on her face said she couldn't imagine why anyone would pay a nickel for any of this junk.

"What do you say?" David asked. "After the dust settles, we set up some of the baby things?"

"Not yet," Ivy said. She rubbed the cobalt blue stone set in the hand-shaped silver good-luck charm that hung from a chain around her neck. The talisman had once been her grandmother's. She knew that it was silly superstition, but she wanted all of the baby things tucked away in the spare room until the baby arrived and had had each of her fingers and toes counted and kissed.

"Excuse me?" said a woman who peered at Ivy from under the brim of a Red Sox cap. She held a lime green Depression glass swan-shaped dish that had been in a box of wax fruit that mice had gotten to.

"You can have that for fifteen," Ivy said. "Not a chip or crack on it."

"Ivy?" The woman with cinnamon curls, streaked silvery blond, had a mildly startled look. "Don't remember me, do you?"

"I . . ." Ivy hesitated. There *was* something familiar about this woman who wore a cotton maternity top, patterned in blue cornflowers and yellow black-eyed Susans. Her hand, the nails polished pink and perfectly sculpted, rested on her own belly. Like Ivy, she was voluminously pregnant.

"Mindy White," the woman said. "Melinda back then."

Melinda White—the name conjured the

memory of a chubby girl from elementary school. Frizzy brown hair, glasses, and a pasty complexion. It was hard to believe that this was the same person.

"Of course I remember you. Wow, don't you look great! And congratulations. Your first?" Ivy asked.

Melinda nodded and took a step closer. She smiled. Her once-crooked teeth were now straight and perfect. "Isn't this your first, too?"

Ivy avoided her probing look.

"I'm due Thanksgiving," Melinda said. "How 'bout you?"

"December," Ivy said. In fact, she was expecting a Thanksgiving baby, too. But Ivy had told everyone, even her best friend, Jody, that her due date was two weeks later. As the end approached, it would be enough to deal with just her and David agonizing over when she was going to go into labor and whether something would go wrong this time.

Melinda tilted her head and considered Ivy. "Happy marriage. Baby due any minute. You guys are so lucky. I mean, what more could you ask for?"

Kinehora was what Grandma Fay would

have said to that, then spit to distract the evil eye. Ivy rubbed the amulet hanging around her neck.

Melinda's gaze shifted to the house. "And of course this fabulous Victorian. Let me know if you ever want to sell it. I work for a real estate agent."

"You collect Depression glass?" Ivy asked, indicating the swan.

"No, but my mother collects swans—or at least she used to. Would have snapped up this piece in a flash . . . but that was before"—Melinda tapped a half-empty Evian bottle to the side of her head— "Alzheimer's. She sold her house here in Brush Hills. Moved to Florida to live with my sister, Ruth. Remember Ruthie? Collects swans, too." The words came out in bursts, and Ivy felt as if a chugging locomotive were bearing down on her as Melinda stepped forward again, narrowing the gap between them to barely a forearm's length.

"This would be so perfect for her." Melinda admired the swan. "For Christmas. Or maybe her birthday. When my mother"—Melinda shifted a bulky white canvas tote bag higher on her shoulder and took a breath—"finally croaks, Ruthie will probably want the whole collection. You don't have a sister, or brother either, do you?"

She didn't wait for Ivy to answer. "Honestly, I didn't recognize this place. Used to come here all the time. We lived practically around the corner, and my mother, she worked for Mr. Vlaskovic. Sometimes. I remember playing jacks on the attic floor and eating red cherry Jell-O powder straight from the package." She pulled a face. "Refined sugar. Might as well be mainlining pure poison. What were we thinking? Have to be so careful now. Eating for two. You going to nurse?"

"I . . . uh . . ." The intimacy of the question startled Ivy. She checked her watch, hoping Melinda would take the hint.

"It's so much better for the baby," Melinda went on, oblivious. "Oh, God, do I sound like an ad for those crazy La Leche ladies or what?"

Over Melinda's shoulder, Ivy saw David talking with a woman who held a pair of brass sconces while four other people were crowded around him, arms loaded and waiting their turn. A young man with spiky black hair was examining the great-coats hanging from a clothesline they'd strung under the porte cochere. The coats, which had been abandoned in a trunk in the basement, flapped in the stiff breeze like monstrous bat wings.

"Did you know that?" Melinda asked.

"Pardon?"

"They put corn syrup in baby formula," Melinda said. Her eyes Ivy recognized, small and intense.

"That doesn't sound good," Ivy said. Now Spiky Hair was trying on one of the greatcoats. "Hang on. I see someone over there looking at some coats. I don't want him to get away."

Ivy hurried off.

"Very dashing," she told the man. The black wool coat fit him perfectly. The mothball smell would disappear after a good dry cleaning. "Fifty dollars gets you all four of them."

The man examined the other coats. She expected him to haggle, but instead he drew his wallet from his pocket, peeled two twenties and a ten from a wad of bills, and handed them to her. He folded the coats over his arm and headed off.

Yes! Ivy pumped a fist in triumph. Then she stuffed the money into her apron pocket.

"Think he's a dealer?" It was Melinda. She'd come up behind Ivy.

Deep breath. With the baby's feet pressing up and into her diaphragm, Ivy was finding it harder to catch her breath.

"I always adored this house," Melinda said. "All those fireplaces. Great for playing hide-and-seek, so many hidden nooks and crannies." Melinda waited. Her inquisitive look felt like probing fingers.

Ivy remembered that Melinda's face had once been pudgy and soft, like if you poked her doughy cheek, it would leave an indentation.

"And those wonderful paint colors you picked," Melinda said. "You always had a great eye. I remember you were the first person at school to get a pair of Doc Martens."

Ivy's smile muscles were starting to wear. *Doc Martens?* She'd bought hers at the Garment District on the Dollar-A-Pound floor. She still had them, somewhere in the back of her closet. Should've thrown them into the yard sale along with the greatcoats.

Melinda's gaze drifted, her eyes dreamy. "Stirrup pants."

"Oh, God," Ivy said. "Can you believe we wore those?"

But Melinda hadn't worn stirrup pants. Her daily uniform had consisted of shapeless skirts and oversize sweaters. She'd eaten lunch alone in a corner of the high-school cafeteria and been herded to and from school by her mother. How utterly transformed Melinda seemed, with her manicured nails and stylish haircut. Slim. Outgoing and confident.

David swooped over. "Guess what," he said. "Someone wants to buy those red drapes." His look said, *Told you so!* "How about you go negotiate?"

"Hi, David. Long time no see," Melinda said. She jiggled her water bottle in the air and gazed up at him from beneath the bill of her cap.

"Hey there. How ya doin'?" David said, returning the greeting without a flicker of recognition.

Ivy excused herself. A balding man with

a barrel chest and intense eyes caught in a tangle of gray eyebrows intercepted her. "You take ten bucks for this?" The black metal fan he held out to her could have done double duty as a bologna slicer. She'd marked it thirty, knowing that electric fans like it were going for fifty on the Internet.

"Twenty-five," she said.

He shrugged and handed her the money.

It had started to drizzle. Ivy glanced over at David. Melinda was saying something to him. He took a step back, looking completely poleaxed. Guess he remembered her after all.

Ivy looked down at her hand. She was holding a twenty and a five. That had been for the fan. She tucked the bills into her pocket.

Now, where had she been headed? Her mind had gone blank. Again.

Somewhere she'd read that women carrying girl babies suffered more short-term memory loss during pregnancy. Something about progesterone levels. If that was the case, then this was definitely a girl. Lately she'd been e-mailing herself reminders to read her to-do list. A week ago she'd even managed to lose her toothbrush.

The greatcoats were gone. Their neighbor, Mrs. Bindel, was reading their copy of the *Boston Globe.* Which wasn't for sale. David was still talking to Melinda and looking just as trapped as Ivy had felt earlier. A woman was shaking out one of the thick red silk brocade panels that had hung—

That was it! Now she remembered where she'd been headed. And she'd scoffed when David had insisted that someone would be willing to buy six sets of fringed drapes that had made the downstairs feel like a bordello or an Italian restaurant.

She went over to the woman, who had on a rock the size of an apricot pit. "We were hoping to get seventy-five for those." What the heck?

"I don't know." The woman pursed her lips. She rubbed the red silk brocade back and forth between thumb and forefinger, then lifted one of the tasseled edges to her nose and sniffed.

Ivy balled her fists and pressed them

into the ache in the small of her back. "Actually, we'd take forty. One of them's a bit faded."

The drapery lady said nothing, just pouted at the fabric some more.

Another tap on her shoulder. "Ivy?" Melinda's fingers were wrapped around the glass swan's slender neck.

"You can have that, my treat," Ivy said. The words were pleasant, but the tone was snappish.

Melinda barely blinked. She tucked the swan dish into her canvas bag.

Ivy cleared a spot on the steps to the side door and sank down. She had heartburn, her morning OJ was repeating on her, she had to pee, and her ankles felt like overripe sausages about to burst their casings.

Thank God, David was on his way over.

"Did you see Theo?" he asked, an anxious look on his face. "I promised him one of those greatcoats."

"You should have told me to save him one. Was he here?"

"Just long enough to leave a campaign sign he wants us to put on the front lawn."

"Sorry, I sold every last—" Ivy closed her eyes as her abdominal muscles cramped.

David crouched alongside her. "You okay?" he said under his breath.

Ivy suppressed a burp. "Just tired."

David pulled over a cardboard box filled with 1960s *National Geographics* and propped her feet on them.

"There's a guy looking for books," he said in his normal voice. "Wasn't there a box that we didn't put out?"

"If there is, it's still in the attic."

David started for the house. He paused midstep and turned back. "Hey, Mindy—want to see the inside?"

Mindy?

"Could I?" Melinda swung around. Her belly bumped into a card table, and a large mirror that had been leaning against the table leg began to topple forward. "Oh, my gosh!" she cried.

Ivy reached over and caught the mirror just before it hit the ground.

"I'm so sorry." Melinda had gone white. She bit her lip, and her face turned pinched. "I mean, what if—"

"It's okay," Ivy said. "Don't worry about it."

"You sure?"

"See?" Ivy set the mirror upright. "No damage done."

"Thank God," Melinda whispered.

"Really, it wouldn't have been a big deal."

"No big . . . ?" Melinda stooped alongside where Ivy was sitting. She gave Ivy a penetrating look as she placed one hand on Ivy's belly and the other on her own. Through her sweatshirt Ivy felt the pressure of Melinda's palm and the tips of those long pink fingernails against her taut skin. "Are you kidding? We don't need more bad luck, do we?"

Ivy felt her jaw drop.

Melinda stood and turned to David. "So did you keep the embossed leather wallpaper in the front hall? And that wonderful statue at the foot of the stairs?"

"You can see for yourself," David said. "Go ahead in. I'll give you the grand tour."

Melinda brushed past Ivy as she climbed the steps to the house. David rolled his eyes and followed.

Ivy rubbed her palms across her belly, trying to erase the feel of Melinda's handprint.

"Hey," Melinda said from the doorway.

Ivy turned.

Melinda mouthed the words, "See you," then turned and went inside, the screen door smacking shut behind her.

Ivy sincerely hoped not.

2

By late that afternoon, all that was left of the yard sale was the lingering scent of exhaust from the truck David had hired to cart away mounds of leftovers. As far as Ivy was concerned, that had been the best part.

She squeezed the telephone receiver between her shoulder and her ear as she straightened the stacks of checks and bills and change on the Formica top of the kitchen table that had been her grand-mother's.

"Twelve hundred twenty-three dollars

and seventy-five cents," she told Jody, who'd called to apologize for not showing up at the yard sale to help. Riker, Jody's little boy, had come down with a virus and kept Jody and her husband, Zach, awake the night before.

"Sounds like you did just fine without me. Don't tell me you sold those Scarlett O'Hara drapes?"

"Can you believe it? A woman actually paid twenty-five bucks for them."

"Did she see where they'd faded?"

"I warned her. Didn't want her showing up and demanding her money back."

"Ferengi Rule Number One of Acquisition: 'Once you have their money, you never give it back.'" As usual, Jody had one foot on this earth, the other firmly planted on the starship *Enterprise.*

"You invented that."

"Google it."

"Anyway, it feels great to have it all gone. Tomorrow I'll clean the attic. Can't wait to get the vacuum up there."

"Yippee," Jody said.

"You think I'm nuts."

"Certifiable."

"You're a fine one to talk. I remember when you were nine months pregnant with Riker. You were up on a ladder washing windows. Not merely insane. Downright dangerous."

Jody laughed. "Never had the urge before or since. Listen, when you're pregnant, it's like being taken over by the Borg—resistance is futile."

Ivy poured herself a glass of milk. "You'll never guess who showed up. Melinda White."

"No kidding. Melinda White from high school? How'd she look?"

"Totally put together. She got her teeth straightened, hair styled and frosted, lost weight. You wouldn't recognize her, not in a million years. Calls herself Mindy. And guess what? She's pregnant."

"Pregnant? Really?" A pause. "Married?"

"I didn't ask. She wasn't wearing a ring." Ivy twisted her wedding ring with its filigree setting and three small rose-cut diamonds. She and David had found it in an antique store in New Orleans. "She kind of freaked me out. It felt as if she knew all about my miscarriages. But how could she?"

"That would certainly creep me out, too," Jody said. "Maybe she heard from someone who knows you. She's still living in Brush Hills?"

"I'm not sure. She said her mother moved away."

"Remember how she used to try to guilt-trip you into being nice, and then if you were, she'd be on you like the Phage?" The Phage? Ivy knew better than to ask about what was probably a foot fungus from some *Star Trek* episode. "Once I was nice to her, and I practically had to scrape her off on a tree."

"You were nice?"

"I'll ignore that remark. We used to call her 'the leech.'"

"We didn't."

"We so did."

"We were awful."

"Cruel, self-centered monsters. Most kids are. I was, anyway. Not you. You were Miss Goody Two-Shoes."

"You make it sound like a character flaw."

"Ivy, there's only one person I know

who's nicer than you, and you married him. Despite that, I love you both. And I'm sure Melinda didn't deserve the abuse we heaped on her. But you gotta admit, the girl offered herself up like a human sacrifice. She was weird."

"Still is," Ivy said. She told Jody how upset Melinda had gotten when she knocked over the mirror. "She turned white as a sheet."

"Superstitious. You should talk," Jody said. "You're forever rubbing that amulet of yours. And you won't even set up the baby's crib. Did I ever tell you about my Great-Aunt Dotty—Beatrice, actually, but we called her Dotty. Now, *she* was truly superstitious to the point of being dysfunctional. Wore rubber gloves all the time and boiled the doorknobs to keep germs from spreading. She thought President Nixon was listening in on their phone line."

"And that was crazy?"

"No. But no one knew it at the time."

"I don't think Melinda's crazy. Just very odd and intense. Needy."

"And desperate. More than a little of that. Also my Uncle Ferd," Jody went on, her thoughts leaping zigzag, as usual.

"He—Speaking of strange, remember Melinda's mother? She and Melinda were practically attached at the hip. Remember how she used to march Melinda to school and back every day? The woman was a fireplug with feet."

Ivy laughed.

Jody sang, *"Dum, da-dum, da-daaaah dum."* The tune was the witch's theme from *The Wizard of Oz.*

"Stop! You're awful."

"If Melinda comes back, invite me over," Jody said. "I'll get rid of her for you. No problem. Just don't ask me to be nice. Or to do any vacuuming."

That night rosemary-scented bath salts filled the third-floor bathroom, the only one with a tub large enough to accommodate Ivy and David together. They reclined, facing each other, her belly rising between them like a great fogbound island. Occasional earthquakes sent water rippling against the sides of the tub.

The bathroom was in the half of the attic that, according to their real estate agent, had been renovated decades earlier to make an oversize bedroom and bath for a mentally deficient son. Ivy had visions of a young man laid out in that tub wrapped in cold, wet sheets, back in the days of ice-pick lobotomies.

Wind whistled through the eaves overhead, and rain pelted the roof like ball bearings. Ivy sank lower, and the hot water rose to her chin.

"Has peace descended in the valley?" David asked. "Feeling better, now that everything has disappeared?"

"Why do I ache?" Ivy asked. "I didn't *do* anything. I just waddled around and accepted money."

The house creaked. Sometimes the place felt alive, like an old person sighing and shifting to find a comfortable position.

"You poor thing, you. What hurts?"

Where to start? Ivy rolled her shoulders, then her head. Her vertebrae cracked. "Ouch. My neck. My ankles. My feet."

"Ah, zee feet. And I have zee magic fingers," David said, wiggling the fingers on both hands and flashing her his half-up, half-down smile. "Scoot back."

Ivy pushed back. David picked up one

of her feet, rubbed it with soap, and massaged gently. She rotated her ankle. The tightness eased.

David's hands were strong, rough and callused from working with his crew digging, clearing brush, and hauling stones. Despite his fancy CAD tools, David insisted that he did his best work in the world of three dimensions. Landscaping was about choices, he said—where to place a specimen plant, how much to alter the natural contour of a plot of land. Spend time in a space and it would come to you, how best to enhance it.

There was a slightly obscene sound as David squished her foot between slippery hands and ran his fingers between her toes, then up her leg. Electricity traveled up and tingled in her groin. Ivy closed her eyes, savoring his touch, as sensual as it was therapeutic.

"Do you think feet qualify as an erogenous zone?" she asked.

"Definitely." He started on the other foot.

She relaxed and surrendered to pure pleasure.

"Backs qualify, too," David said, handing her the soap. He hoisted himself, pivoted 180 degrees, and sank into the water again so he was sitting between her legs, facing away from her.

Ivy sat forward and soaped David's back. He had the shoulders of a football player, but the skin, with its dusting of freckles, was smooth and baby soft.

"Mmm. That feels great." David hunched forward. "In my next life, I'm coming back as a cat."

"I thought you told me you wanted to be a sea otter. And float on your back, dining on oysters."

"That sounds good, too. Maybe that'll be my *next* next life."

Ivy pressed her lips to David's spine. Then she soaped up a washcloth and spiraled it around and across his shoulders and down into the small of his back.

"It was weird seeing Melinda White again," she said. Odd that she'd shown up pregnant with a due date identical to Ivy's. "Here we've been living in the same town and never run into her before." Ivy soaked the washcloth and began to rinse his shoulders. "Did you—"

David straightened and started to get up.

"Hang on. You're still soapy."

"That's okay." He stepped out of the tub and reached for a bath towel.

Ivy stretched her legs and leaned back. Just her head and belly button, now an outie, stuck out of the water. "I didn't realize that she had a sister. Her mother I can still picture. Remember how she—"

"Don't ask me," David said as he rubbed himself down. Then he anchored the towel around his waist. "I barely remembered her at all."

Ivy sat up. Water sloshed against the sides of the tub. "I thought you recognized her."

"I thought *you* did."

"But you looked so surprised—"

"Yeah, sure I was surprised. I mean, what did you make of that story? She used to *play* in this house? Who with? Vlad?"

"So why'd you offer to show her around?"

"Because you looked as if you were about to drop-kick her into the street."

"It was that obvious?"

"Besides, I had to go in anyway."

"I admit, she made me very uncomfortable. She was going on and on about Doc Martens. And stirrup pants."

"What?"

"Never mind."

David offered Ivy his hand and helped her to her feet. As she stepped onto the damp bath mat, she caught a glimpse of herself in the misty bathroom mirror. Only months earlier she'd had a slim runner's build—long arms and legs, sinewy torso, solid thighs.

Now she was a gigantic jelly bean. But it wasn't just that amazing pink abdomen with the dark line running down from her belly button to her groin that gave her pause. It was those breasts—out of nowhere, *bazooms!*—that overflowed her usual A cup.

She ogled them in the mirror. Marvels of nature. Too bad they were so tender and achy—took the fun out of having them. She pressed her arms against her sides, bunching up magnificent cleavage. Who'd have thunk she'd ever have some of that?

Ivy dried off, wishing she'd invested in supercolossal-size towels rather than merely extra large. The towel snagged on the chain of her necklace.

"Damn." She tugged at it and tugged again.

"Stop. Here, let me," David said. His fingers tickled her neck as he worked it loose. "Uh-oh. Looks like the clasp got bent." He set the chain and the hand-shaped amulet on the bathroom vanity. "I'll leave it here. I can fix it for you later."

The room had turned drafty. Ivy shivered and slipped into her thick terry-cloth robe. She padded out of the bathroom and across the darkened bedroom. The cavernous space, with its cathedral ceiling, dwarfed the daybed that had been the couch in their first apartment and the maple bureau and floor lamp that had been Ivy's ever since she was little.

The green-flecked linoleum felt cold and smooth under her bare feet. Melinda was right; it was the perfect surface for playing jacks.

Ivy was halfway to the lighted stairwell when she felt a stabbing pain in the ball of her foot.

"Ow!" She set the foot down gingerly and felt the pain again. She hopped, then limped to the wall and leaned against it. When she ran her finger lightly across the bottom of her foot, she could feel a sharp point sticking out from it.

"What's wrong?" David asked.

She tried to pinch the splinter and pull it out. "Ouch! Damn. Something's stuck in my foot."

Ivy tried to see what was there, but getting a good look at the bottom of her own foot was no longer a trivial matter. Besides, it was too dark to see anything.

"Stop picking at it. You want to drive it in farther? Stay there, and I'll get something to pull it out."

Bare-chested, with the towel wrapped around his waist, David left behind a trail of damp footprints as he crossed the room and started down the stairs.

"There's a pair of tweezers on my bureau," Ivy called after him. "Or maybe it's in my cosmetic bag on the back of the toilet." She couldn't make out his grunted reply. "And bring up the rubbing alcohol. I think it's under the sink in the kitchen. Or—" When was the last time she'd used the alcohol? Ivy couldn't remember.

She eased herself down to the floor

and slid back until she was pressed up against the wall. Her foot throbbed. She felt more than heard a scuttling from the other side of the wall where the attic was unfinished. Mice, probably, wondering where all the old furniture and delicious wax fruit had disappeared to. She'd get David to set more traps. Fortunately, she had the baby's things stored in the spare room.

The rain had let up. Bathwater gurgled in the drain as David clumped down the stairs. Ivy pulled in her feet and just managed to hug her knees.

"Can you hear me now?" David's voice came from the dumbwaiter just a couple of yards away. His spooky chuckle seemed amplified. It was amazing how well sound traveled up and down the shaft.

Ivy bumped over and pushed up the sliding panel that covered the dumbwaiter opening. In the dark she could just make out the twisted-metal cable that ran up and down the shaft, still intact, though the dumbwaiter itself lay dormant at the bottom of the shaft in the basement.

"Loud and clear," she said.

"Ain't technology grand?"

"Would you stop playing games? This hurts."

"Any other ideas on where you hid the alcohol?"

"Try the downstairs john. In the medicine cabinet, maybe. Or under the sink. If you can't find it, there's probably a bottle of hydrogen peroxide somewhere."

The dumbwaiter panels operated like old-fashioned double-hung windows, and Ivy had done most of the work refinishing them. Soon after that, she'd scored some funky chrome ceiling fixtures at a yard sale. "Retro-chic," Jody had proclaimed them. Tired of waiting for David to get around to installing them, Ivy had gotten a book on home repair out of the library and tackled them herself. It had been a proud moment when she flipped the kitchen switch and the lights came on. No blown fuses, no scorched-wire smell.

"Bingo!" David's voice was barely audible. There was a pause. "Hang on." Louder. "Here comes the cavalry."

Ivy heard his footsteps in the stairwell, saw his shadow growing long in the frame of hallway light cast on the linoleum floor. Then he appeared, holding a flashlight under his chin, his face transformed into a Kabuki mask.

"Eet's Vlad. I've come to suck your blood."

In spite of herself, Ivy felt an adrenaline surge, and her heart raced. "Would you stop being a jerk and get whatever this is out of my foot?"

"The lady wants to play doctor? I can do that, too." David sat beside her, aimed the light at the bottom of her foot. "Here, Stretch. Make yourself useful." He handed her the flashlight and pulled the tweezers from his pocket.

She aimed the beam.

"Aha! I see. A little this way." He gestured with his chin. Then he hunched over her. "Hold still." With a swift, sure motion, he touched the tweezers to the tender spot, closed down, and gave a firm yank.

Ivy felt the pinch and a stab of pain. She strained to see the bottom of her foot. In the spotlight was a bright red carbuncle of blood. Ivy touched it with the hem of her robe, and the blood wicked into the terry cloth. She squeezed out some more blood and then pressed the fabric against the spot to stanch the bleeding.

"And here," David said, holding up the tweezers, "we have the culprit."

The half-inch-long sliver of glass glowed lime green in the flashlight's beam.

3

The Sunday paper isn't even here yet," David grumbled the next morning as he thumped and dragged the canister vac up to the third floor, the tube draped around his neck like a languid boa constrictor. He was still in his pajamas. "Sheesh, and the sun's not even over the yardarm, whatever the hell that is. Have I mentioned that I think you've gone more than a little nutty?"

"That's what Jody says." Ivy followed him into the attic, trying to keep the weight off the sore ball of her foot. "And I'm sure that in a few weeks vacuuming will be the last thing I'll feel compelled to do."

"But for now you've decided to suck it up"—David wasn't too sleepy to crack a truly dreadful pun—"and you'd advise me to do the same."

David set the vacuum cleaner at the top of the stairs and gave her a weary salute. His face was still creased from sleep, and a herd of cowlicks stood at attention on the crown of his head.

"Go back to bed, you handsome thing, you," she told him.

She plugged the cord into an outlet on the landing, then pulled the machine into the unfinished half of the attic and turned on the light. There was a rough floor and, overhead, bare roof timbers. Pink insulation was tacked between the studs in the walls and the ceiling joists.

Two days ago the space had been filled with what had once been other people's possessions. Now only a box of books remained.

She kicked the switch, and the machine roared to life. There was something satisfying about how cobwebs shot onto the mouth of the vacuum, something Zen-like about how grit crackled on its way to oblivion. The occasional sharp *tink* and the ache in her foot reminded her of the piece of broken glass that had gotten stuck in her. She wondered what had broken as she worked around the edges of the room and then crisscrossed the middle.

Ivy turned off the machine, anchored her hands on her hips, and massaged her lower back with her thumbs. Then she dragged the vac into the finished half of the attic. She knew from early photos that the room had once had double-hung windows. Now the openings were covered over inside with sheets of wallboard, a clumsy repair, and shingled over outside. Maybe the previous owners had wanted to be sure that the young man who'd been cared for up there didn't throw himself out a window. One day, if Ivy and David ever had cash to burn, they'd have the windows restored.

Ivy kicked the machine on again. Despite the boarded-up windows, light streamed in through the arched window set high in the eaves. As she worked, she noticed the dings and dents in the linoleum floor. Like skid marks on a highway, they testified to a past. Six deep gouges formed a rectangle against one wall— probably from a bed. Four circular indentations in the room's center. From a heavy table of some kind? She envisioned a mahogany pool table, green fringe hanging from the edges, in pride of place in the center of the room—though she couldn't imagine how anyone could have gotten it up the stairs.

When she was done, she took a deep inhale and blew out. *Cleansing breath.* That's what Sarah, their childbirth instructor, said to do after she and David had hut-hut-hutted their way through breathing exercises for transition, the dreaded period of intense contractions between active labor and pushing.

Everyone's labor is different—that was the popular wisdom. What would hers be like, she wondered. Long or short? Would there be sharp pains, as she'd suffered during her miscarriages? Or merely "discomfort," the benign term Sarah favored. Would any of the exercises they'd practiced help? Ivy had no problem asking for pain medication, but she'd rather manage without if it meant that the baby would come through even a little bit healthier.

How had it been for her mother—

Ivy stopped the thought in its tracks. It would be a sure sign of dementia to think that her mother would be anything but trouble if she were still alive.

Ivy had been ten years old when her mother started going downhill. That was when they found out that Ivy's father had pancreatic cancer—a diagnosis that made people avert their eyes. Something like 96 percent of those who got it died within five years. Her father had suc-cumbed in six months.

Ivy realized now, and even a little back then, that getting drunk was how her mother numbed herself. But what had started as a coping mechanism turned into a way of life, and her mother didn't stop drinking for more than a week or two until, a decade later, she ran her car off the road and into a tree. Ivy had been twenty-one when the call came, fall semester in her junior year at UMass.

Years before that, she and her mother had moved in with Grandma Fay. "Just temporary," her mother had assured her.

But by then Ivy had stopped believing the fantasy that they'd ever move back into the charming Victorian house she remembered from her childhood, or the small ranch-style home they'd moved into after her father died, or the condo they'd lived in after that, or even the one-bedroom rental on the top floor of a triple-decker that they'd been evicted from by a landlord who'd expected to be paid.

Ivy had stood in the ICU with Grandma and watched her mother fade. She could still smell the sweet antiseptic, hear the hums and hisses, the beeps and clanks of all that equipment designed to keep alive people who were trying to die.

"Admit that you are powerless *over the alcoholic*"—Ivy had whispered her own version of Al-Anon Step One. Then her corollary: "Just because she's your mother doesn't mean you're going to become her."

For days and on into weeks, they waited for her mother's labored breathing to stop. It had been like waiting for zeros to queue up on an odometer. Ivy had been afraid to look away.

And then, just like that, it was over. Her

mother was dead. No more crazy middle-of-the-night phone calls. No more ruined holidays followed by tearful apologies that Ivy knew were heartfelt and accompanied by promises that, time after time, Ivy let herself believe.

The baby shifted, pressing what must have been a foot into Ivy's ribs and bringing her back to the present. She hoped that this little girl she carried would never feel the emptiness toward her that Ivy felt toward her own mother. Because by the time her mother died, that's all she felt. Well-meaning friends had assured her that one day she'd grieve, but she never had.

Ivy could see Grandma Fay shaking her bony finger. *Focus on what you can control, let go of what you can't.* That had to be what this cleaning frenzy was all about. Because normally Ivy was a distracted housekeeper at best, impervious to clutter and content to let piles of dishes overflow the sink. Yes, indeed—she poked the vacuum nozzle under the bureau—when the spirit moved her, she could vanquish dust balls with the best of them. A regular Martha Stewart.

When she was done, she gazed about the room. Short of hosing down the place—and then David would have been justified in calling in the white-coated men—she'd done what she could.

She sneezed, and a second later the baby kicked. *Bada-boom, bada-bing.* Sometimes it felt as if she were playing straight man in a comedy duo.

Later, maybe that afternoon, she'd tackle the basement.

Then what? Ivy closed her eyes to stave off a wave of panic. Her maternity leave officially started that day. Symbolic of the disconnect, when she got home Friday she hadn't even bothered to bring her laptop in from the car. Her PalmPilot said it all—on her normally long to-do list were only doctor appointments, a baby shower at Rose Gardens on Tuesday afternoon, and a lunch date with Jody the following week. Period.

Not that she was going to miss getting up every morning at six and fighting her way into Cambridge. Not that her colleagues weren't perfectly capable of writing updates for the Web site and issuing press releases without her for the next eight weeks at Mordant Technologies, one of the few dot-com survivors.

She sneezed again, wiped her hands on her jeans, and headed down to the master bedroom. She pushed the door open. Warm air oozed out, and she inhaled David's musky presence. The top of his head was barely visible under the quilt.

Give the poor guy a break—once the baby was born, it would be a rare morning that either of them would be sleeping in.

She left the door ajar and went downstairs. At the base of the stairs, a foot-high bronze statue of a woman was mounted on the elaborately carved newel post. David's cap with its sweat stains and Rose Gardens logo hung from the statue's upraised arm. Ivy ran her finger through a dust-filled groove in the figure's flowing gown. She'd been meaning to remove Bessie, as David called the figure, from her perch and rinse her down. Maybe later.

She continued into the kitchen and chugalugged milk straight from the carton. Amazing how the human body craved what it needed. She grabbed a handful of salted nuts. What essential vitamin or mineral in cashews made them this year's chocolate, while her favorite dark, dark chocolate bars made her gag?

The green and white placard that Theo had dropped off was propped against a lower kitchen cabinet. SPYRIDIS FOR STATE SENATE, it blared. In the upper corner was a head shot of Theo, reeking gravitas and somber determination. Theo, trying not to look like the supreme egotist that he was. Theo, drained of his individuality and stripped of his best and worst traits. He'd even cut off his long ponytail in preparation for the senate run.

"Where did you find that impostor to pose for your picture?" Ivy had asked him.

"Didn't you know? I have an evil twin," Theo had said with a wink and a grin.

Ivy picked up the campaign placard and carried it to the front door. She stepped out onto the front porch. The sky was cloudless, and the air had the kind of crystalline clarity that only fall brought to New England.

She planted the sign in the grass, shaded her eyes, and looked back at their home. Eyesore indeed. When the real estate agent first showed them the house, the exterior hadn't been touched by anything but weather for so long that it had looked sandblasted. Fresh paint—three layers of it—had done wonders. Chelsea Mauve around the windows; Corn Silk for a band of fish-scale shingles between the first and second floors; Smoke Green for the latticework under the porch and in the roof peak over the magnificent arched, multipaned window that looked out on the world like a beneficent eye.

The interior had been something else entirely. As the newspaper ad had promised, the condition was "pristine." That was because decades earlier, like some light-averse mole, the former owner, Mr. Vlaskovic, had retreated to the kitchen. There he'd set up a cot and a wood-burning stove and made do with a single lightbulb. He shut off the water and electricity to the rest of the house. The annual electrical bill for the enormous house had come to a whopping $96.31 the year before the house went on the market. The water bill was even less.

Three years ago Ivy and David had moved in with no clue what it would take to heat the place. They couldn't even flush the upstairs toilets or bleed the cast-iron radiators before signing the Purchase and Sale. Making the down payment that wiped out their savings had been a huge leap of faith.

Ivy picked up the newspaper from the lawn and returned to the porch. She dragged the rocker to a sunny spot and lowered herself into it. She closed her eyes and leaned back. The insides of her eyelids glowed red, and her muscles relaxed and expanded in the sun's warmth.

Though they lived in a busy suburb, on a Sunday morning the occasional whoosh of a car going by couldn't compete with the cacophony of birds. There was the whistled call and response of a pair of cardinals. The raucous cawing of crows. Chickadees chattered from a neighboring yard, and from far away came the bell-like chime of a blue jay.

Ivy opened her eyes. Insects hovered about the shimmering white flowers of the rose of Sharon bushes that David had planted in front of the porch. He'd dug out overgrown yews and replaced them with these, shrubs he'd propagated from cuttings he'd taken years earlier from specimens he'd been stunned to find growing

wild along a streambed in New Hamp-
shire.

Across the street a woman pushed a
double stroller with toddlers, like a pair of
Pillsbury Doughboys, bundled up in it. Ivy
recognized her from the yard sale. The
woman waved, and Ivy waved back. She
really should get up, introduce herself, and
chat. Other than elderly Mrs. Bindel who
lived next door, Ivy barely knew any of her
neighbors.

So why was she opening the newspaper and hiding behind it?

Once Sprout was born and named and
Ivy was out there pushing her own stroller,
she rationalized, there'd be plenty of time
to get to know the local stay-at-home
moms. For now her center of gravity lingered in the working world with friends
who were busy at their desks the whole
week, friends whom she'd begged not to
call with questions about whether she'd had
the baby yet. "Yet," she'd instructed one
and all, was not a word to be uttered in her
presence. She and David would e-mail
just as soon as the newest Rose had made
her entrance into the world.

Ivy had just started reading the paper

when she heard *screech-scritch, screech-scritch.* Then a pause. The sound came again, another pause.

Next door, Mrs. Bindel backed into view. She was hunched over and, in spurts of effort, tugging a wicker trunk down her driveway. Poking along at her heels was Phoebe, a dog of indeterminate breed with a fat sausage body, skinny legs, and the black jowls of a bull mastiff. The dog's snout was studded with white whiskers, and her fur was brown and threadbare in places, like a well-loved plush toy.

Ivy put down the paper. "Good morning," she called out. "Need help with that?"

Not waiting for an answer, she got up. The dog listed to one side and did her snort-grunt routine at Ivy as she walked across the lawn and up her neighbor's driveway. Phoebe was lame, nearsighted, and usually even-tempered, but those jaws were designed to crunch bones. Ivy would have to watch out when her daughter, God willing, got to the ear-pulling stage.

"Hello, you little monster." Ivy leaned forward and held out a tentative hand, ready to whip it back if Phoebe snapped instead of slobbered. "Remember me?"

Phoebe sniffed at Ivy's hand and wagged her stumpy tail. The dog's one redeeming virtue was that she didn't sniff Ivy's crotch. Maybe, after a certain age, dogs no longer needed to scratch that particular itch.

"You . . . inspired . . . me," Mrs. Bindel said between efforts, her platinum bouffant slightly askew.

Phoebe tacked sideways, supervising, as Ivy pushed the basket from behind and Mrs. Bindel tugged from the front. They wrestled the trunk out to the street, leaving white scuff marks on the asphalt driveway.

Mrs. Bindel held her hand to her chest. "Don't . . . know . . . why," she huffed, pink from exertion, "I've been holding on to . . . these old things." She pulled a tissue from the sleeve of her sweater. "Where's a man when you need him?"

"Sleeping," Ivy said. "But I'm sure he'll be glad to come over later and help if you've got more stuff to drag out."

"No. Thanks." Mrs. Bindel took off her glasses and cleaned them with the tissue.

She dabbed at her forehead. *"Phew!* This is the last of it."

Phoebe sniffed at the cardboard boxes already lined up in a tidy row on the strip of lawn between the sidewalk and the street in front of Mrs. Bindel's house. One box had the handle of a frying pan sticking out of it; another overflowed with lengths of pipe and white porcelain plumbing fixtures. A third was filled with a lifetime supply of neatly nested plastic deli containers.

None of it was nearly as intriguing as the wicker trunk, its back wall slanted as if it had been designed to fit into a ship's hold. A pair of metal hinges along one edge fastened the trunk lid to the base; the opposite edge had a padlocked metal hasp.

Ivy bent closer to read a tattered, yellowed tag, a shipping label handwritten in Cyrillic characters and tied to the hasp.

"Looks pretty old," she said.

"It was old already when Paul's father asked us to store it in our garage for him, and that was years and years ago."

Paul? It took a moment for Ivy to realize that Mrs. Bindel was referring to Paul

Vlaskovic, the previous owner of Ivy and David's house.

That seemed odd. Their huge Victorian had much more storage space than Mrs. Bindel's trim ranch house with its replacement windows and pale blue vinyl siding, which she hosed down every spring and fall.

"Mr. Vlaskovic didn't want this back when he moved?" Ivy asked.

"I never asked. Too late now." Untroubled, Mrs. Bindel picked up a little sign made from a shirt cardboard and a stick and planted it in the grass up against the wicker basket. The sign read FREE HELP YOURSELF. "This trunk must have come over from the old country with Paul's father, back in the twenties."

Ivy's mother's family had come over from Russia in the early part of the century, too. Ivy had recorded her grandmother's voice telling of the difficult crossing, of their five trunks, including one filled with zwieback because Ivy's great-grandmother knew they'd find nothing kosher to eat on that boat. They'd arrived with only the clothes on their backs, because by the time they reached Ellis Island, Ivy's great-grandmother had had to sell the trunks and everything in them in exchange for water. Another week and they'd have died of thirst, like some of the others.

Ivy had listened to that recording over and over, and she could hear Grandma Fay's voice telling how the men in the dark uniforms and caps had pushed them along, trying to get them up the ramp and into the big building. "But my mother stood there watching our trunks come off the boat. They didn't belong to us anymore, and we needed like a hole in the head to be standing there in the freezing cold. 'Come on,' I begged her. And the men were scowling at her and scolding and shouting at us, words that I didn't under-stand."

Would the wicker trunk contain lace tablecloths and hand-embroidered bed linens, like the ones her great-grandmother had sold to save her family? When Ivy's great-grandmother had cried over what she'd lost, her great-grandfather had scolded her, "Don't worry about those old *schmattes.* This is America. Here we get everything new."

"What's inside?" Ivy asked Mrs. Bindel.

"I don't know. It's locked."

Weird logic—Mrs. Bindel could throw it away, but she couldn't break it open. It wouldn't be hard. The trunk fittings were rusted and not all that sturdy to begin with.

"You're not even a little bit curious?"

"You want it?" Mrs. Bindel asked with a hopeful, upturned inflection.

"Well . . . I guess. . . ." *What are you, nuts? A hectoring voice sounded in Ivy's ear. You just got rid of Mr. Vlaskovic's old junk, and now you're acquiring more?* "I just wanted to—"

"So!" Mrs. Bindel beamed and clapped her hands together. "You'll take it all."

Before Ivy could muster a protest, Mrs. Bindel had yanked the little sign from the ground and tossed it into one of the boxes. She pivoted and started back toward her house.

"Settled!" Mrs. Bindel said, pointing a finger toward heaven.

4

I get the pipes and empty paint cans—you can never have too many of those," David said later that morning, poking the toe of his work boot into one of the boxes now amassed in front of their house. "But remind me why we need a burned frying pan?"

"Burned and dented," Ivy said. "I wanted to see what was inside the trunk. She made me take it all."

"Made you? That woman drives a hard bargain." He leaned closer to the trunk and sniffed.

"I know. It's stinky. The thing's been

stored in Mrs. Bindel's garage for decades. God knows what vermin have gotten to it. It belonged to the Vlaskovics."

David eyed the trunk with new interest.
"So this was Vlad's. One of his boxes of
earth?"

"It was his father's. Besides, it's not that
heavy," Ivy said. The vampire jokes were
getting stale. "Think you can pry it open?"

David got a crowbar from the toolbox in
his pickup truck. It took seconds to jimmy
the trunk's hinges.

"Ta-DAH!" he said with a dramatic sweep
of the hand as he raised the lid.

The wicker creaked. A powerful wave of
mildew rose from the open trunk. Ivy put
her hand over her nose and peered inside.
She felt a tremor of excitement. It was full
to the brim.

"Oh," Ivy said, picking up a once-white
cotton infant's jacket with pale blue picot
embroidery along the edges and a narrow
satin ribbon at the neck. Alongside that
was a baby's gown with tiny pin tucks
across the chest and lace insets in the
sleeves and around the hem, and a matching bonnet. "Aren't these sweet?"

She took out the gown. The fabric felt

dry and brittle. Out dropped a lock of fine dark hair, tied with a pale blue ribbon. Baby's hair. Surely whoever had packed this trunk and nestled the lock of hair so carefully into the infant's clothing hadn't meant for it to end up getting pawed over by anonymous neighbors.

Beneath a layer of baby clothes was a woman's white dress made of semi-sheer fabric. It had a high neck, and there were delicate ruffles across the shoulder and down the front. A wedding dress? Such a shame it was covered with tea-colored spots.

Ivy dug through the remaining contents of the basket. There were other women's dresses, one of navy wool with a white scalloped collar and small pearl buttons. Ivy lifted it out. No waist, just a tie in the back. The fabric was riddled with moth holes.

"What do you suppose . . . ?" David said, lifting out what looked like a coarse piece of white sailcloth. He turned it over. It was a shirt, its tapered sleeves sewn together at the cuffs. A thick leather strap was sewn to the end of one sleeve, and a sturdy-looking metal buckle was sewn to the end of the other. Instead of buttons to fasten the front—or was it the back?—there were smaller straps and more metal buckles. A straitjacket, Ivy realized with a jolt.

"That story about a crazy son in the attic," David said. "Maybe it's true."

The front was covered with stains, some dark brown and some yellow. Ivy looked away, feeling as if this was something obscene. Too personal to be held up in public.

"Put it back," she said.

"Hang on," David said. "This looks interesting." He handed Ivy a bundle wrapped in ecru lace.

It was heavy. Unrolling the musty layers, Ivy found a tarnished silver hairbrush. Then a matching hand mirror and a cut-glass jar that fit in the palm of her hand. The jar's silver lid had a hole in the middle.

Ivy pried the jar open. Inside was coiled . . . what? Thread saved by a thrifty housewife? Ivy poked at it. Not thread. Hair.

The final item in the bundle was a notebook. Flakes from the pebbly black leather cover came off on Ivy's hand as she opened it. She riffled through lined pages of dated handwritten entries. Between the pages was a piece of thick folded paper. Ivy took it out and opened it. It was a sepia-tinted photograph.

To one side of the crease stood a young woman with a long, expressionless face and shadows around her eyes. She wore a dark dress with a white collar—the dress from the trunk. Her spider-leg fingers seemed to float over the stolid shoulder of a stern-faced man with a brushy mustache who was seated in front of her. He was dressed in a dark suit and sat with one arm poised, rigid around a bright-eyed little boy. The youngster couldn't have been more than five years old, but he sat there on his father's knee, somber and straight-backed as an adult in his short pants, jacket, and tie.

The photograph broke apart at the fold, and Ivy was left holding just the woman. As she gazed into the emptiness of the young woman's eyes, she felt overpowering sadness.

"I'm sure the Vlaskovics never intended for these things to be thrown out," Ivy said

as she stood at the kitchen sink that evening, waiting for the running water to get
warm so she could rinse the tarnished silver pieces. "I don't feel right keeping
them."

David grunted. He sat at the table with
a dictionary, working a crossword puzzle.
Vocabulary was David's latest self-
improvement jag, triggered by a tart
remark from Rose Gardens' office manager, Lillian Bailiss, that had sent him to the
dictionary for the definition of "philistine."

Ivy yawned. It was barely nine-thirty,
still too early even for her to turn in. "We've
got Mr. Vlaskovic's contact information
somewhere. I'll call him and find out if he
wants these back."

Even without a personal connection, Ivy
had also kept the notebook, the photograph, and the lock of baby's hair from the
trunk. It was odd, the things one could so
easily pitch and the things one couldn't.
Without a qualm, Ivy had bagged and
given away Grandma Fay's clothing, her
pocketbooks and costume jewelry. What
she couldn't part with had been, of all
things, her grandmother's reading glasses
and her rubber-band ball.

Ivy got out a jar of silver polish from under the kitchen sink. Before she started to work, she squinted through the kitchen window. At first all she could see was her own reflection—the fullness of her cheeks, something new with the weight gain of pregnancy, made her nose seem less like an exclamation point down the middle of her face.

Her eyes refocused, and she could see the trunk. She and David had left it with its remaining contents out at the curb for Wednesday's garbage pickup. It was still out there, looking forlorn and hopeful in the dappled glow of the streetlight.

David had appropriated Mrs. Bindel's sign proclaiming it free for the taking. Apparently many folks had found that irresistible, because all afternoon and into the evening a virtual cavalcade of garbage pickers had stopped to check it out. A young blonde, who reminded Ivy of Britney Spears on a good day, had helped herself to the white dress. The woman who'd been at their yard sale and whom Ivy had seen that morning, pushing her two kids down the block, had taken the baby clothes. At twilight Ivy had seen a man with a tall, thin silhouette out there rummaging through what remained. Later she noticed that the box of plumbing in-nards had disappeared. At one point even Mrs. Bindel was out there looking into the trunk. Giver's remorse? Ivy won-dered. Too bad the bottom was such a mess, or someone would have taken it for refurbishing.

Ivy ran warm water over the silver back of the hairbrush.

"Repoussé," she said. It was a lovely, voluptuous word that perfectly described the ornate, raised design of flowers and hummingbirds.

"'Pushed back.' Eight letters, half of them vowels." David licked his index finger and made a hash mark in the air. "Now, hush. I'm trying to concentrate."

She removed the remaining hair caught in the bristles of the brush.

"You know that glass dish with the silver lid?" Ivy said. She tucked the strands of light brown hair through the hole in the lid of the jar. "It's a hair receiver. Victorian la-dies saved hair to stuff pincushions and make jewelry. One a lot like this one recently sold for over a hundred dollars on eBay."

"Sounds like we still need to hit the lottery."

Ivy gouged silver polish from the jar with a damp cloth and began to rub the back of the hairbrush. Black appeared on the cloth as tarnish disappeared from the raised surface.

"A complete dresser set would be worth a whole lot more," she went on. "There would have been a half dozen more pieces. Probably a comb, a buttonhook, a . . ."

David picked up his puzzle and dictionary and left the room.

Ivy switched to an old toothbrush, working away at the final traces of tarnish. Then she picked up the hand mirror. Her face looked back from the streaky glass. Chipmunk cheeks aside, she still resembled Morticia Addams, with her long straight hair and bangs, especially at the end of a busy, tiring day.

She polished the mirror back. Then she went to work on the lid of the hair receiver. She rinsed the pieces and buffed each with a dish towel. Finally she lined them up on the counter and admired the results.

She remembered the bronze statuette mounted at the base of the stairs. Might as well give it a cleaning while she was at it. She went to the entry hall and lifted Bessie off her perch. A six-inch bolt that stuck down into the newel post was all that kept the heavy statue anchored in place.

As Ivy carried the figure into the kitchen, she remembered the first time she and David had stepped over the threshold of their new home and how Bessie, with her arm raised, seemed to welcome her personally. Ivy had been overwhelmed by a sense of déjà vu—the house had felt so much like the more modest Victorian where her family had lived before her father died. Before her mother started drinking.

She set the statue on the kitchen counter. She'd seen enough episodes of *Antiques Roadshow* to know that polishing old bronze was a terrible idea. That poor woman who'd taken Brasso to a Tiffany lamp base had dissolved into tears when she was told that she'd polished away ten thousand dollars' worth of patina.

Ivy was wiping the statue with a damp cloth, clearing each of its dust-lined crevices, when she heard a sound from outside. A dry squeak. A moment later there it was again. Sounded as if yet another customer had stopped to see what wondrous items could be had for free.

Ivy glanced at the clock. After ten. She dimmed the kitchen so she could see out. Beyond the lawn, past Theo's campaign sign, out at the curb, the lid of the wicker trunk was raised. It lowered a bit, and Ivy could see the head and shoulders of someone out there. A car drove by, and its headlights strafed the shadowy figure. A woman.

The lid lowered a bit more. Ivy felt a jolt of recognition. Long dark hair. Bangs. Sunglasses.

If she didn't know better, she'd say she was looking at herself.

With a loud clatter, the statuette fell into the sink, and Ivy reached for her throat, groping for her grandmother's necklace and the hand-shaped good-luck charm that should have been hanging there but wasn't.

5

Stop chasing your tail and think. That was what Grandma Fay would say whenever Ivy ran around the apartment looking for misplaced homework or house keys. *Dollars to doughnuts, it's wherever you think it is.*

So where should it be? Last night the necklace had gotten caught on her bath towel. David had broken the clasp getting it unstuck, and he'd left it on the sink in the third-floor bathroom.

But it wasn't there. Not on the bathroom counter, not in the sink, not on the floor or in the wastebasket or behind the radiator or anywhere else in the room.

Had she inadvertently vacuumed it up? She found the vacuum cleaner, still in the attic bedroom. She removed the dust bag, tore it open, and dumped the contents onto some newspaper. But when she picked through, she found no necklace.

Methodically, she searched the rest of the house, top down, becoming increasingly ticked off at herself. An hour later she found David watching TV in the den. She stood in the doorway and swallowed a ragged sob.

David looked over. "Stretch?"

It was ridiculous. Just because she couldn't find her grandmother's amulet . . . Ivy put her hand to her mouth and sobbed again.

David sprang to his feet and came over to her. "What's wrong?" He wiped away a tear from her cheek. "Hey, what's this about?"

She told him.

"That's it? You misplaced your necklace?"

"It's so frustrating. I'm losing things. Seeing things."

"Seeing what?"

Ivy told him about the woman she'd seen standing outside at the curb.

"Hey, we'd hoped people would stop and help themselves, didn't we?" David asked.

"But she looked just like me."

David blinked. "Sounds like you were seeing your own reflection—"

"I'd turned out the light. And I was not wearing sunglasses."

"She had on sunglasses?"

"That's what I just said!"

David raised his eyebrows. "Show me."

She walked him to the dark kitchen, and they stood looking through the window. Outside, the wicker trunk sat closed at the curb.

"Wraparound sunglasses," Ivy said.

"It's pretty dark out there."

"A car drove by with headlights. I saw what I saw."

David turned to face Ivy. "Okay. So a woman wearing sunglasses walks by, stops to have a look in the trunk. Maybe she even takes some stuff." He put his hands on her shoulders. "Big deal."

Ivy sighed. "Of course. You're right. It's

just that"—she hiccupped a sob—"and now Grandma Fay's necklace is—" The final word caught in Ivy's throat. "I'm sorry. I don't know what's the matter with me."

Of course, she did know. Up past her bedtime and nine months pregnant.

"Did you look in the—" David started.

"I looked everywhere." The words came out loud and whiny. Pregnancy had permeated every one of her defenses.

David recoiled. "Hey, it's probably out there partying with my orphaned socks and your missing toothbrush."

Ivy snagged a tissue and blew her nose.

"Want me to help look?" he said. "You know what they say about two heads."

"Better than none."

She let David lead the way through the house, to all the spots she'd already checked and others that she hadn't.

"I told you, it's gone," she said when it still hadn't turned up.

He put his arm around her waist. "Silver's not biodegradable. I guarantee, it's got to be somewhere. In the meanwhile you need someone to tuck you into bed. You've been up since dawn."

Gently but firmly, he propelled her up the stairs.

Feeling too anxious to fall sleep, Ivy sat up in bed. She opened the small leather-bound book that she'd found in the wicker trunk. She ran her fingertips across a dry, brittle page, over words written in ink from a fountain pen.

Emilia V. – May 23, 1922

Emilia. That was an old-fashioned name. The *V* must have been for Vlask-ovic. *1922.* Between the wars and around the time that Ivy's grandmother and great-grandmother had left Europe.

New journal, new beginnings. Today we moved into this beautiful house on Laurel Street. It is past midnight, but I am too ex-cited to sleep.
For the first time, this afternoon I stood on the porch, __my__ porch. The meadow across from us is covered with buttercups.

Across the street there'd been a field? Amazing. Ivy read on.

As I watched the man that Joseph hired carry in the table Mother and Father gave us, I felt the baby move. I wanted to call out to Mother and Matilda, but my letter will take a week to get to Toronto.

The baby had been a boy, Ivy was sure of it—just as she was sure that Emilia V. was the long-faced, somber woman in the photograph, and that Emilia's fingers had tied the narrow blue satin ribbon around the lock of baby's hair Ivy had found tucked in this notebook.

As Ivy read through page after page of dated entries, written in flowing script, the flickering ghost image of a woman solidified into one of flesh and blood, one whose days were filled with making a home, waiting for her first child to be born, and yearning for the friends and family she'd left in Canada. Ivy had nothing like this diary to document her own family's past.

By July the writing had become tight and crabbed. Ivy imagined Emilia pregnant, writing at a drop-front desk in the living room, clutching her pen, her face pinched.

Ivy read the entry for August 20 twice.

When I returned from my walk, I studied myself long in my looking glass. I saw just what I expected. My face is too thin, my nose too large, my complexion pasty. My hair is too short to be described as luxurious tresses and the color is neither blond nor brown. My fingers are blunt and stubby instead of tapering. No wonder Joseph can hardly bear to look at me.

Poor thing. There she was, about to give birth, stranded in Brush Hills with the clueless Joseph. No Lamaze classes where she could meet other young couples. No "friends and family" phone deals. No e-mail. No MySpace.

Count your blessings, Ivy heard her grandmother's voice say. Even though at nine months pregnant Ivy had all the grace of a 1966 Bonneville station wagon, David made her feel like what Grandma Fay would have called a "hot tomato." She had friends, colleagues, and a job to go back to.

Ivy rested her hands on her swollen belly. Soon she'd have a child. Even *she* was starting to believe that.

Ivy yawned and closed the book. She

switched off the light, turned over on her side, and shut her eyes.

An hour later she was still awake, with David snoring gently alongside her. The smell of mildew seemed to have infested her sinuses. Her mind leapfrogged from the painfully crabbed handwriting to the haunted face that had stared back at her from the sepia photograph to the woman she'd seen through the kitchen window— long dark hair and bangs framing a pale face, partially obscured by dark glasses. Morticia II.

Ivy covered her head with her pillow, as if muffling sounds would smother the images that crowded into her head. She conjured the charming pen-and-ink drawing on the first page of *Madeline*—an old house in Paris with vines crawling over the front walls, two chimneys puffing jaunty smoke swirls perched on its tile roof. Her father had read that children's book to her so many times that she knew it by heart. She'd always found it calming, when she couldn't fall asleep, to meander through the whimsical illustrations and rhyming text.

At last it worked its magic, and when it

did, Ivy dreamed that she was in the attic of Madeline's Paris school, an attic awash in mildewed wicker trunks, filled to the brim with rotting feather beds and linens. From somewhere in one of the trunks came an infant's screams.

6

Ivy lay on the examining table in Dr. Shapiro's office late the next afternoon, listening for the baby's heartbeat through a stethoscope. A small device that attached to a fetal monitor lay heavy on her belly, where the doctor had slathered icy-cool petroleum jelly.

Lub-dub, lub-dub. The sounds came against a sloshy background. Ivy's insides grew warm, and she felt a smile melt across her face.

David listened, too, hooked up through a second stethoscope, his eyes wide. "That's a baby? Sounds like a Mack truck."

"That," said Dr. Shapiro, a robust older woman with sensibly cut salt-and-pepper hair who looked like she should be wearing golf shoes and swinging a nine iron, "is what we call a good, strong heartbeat."

Dr. Shapiro picked up Ivy's hand and squeezed it. She'd done an internal exam, Ivy's first in months. When she'd announced that Ivy's cervix was becoming effaced and was two centimeters dilated, David had gone white.

"Perfectly normal. Just means you're nearing the end," she'd explained. "But you don't need me or any of these fancy gizmos to tell you that."

With a practiced eye, Dr. Shapiro examined Ivy's knuckles and palpated her wrist. Checked her ankles. It was Dr. Shapiro who'd told Ivy that the baby she'd miscarried over a year ago had been a little girl.

"Now, neither of you should get concerned if this one quiets down a bit. They do that toward the end. It's getting pretty snug in there."

"You're telling me," Ivy said. "When do you think . . . ?"

"Could be any day, or it could be several

more weeks," Dr. Shapiro said. "It's not a science."

Any day? The thought was terrifying. But weeks more of feeling like she'd swallowed a hippo? If men got pregnant, they'd have figured out how to fast-forward past this part to the end.

"She's been cleaning," David said, unhooking the stethoscope from his ears.

"And hallucinating," Ivy added.

"Really?" Dr. Shapiro said.

"Not really," Ivy said.

"It's good to stay active," Dr. Shapiro said, moving on briskly. "Follow your normal routine. Cleaning is fine, as long as you're comfortable doing it and as long as you drink plenty of liquids and go easy on salt. And be thinking about names, because this baby is ready to boogie."

"Boogie Rose," David said as he drove them home in Ivy's car. Traffic on the highway was starting to congeal as the evening rush began in earnest. He glanced over his shoulder and shifted lanes. "What do you think? Works if it's a boy, works if it's a girl."

"Works if it's a band," Ivy said.

"Well, we can't keep calling her Sprout."

"Gwyneth Paltrow named her baby Apple."

David tipped his head back and smacked his lips, as if he were tasting the name. "Not bad. Or better yet, how about we name her for a food I really like?"

"Forget it. We're not naming this kid Sam Adams. Besides, it's a girl."

"You don't know that for sure."

"Betcha a million bucks."

David snorted. He took the exit ramp and pulled up at the end of a long backup of cars at the first light. "Beer Rose. Has a certain . . . cachet."

"The first name can't end in *r*."

"Why not?"

"Because our last name starts with *R*. Beerose," Ivy said, running the words together. "People will think her last name is Ose."

"Or her first name is Bea."

"And a one-syllable first name is out," Ivy went on.

"Ah, Rule Number Two," David said. "You're just full of rules, aren't you?"

"Jane Rose. Jill Rose. A one-syllable

first name sounds kind of stumpy with Rose for a last name."

"Stumpy Rose."

"Tah-dum Rose. Or Tum-te-de-dum Rose. And—"

"Lily Rose? Honeysuckle Rose?" David signaled to turn.

"Lily's not bad, actually. But don't you think two flowers are a bit much? *Ivy* Rose is bad enough."

David turned the car onto their street. "Hey, one flower has always seemed a bit much to me, but nobody ever asked my opinion. Besides . . ." His voice died. A police cruiser was pulled up in front of their house. "What the . . . ?"

Ivy's immediate thought was Mrs. Bindel. A heart attack? A stroke? But there Mrs. Bindel was, standing behind her storm door, her cardigan pulled tight around her narrow shoulders, knuckles to her mouth.

A uniformed police officer was in front of their house, crouched alongside the wicker trunk, talking into his cell phone. The trunk lid was raised. He looked up as David let the car roll to a stop at the curb.

The officer closed his phone, lowered the trunk lid, and stood, unfolding long and lean, like a praying mantis.

David got out of the car. Ivy followed.

"You folks live here?" the officer asked, jerking his head in the direction of their house, his expression somewhere between a smile and a grimace. His eyes drifted down to Ivy's pregnant belly.

"We do," David said.

With the heel of his hand, the officer tipped back his cap. His thinning hair was the color of straw.

"Officer Fournier. Brush Hills Police." He flashed his badge and then showed them a photograph. "Has either of you seen this person?"

Ivy recognized this version of Melinda White—a pudgy young woman, posed against a painted background of clouds and blue-blue sky and giving the camera a closed-mouth smile.

"That's Melinda White," she said.

"So you know her?" Officer Fournier asked.

"Sort of," Ivy said. "Not well. We went to school with her."

"And you last saw her?"

"She was here this weekend. Saturday morning," Ivy said. Ivy couldn't read the tense look David shot her. "We had a yard sale."

"Why? Did something happen to her?" David asked.

Officer Fournier pocketed the picture and drew out a pad. He pulled out a pen and clicked it open. "That's what we're trying to determine."

He took their names and jotted a few notes. Then he squinted into the setting sun. "So you folks talked to her? Saw her leave?"

David opened his mouth, but nothing came out.

"I talked to her," Ivy said. "She bought a swan dish . . . you know, a green glass swan. Depression glass. Actually, she didn't buy it. I gave it to her. She said her mother—or was it her sister?—collected swans and . . ." Ivy realized she was babbling. "She was here. Yes, we talked to her. She likes to be called Mindy now, and she looks a lot different from that picture."

"Different? How?"

"Hair's lighter, straighter, shortish." Ivy held the side of her hand just below her ear to show how short. Officer Fournier took some more notes. "She's not so frumpy, if you know what I mean."

Officer Fournier stopped writing, glanced up from his pad and gave her a blank look.

"Frosted hair. Manicured nails," Ivy added.

"Do you remember what she was wearing?"

Ivy said, "Baseball cap. Dark pants. A blue and yellow flowered maternity top. Black-eyed Susans."

David gave her a surprised look. What could she say? She noticed clothes.

"Maternity top? She was pregnant?" Officer Fournier asked.

"Very. And she was carrying a white canvas bag, about the size of a shopping cart," Ivy said.

"And you're certain this was the woman you saw?" Fournier asked.

"She introduced herself," Ivy said.

"Neither of us would have recognized her if she hadn't," David added. "We haven't seen her since high school."

"Like I said, she's changed," Ivy said.

"How did you know she was here?" David asked the policeman.

"Her sister reported her missing, and we located her car. It was parked down the block. There was a copy of the *Weekly Shopper* on the front seat, with your yard-sale ad circled." Officer Fournier paused. "She never made it home, and her apartment looks as if she had every intention of coming back. She left her coffeepot turned on."

Officer Fournier said nothing more for a few moments, his gaze shifting from Ivy to David. "She didn't go to work and didn't phone in sick. Her sister's been calling and calling. Quite distraught, as you might imagine."

Ivy's neck prickled as he continued to watch them closely.

"So let me see if I've got this right," he went on. "Yard sale starts at nine. Melinda White shows up. What time was that?"

"Early," Ivy said. "Must've been a few minutes after nine. We'd just opened up."

"She introduces herself?"

"Right," Ivy said.

"Either of you notice her talking to anyone else?"

"I didn't," David said. Ivy agreed.

Officer Fournier scratched his head. "So she's here for what—five, ten minutes?"

"More like twenty or thirty," Ivy said. It had felt like an eternity.

"Maybe you noticed her leaving with someone?"

"She . . ." Ivy was about to say that David had taken Melinda into the house, but something in David's look stopped her. "I didn't notice when she left," she said, biting her lip.

"No one followed her?"

"The place was hopping, Officer," David said. "We were selling off a huge accumulation of junk, left here by the former owner, and there were people crawling all over the place."

"Perhaps you know some of Ms. White's friends?"

"Sorry," David said. "You see, we don't really *know her* know her. We just went to the same high school. Ages ago. Brush Hills isn't that big, but there were over a thousand in our graduating class. I was never friendly with her. You either—right, Ivy?"

Ivy nodded.

"Mmm," Officer Fournier said, shutting his pad. "And this belongs to you?" He jabbed his pen in the direction of the wicker trunk.

"No . . . yes," David said. "I guess it does now. Our neighbor"—he jerked his head toward Mrs. Bindel, who was still watching from behind her screen door—"sort of gave it to us."

"Sort of?"

"She was throwing it out," Ivy said.

"And now you're throwing it out?"

"Right," David said. "Long story."

Officer Fournier clicked his pen open and shut and waited.

"It's a neat old basket," Ivy said. "I was curious to see what was inside. I thought maybe there'd be some things in it worth saving."

"And were there?"

"Some. And at first I thought I might be able to refurbish the basket itself. But the bottom's rotted, and it stinks."

"I see," Officer Fourier said. "So you left it out at the curb for garbage pickup?"

"That's right," David said. "If there's a problem leaving it out until tomorrow, we can drag it into the garage—"

"No, no problem," Officer Fournier said. "Not under normal circumstances. However . . ." He pocketed his pad, then reached out and raised the lid of the wicker trunk. With the end of his pen, he hooked something from inside and lifted it.

Ivy recognized the blue cornflower and black-eyed Susan pattern. The fabric had been crisp and clean when Ivy had seen Melinda White wearing it.

Now it was crumpled and stained with splotches of rusty brown.

7

The ground felt as if it were tilting sideways, and Ivy's head filled with a metallic smell, like the inside of a soup can. She tried not to gag as Officer Fournier dangled the stained blouse from his pen for inspection.

"Any idea how this got in there?" he asked.

"What the hell is that?" David said. "It was *not* in there yesterday, when we put the trunk at the curb."

"It wasn't?" Officer Fournier asked, deadpan.

"That's right. I repacked it myself," Ivy

added, surprised that her voice sounded calm and steady. "Lots of people stopped to check it out. Someone else must have put that in there, because we certainly didn't."

"Someone else? Right." Officer Fournier let the blouse fall back into the trunk, dropped the lid, and stood. "How about we go inside?" He squinted toward the house, then at David. "I've got a few more questions, and I'd like to have a look around, if you don't mind."

David folded his arms over his chest, and his jaw stiffened. "Actually, I do. This is our home. We've done nothing wrong."

"What's the problem?" Officer Fournier's polite tone had taken on a hard edge. "That is, assuming you've nothing to hide—"

"And I don't like your implication," David said.

"I understand. Of course it's your pre-rogative. But here's the thing: Either I go inside now and take a quick look around, or I get a warrant and bring in a team that will search your house. Thoroughly. If I'm not mistaken, any judge would agree that *this*"—with his knee he nudged the trunk lid up a few inches and eyed the blouse with detached interest—"is more than sufficient for probable cause."

What would have happened next, Ivy wondered, had David simply said, "Sure, whatever," or "Be my guest," when Officer Fournier had asked to come inside? An hour later she felt trapped in a surreal replay of the yard sale with the "mute" button engaged. Only it wasn't morning, and those weren't buyers assembled at the end of the driveway, eager to surge in. They were gawkers, keeping their distance but tethered by morbid curiosity, their movements herky-jerky in the blue and white police strobes.

Cars slowed as they drove past. Across the street, neighbors watched from lit windows. A stranger with a bicycle had his cell phone turned toward them. Transmitting a picture?

Ivy felt sick to her stomach, caught at the wrong end of the viewfinder. She desperately wanted to run into the house and slam the door, but a uniformed officer stood barring the way.

Right away, David had called his friend Theo, an attorney. Theo's terse instructions had been, "Cooperate. Be polite. Don't argue. But do not—repeat, *do not*—answer any questions until I get there."

The crowd across the street seemed to grow larger by the minute, and now the man on the bike was talking into his cell. A gold Crown Victoria pulled up. The headlights flicked off, and a man wearing a dark suit emerged. He did a squinty-eyed 360, surveying the tree-lined street and houses, and conferred briefly with Officer Fournier. Then he strode over to Ivy and David.

Ivy barely registered the badge he showed them, barely heard him introduce himself. She was focused on the papers he handed David.

David cursed and crumpled the pages in his fist. "Search warrant," he said. "Where the hell is Theo? His office is just around the corner, for Chrissakes."

Tight-lipped, David climbed the steps and unlocked the front door.

The newcomer and the uniformed officers swarmed into the house, leaving a single patrolman outside to guard the entrance.

David and Ivy retreated to under the porte cochere. Waiting in the gloom, at least they were sheltered from prying eyes. There was a nip in the early-evening air, but the bone-chilling cold Ivy felt was more than that. David had his arm around her, but he seemed disconnected, radiating little warmth as he watched, tensing each time a car approached and drove past.

At last a black Lexus pulled up. Theo climbed out. Looking thoroughly corporate in his dark suit and overcoat, he gave an uneasy glance at the crowd gathered on the street.

"Thank God. It's about time," David said, waving him over.

Theo walked toward them. He set down his bulging cordovan leather briefcase. "I've heard of police vigilance, but this is ridiculous," he said, sputtering under his breath. "I'm sorry you have to go through this. Especially now." He gave Ivy a sympathetic look and hugged her, enveloping her in musky cologne.

Ivy felt a rush of gratitude and relief.

David handed Theo the crumpled search warrant. Theo smoothed it and scanned the contents. He looked up. "You haven't answered questions, have you?"

"We had no idea we were 'answering questions,'" David said, drawing quotation marks in the air, his voice low and intense. "We get home and—"

Theo put up his hand. Ivy followed his gaze to the street. A media van had pulled up in front of the house. "Hang on."

Theo approached the officer guarding the front door and a moment later disappeared inside. A few minutes later, the side door opened, and he stuck his head out.

"Come on in. They're done in the kitchen."

Ivy climbed the steps and entered the house. She crossed the little mudroom, where layers of coats hung on hooks behind the door, and went into the kitchen. Quickly, she lowered the window shades and shut the drawers and cabinets that the police had left open. She leaned back against the counter, pulled her jacket around her, and stood there shivering, her arms folded across her belly.

"I feel like we've been ambushed," David said, grinding a fist into the refrigerator door.

Theo tossed the search warrant on the table. He pressed the door to the dining room firmly shut and took a seat at the table.

David paced up and back. "What in the hell is going on? They're treating us like—"

"Stop. Sit," Theo said. "We need to talk."

David and Theo exchanged a long look. Then David drew a deep breath and ran his hand back and forth through his hair. He shrugged off his jacket, hung it over the back of a kitchen chair, and sat.

"You, too," Theo said, looking at Ivy.

Ivy slipped into a chair.

There was a sound like someone was playing the theme from the old TV show *Dragnet* on a toy piano. Theo fished his cell from his pocket, flipped it open, and looked at the readout. He turned off the phone, and the sound died.

"Why are they doing this?" David asked. "Treating us like criminals."

"These days no one gets cut any slack. Not since the JonBenét Ramsey case."

Theo explained that ever since the Boulder police had famously screwed up the investigation of the murder of the little girl, police everywhere were going by the book, "especially when the case involves a white suburban household. It's nothing personal."

Theo read through the search warrant, then pulled a silver pen and a pad of yellow lined paper from his briefcase. "Okay, from the top. The missing woman?" Theo's brow creased. He loosened his tie and shot David a questioning look. "We're talking Melinda White—as in Melinda White from high school?"

"Right." David explained how police had tracked her to their yard sale.

"Okay. Her sister reports her missing," Theo said. "They find her car. Your newspaper ad brings them here. So how'd that get them a search warrant?"

David told him about Mrs. Bindel's wicker trunk, left out at the curb for garbage pickup. How the police officer had found Melinda's clothing inside.

"Can they do that, Theo? I mean, isn't that invasion of privacy?" David asked.

"Anything out in the open on the street

like that is fair game. It's entirely legal for the police to open it up and look inside."

"That blouse was not in there when we put the trunk out Sunday night," David said, glancing at Ivy for corroboration.

"Of course it wasn't," she said.

"You don't have to convince me," Theo said. "I'm your attorney." He looked long and hard at David. "And I'm also your friend."

The ceiling creaked. The police were probably up there searching their bedroom, pawing through Ivy's underwear, running their hands through the bedding.

"Ivy saw lots of people stop by and rummage around in it," David said. "Any one of them could have put that blouse in there."

Theo took notes. "What kinds of people? How many?"

"Our neighbor," Ivy said. "Another woman who lives in the neighborhood. Some tall guy, but by then it was too dark to see who he was." Ivy picked up a salt shaker from the table, a little ceramic frog she'd found at Goodwill. She ran her thumb over its smooth head and tried to keep her teeth from chattering. "There must have been others, too. I wasn't watching every minute."

"We thought they were taking stuff," David said. "Which was fine, because we'd been hoping the whole thing would disappear by morning. I mean—we'd been hoping . . ." David stammered.

"Garbage pickers," Ivy said. "Better to have someone take stuff and put it to good use rather than us throw it away."

Now Theo looked baffled. Ivy flashed an image of Theo's apartment, all chrome and glass and white Berber carpeting. Theo could no more imagine dragging someone's discarded wicker trunk into his home than he could imagine wearing a Timex or drinking wine from a screw-top bottle.

"Ivy got a little freaked when she saw a woman out there, late that night," David said, lowering his voice.

"And?" Theo asked. "Ivy?"

"I heard a sound. I looked out the kitchen window and saw her."

"This woman, did you recognize her?" Theo asked, taking more notes.

Ivy swallowed. "She looked like me."

Theo stopped writing.

"She had hair like mine anyway," Ivy added.

"Pregnant?" Theo asked.

Ivy closed her eyes and tried to remember. "I . . . I don't know. The trunk lid was up."

"Have you told the police about these people you saw out there?"

"They never gave me—" Ivy started.

"Good," Theo said. "Because you can imagine what they'll think if you tell them you saw someone who looks like you. Sounds like you were out there yourself, and you're trying to establish an explanation in case another witness who saw you comes forward."

"But it wasn't me!"

"Of course it wasn't. I know that," Theo said in a harsh whisper. He held a finger to his lips and jerked his head in the direction of the door to the dining room. "I'm just saying—"

"That they're going to assume I'm lying or that I'm a crazy pregnant nut job."

"You're not crazy," David said, his voice shaking. "Melinda's the crazy pregnant nut job. I wish to hell I'd never—" David's words died as Theo sent him a withering look.

"Okay. Back to Melinda." Theo looked from Ivy to David. "When did you guys see her last?"

David stared down into his lap.

"Hon?" Ivy said.

"What?" Theo said.

David looked pale and tired as he sat slumped in the chair. "I guess I'm the one who saw her last," he admitted. "I showed her around inside the house."

"He was going in anyway," Ivy added. "To get the last box of books. Melinda kept asking what we'd done with the interior, so he offered to give her a tour."

David stared down at the table. "She said she used to play in the house when she was little. Her mother worked here, or something like that. It was obvious that she was making Ivy uncomfortable."

"Okay. So you do the *House Beautiful* tour. Then what?"

"Then nothing. Downstairs, up—that was it," David said.

"You saw her leave?" Theo directed this to Ivy.

Ivy shook her head.

"Did anyone else see her leave?"

"The yard sale was in the driveway, up the side of the house," David said. "I guess someone must have. I was in a hurry to—"

There was a light knock at the door.

Theo leaned toward them. "Okay, here's the drill," he said under his breath. "Very simple. You don't answer questions unless I say it's okay. Refusing to answer police questions is not a crime. And no, it does not make you look as if you have something to hide. It makes you look as if you're listening to your attorney, who's looking out for your best interest."

Theo stood. "Anything, and I do mean anything, you say can be used against you. Something you think is completely innocuous can be twisted and made to look incriminating. Okay?"

He straightened his tie, smoothed the sides of his hair with his palms, and shot his cuffs. "Okay?" he repeated.

Hunkered down into her jacket's up-turned collar, Ivy nodded. She was so cold.

8

Lawyered up, have they?" The man who'd arrived in the Crown Vic and brought the search warrant made their kitchen table and chairs look like doll furniture. He had to be at least six-three. He'd introduced himself as Detective Blanchard, and he had a uniformed officer with him.

"We'd like to get DNA swabs from you both," he went on, talking in a raspy smoker's voice. "That way we can eliminate—"

"I'm advising my clients against it," Theo said, cutting him off.

Detective Blanchard's mournful look said they'd disappointed him personally.

Ivy pulled her jacket tighter around herself.

"We've interviewed some of your neighbors," Blanchard went on, "trying to find someone who saw Ms. White leave your house. So far, we—" He stopped. "Mrs. Rose? Are you all right?"

"I'm . . . just c-cold," Ivy said, trying to keep her teeth from chattering.

David took her hands in his—his palms felt hot.

"Would you go kick up the thermostat?" Blanchard told the uniformed officer.

"Thermostat's in the living room," David said.

"We know that," Blanchard said with a wry smile.

"Do you want to make yourself a hot drink?" Blanchard asked.

Glad to have something to do, Ivy stood. A wave of dizziness surged up to meet her, and she steadied herself against the table. When it passed, she got down a mug and some chamomile tea.

The furnace in the basement thunked on.

Ivy's hands trembled as she filled the

kettle and set it on a burner. She turned on the stove and stood close by, absorbing warmth from the gas flame.

Eating something might help. She got out a saltine cracker and took a bite. Sawdust. She choked down the mouthful.

Ivy turned off the burner as the kettle started to emit its two-toned whistle. Blanchard waited, all the patience in the world, until she had a steaming mug of tea and had settled herself against the cast-iron radiator that was starting to heat up.

"Like I was saying, we're looking for anyone who saw Ms. White leave your house. We know she didn't move her car, and it seems as if she never made it back to her apartment. She must have gone somewhere. It would be very helpful if you could give us names, or even just descriptions of the people who were at your yard sale at the same time." At that moment Detective Blanchard reminded Ivy of her Uncle Bill, her father's brother and the only person in the world who could coax her into cleaning her room when she was eleven.

Theo gave a cautious nod, and the tension in the room seemed to ratchet down a notch.

"There must have been at least twenty people at the yard sale when she was there," David said. "Most of them strangers."

"Anything you can tell us will help."

David enumerated neighbors who'd been there. Ivy retrieved the checks she'd been given. She described everyone she remembered, including the yard-sale regulars who'd shown up.

"And I understand you saw some people, later that day and into the night, looking into the trunk after you'd left it outside?" Blanchard said.

Ivy described everyone she'd seen. Theo's raised index finger reminded her that the police didn't have to know how much the woman with long dark hair and sunglasses had reminded Ivy of herself.

"Thanks," Blanchard said. He snapped his notebook shut. "Just one final thing. I was wondering when either of you was last up in your attic."

Gentle, coaxing Uncle Bill had evaporated. Ivy didn't need Theo's clearing his throat to get the message.

"Mmm," Blanchard continued. "Well, I ask because there's a vacuum cleaner up there now, in that half that's unfinished. Mrs. Rose, you must be quite a fastidious housekeeper. And it's odd, isn't it, that the dust bag's been removed? I can't help wondering why, when it wasn't nearly full. We found it in the rubbish bin outside. Someone had sliced it open."

Even if Ivy had allowed herself to respond, she'd have been at a loss for words.

David looked as if he were about to explode. "The whole point of throwing a yard sale was to clear out old junk and clean out the attic, and the basement, and wherever else the former owners had squirreled it away." He put his hands on the table and half stood from his seat. "My wife—she's pregnant, in case you haven't noticed—she's been doing a lot of cleaning lately."

Theo put his hand on David's shoulder. David sank back, folded his arms across his chest, and leaned the kitchen chair up on its back legs. A muscle twitched in the corner of his jaw.

The detective gave a sympathetic smile.

"Hey, I hear you. Been there." His face turned hard again. "Actually, I wondered if it was *you* up there vacuuming and cleaning, Mr. Rose. No matter, because despite your efforts to clean up, we did find at least one very interesting item."

Blanchard dropped a small evidence bag on the table. It landed like a stone in a still pond. Ivy felt herself pulled forward as she tried to make sense of what she was seeing. Visible through the clear plastic was a marble-size piece of green glass.

"Mrs. Rose, you told Officer Fournier that you gave Ms. White a green glass dish, shaped like a swan?" Blanchard said.

The mug slipped from between her hands, and hot tea erupted when it hit the floor.

"That's it. We're done," Theo said.

The police spent another hour in the house. After they left, Ivy and David and Theo sat in the kitchen. Ivy had changed pants, but the insides of her legs still stung from where she'd been splattered with hot tea.

She reached for the search warrant that Theo had tossed onto the table, pulled over the form, and read.

Evidence to be seized: Any and all items that may have contributed to the disappearance of Melinda Jane White, DOB: 05/18/76.

The list of possible finds included:

blood; tissue; fibers; hair; bodily fluids; material; clothing; drugs; any weapon, including, but not limited to, any cutting instrument, knife or knives; firearm(s); blunt objects; wires and/or cords.

Glass swan head. The police had taken that with them. They'd been through the bathroom hamper and bagged up towels and the clothing that Ivy and David had worn on the day of the yard sale. She wondered how they'd known what to take. Probably from Mrs. Bindel.

The police had taken the wicker trunk, too, and no doubt Ivy's bathrobe, noting the bloodstain at the hem where she'd soaked up her own blood after David removed the glass splinter from her foot. Now she knew where that shard of green glass had come from.

"I'm sorry," David said. He reached for Ivy's hand and made eye contact for the first time since the swan's head had landed on the table. "I should have told you earlier."

Ivy's skin prickled. "Told me what?"

"The thing is, I didn't see Melinda leave." David rubbed his hand across his mouth. "When we got up to the attic—"

Theo stood and reached for his brief-case. "Maybe I shouldn't hear this."

"You idiot." David grabbed his arm. "Put that down. And stop looking at me like that. Nothing happened! Well, nothing like whatever it is that you're thinking might have happened."

Theo lowered himself into the chair.

David took a deep breath and then began. "We get up to the attic, and she starts walking around the room, running her palm across the wall, practically caressing the doorknobs. She makes a complete circuit, then plops herself in the middle of the floor, cross-legged, cups her hands together, and shakes them up and down, singing 'Onesies, twosies, threesies, four-sies.' Then she pretends like she's throw-ing a ball and picking up jacks."

As Theo listened, his mouth dropped open.

"You think I could make this up?" David said. "She tells me how she used to play in our house when she was a kid. And I'm like, o-kaaay. Then she starts talking about her mother, and her sister, and how hard high school was for her. She gets herself more and more worked up." He closed his eyes and rolled his head back, the vertebrae in his neck cracking. "Then she starts to cry. I thought, Jesus Christ, get me out of here." He looked at Ivy. "That's when she threw it."

"The dish," Ivy said.

David held his hands open in a gesture of helplessness.

"Why didn't you tell me before?" Ivy asked.

"She's crazy. I figured you didn't need the aggravation." David came up behind her and put his arms around her. "Why should both of us be upset?"

Ivy pulled away. "Any other details you don't think I can handle?"

"Ivy, that's not what I meant."

"What happened next?" Theo asked.

David shoved his hands into his pockets. "I got her a glass of water and some tissues, and then I went downstairs to get a broom and the dustpan to sweep up the glass."

"And then?" Theo said.

"Then nothing. When I got back, she'd gone."

9

Anxiety scraped the inside of Ivy's rib cage as she climbed the stairs, exhausted and confused, leaving David and Theo talking in the kitchen.

Why should both of us be upset? The explanation was plausible. But since when had Ivy turned into someone David needed to protect? Hadn't they always been honest with each other?

She stood in the bedroom doorway. It was obvious that the police had searched the room. Bedding was pushed back. The closet doors had been left open and clothing shoved to the sides. Items on her bureau top had been rearranged, and the smell of sandalwood and spicy clove hung thick in the room. The scent she'd once loved told her that they'd opened her bottle of Opium perfume, though she couldn't imagine why.

The middle drawer of her bureau was ajar. She pulled it open. Her nightgowns had been put back upside down and on the wrong side of the drawer. She lifted one out, shook it, and sniffed. All she smelled was laundry detergent.

She picked up the silver Victorian mirror she'd rescued from the wicker trunk. A disk of Tinker Bell light skittered across the ceiling. She looked at her own reflection. Her eyes revealed the exhaustion that she felt, and her hair was in tangles.

She reached for the matching hairbrush. The burnished silver had a warm glow. A few strands of dark hair were caught in the bristles.

Deep inhale, exhale. Ivy looked down at her belly. She was still feeling enormously pregnant, but something had changed. Shifted south.

She placed her hands on her abdomen

and could actually feel her top ribs. The baby must have dropped. That was supposed to happen now, near the end. No wonder she hadn't been burping and feeling uncomfortably full. That explained why it felt as if the baby were sitting directly on her bladder.

She went into the bathroom and peed. Out of habit she went into her office to check her e-mail. A wave of panic stopped her when she saw the empty surface of her desk. Had the police confiscated her computer?

Then she remembered—her laptop was still in the car. Thank God for small miracles.

Ivy went downstairs. David and Theo fell silent as she passed through the kitchen. She went out the side door and retrieved her briefcase from the trunk.

Back in her office, she hauled out the laptop, plugged it in, and started it up. As usual there was a message from kamala@ nextgen.com. Kamala was "the perfect mate" from one of Jody's favorite episodes of *Star Trek: The Next Generation.*

Ivy opened the message.

So? I know you don't want me to call and
ask, but anxious friend is dying to know.
xx
J

It took a moment for Ivy to realize that
Jody was asking about her doctor's appointment. It felt like days ago, not just
hours ago, that she'd been on Dr. Shapiro's examining table and listened to the
baby's steady heartbeat.

Ivy started a reply:

Went fine. Confirmed, giving birth to a water buffalo. ETA April 1.

She paused. *Guess what? Melinda
White disappeared, and her bloody
clothes showed up on our front lawn.*

She couldn't type those words. She'd
see Jody tomorrow at the baby shower.
With any luck by then the mystery of Melinda White's disappearance would be
resolved.

Ivy lay in bed a short while later, listening to Theo's and David's voices floating
up from downstairs. Drinking buddies,
poker buddies, high-school quarterback

and wide receiver—the two had shared adventures that went back to childhood. It sounded as if they were arguing.

She forced her eyes shut. Other sounds seemed to swarm around her. A steady thrumming and then the thud of water running and being turned on and off. A squeak and a ratchet, like the sound of a wicker trunk lid being raised. Probably the maple tree outside her window, swaying in the wind. A wheezy inhale and exhale, and a barely audible *thumpa-thump-thump.* Then sounds like stealthy footsteps kicked her heart into high gear.

A moment later she realized what it was. Water dripping.

She got out of bed, padded to the bathroom, twisted the faucet shut, and left a washcloth over the drain to muffle the occasional drip. She returned to bed, rolled onto her side, and sandwiched her head between pillows. Behind closed eyelids she replayed the reassuring steady pistoning of the baby's heart. *A good, strong heartbeat,* Dr. Shapiro had said.

Her mind veered to when they'd come back to the house and found a police officer standing at the curb, how he'd disarmed and entrapped them. Her mind veered again, and she saw the figure standing by the open trunk, only now she wasn't as sure that it hadn't been her own reflection. Again her mind veered, and she saw the bicyclist with the camera phone pointed at their house.

Ivy tried reciting *Madeline,* but picturing the story's Miss Clavell in her long nun's habit with a cross hanging over the front reminded her of her lost amulet.

She shifted to her other side, the pillow cool against her cheek. Where could Melinda have gone? If Melinda had been crying and distraught when she left their house, she might not have noticed someone following her. Had her car been parked on their street since Sunday, or had it been driven away and returned later? Were the police talking to Melinda's friends and co-workers? Were they trying to identify the father of her unborn child?

More questions flooded Ivy's mind. How the hell had Melinda's maternity blouse found its way into the wicker trunk? How long would it take for the police to determine whether the stains on it were Melinda's blood?

Her brain would not shut down.

Finally Ivy turned onto her back, stuffed the pillows under her head, reached for the remote, and turned on the TV. She flipped past cooking shows that made her sick to her stomach, past crime shows that on any other night she'd have been content to settle down to watch. Murder had lost its entertainment value.

She whipped by a news broadcast, and then flipped back to it. There was a woman commentator, solemn-faced in a form-fitting pale blue suit, standing in front of their house. Ivy propped herself up on her elbows, now wide awake.

"A Brush Hills woman remains missing at this hour. Melinda White was last seen Saturday morning at a yard sale at this home." The camera panned sideways, showing their front door being guarded by a police officer.

Ivy sat up and threw off the covers.

"She is pregnant with her first child." A photograph of a pudgy woman, all cheeks and chin and dark eyebrows, filled the screen. It was the same picture the police had shown them—Melinda in high school. "Anyone with information is urged to call this number." A phone number appeared at the bottom of the screen.

A moment later a cheery weatherman came on. "Well, we're in for a period of un-settled weather. . . ."

No kidding.

Ivy snapped the TV off. She hung her legs over the edge of the bed and pressed her fingertips against her eyes. Then she got up, crossed the upstairs hall, and went into her office. On the top shelf of the floor-to-ceiling bookcase, she found the Brush Hills High School 1993 yearbook. She opened to the back.

There it was, among the last entries in the index: WHITE, MELINDA. Beside the name were five page numbers.

Ivy turned to the first page listed. It had Melinda's graduation picture, the same photo the police had shown her and the one Ivy had just seen on TV. She turned to the next entry. Melinda was part of a two-page who's who—she'd been voted Friend-liest. Ivy winced at the memory of the cruel joke that only Melinda hadn't gotten.

David was there, too, on the opposite page. Best Physique. He was giving the camera a hunky muscle-man pose while he ogled the abundantly endowed Marla Ward.

Ivy wasn't there at all. Smart, but not the smartest. On the track and the soccer teams, but no star athlete. Ivy had also written for the yearbook, started the school's first chapter of Amnesty International, and painted scenery for Drama Club.

David had been a jock, Ivy a geek, and Melinda an untouchable. In the petri dish of Brush Hills High, where cliques bred like colonies of toxic fungi, it was a near miracle that Ivy and David had ended up paired. In fact, it had been a total fluke.

It was in the late fall of their senior year, and the boys scrimmaged on the field while the girls' relay team practiced on the surrounding track. Ivy hadn't seen David throw the pass, hadn't seen the receiver running backward, backward, didn't hear the shouted "Heads up!" The football hit her hard and square between the shoulder blades, literally knocking the wind out of her.

Next thing she knew, she had a mouth full of dirt and there was David, the sun bright behind his head, bending over her. "Are you all right? Are you all right?"

That night he'd called her on the phone. Three hours later they were still talking. Ivy sighed, remembering those sweet early days and the surprised looks they'd gotten later when they'd first walked, hand in hand, through the school hallways.

The next page with Melinda White's picture was French Club, its main claim to fame an annual cheese party. There was Melinda in the front row, her hand over her mouth, hiding those teeth that she'd since gotten straightened.

Ivy flipped to the next entry. Marching band. Melinda was at the end of the back row, wearing one of those feathered hats and a jacket with brass buttons and epaulets the size of flapjacks. Why, with everything Melinda *didn't* have going for her, would she choose to play the tuba? She did seem to be, as Jody had suggested, a willing human sacrifice.

Ivy turned back to Melinda's graduation picture. Below it was her "senior will." It began, "I, Melinda White, am so glad to be out of here." Maybe not so clueless after all.

Ivy read on:

I leave a huge thank-you to Mr. Ball for being the best teacher ever and to Mrs. Markovich for all the times that I needed you and you were there. To the team, thanks for the memories.

What team? Ivy wondered as she touched Melinda's picture. Anger welled up inside her, and she had to tamp down the impulse to gouge her fingernail into that simpering, closed-mouth smile.

"Where the hell are you?" Ivy whispered. Why couldn't she have disappeared at someone else's yard sale?

Ivy slammed the book shut and turned off the light.

She crossed the landing and entered the corner room they'd fixed up for the baby. She ran her hand across the wall's cool surface, which she'd painted a cheery yellow, barely able to feel the ridge where she'd filled in and smoothed over an enormous crack in the plaster. She gazed up at the border of blue sailboats she'd stenciled along the ceiling. She walked to the front window, her palms on her belly, trying to calm herself and channel some semblance of serenity the baby's way.

The crowd outside was gone. So was Theo's campaign sign. Maybe someone had taken it as a souvenir, or maybe Theo had removed it himself, not eager to have his name emblazoned front and center on the evening news with a story about a missing pregnant woman.

Ivy shifted to the side window. Below, light glowed from the living room of the house next door. Mrs. Bindel sat, as she often did, in a wing chair pulled up to the window. She had a newspaper folded in her lap, and she sat very still, with her eyes closed and her head tipped forward, her mouth hanging open.

"I'm the neighborhood burglar alarm," Mrs. Bindel had once boasted to Ivy.

Mrs. Bindel shifted in her chair, yawning. Then she leaned forward and seemed to stare straight up at Ivy.

10

By daybreak Ivy was exhausted. Co-cooned in warm quilts as she was, the last thing she wanted to do was get out of bed. But there was no way around it. She had to pee. Again.

She dragged a quilt to the bathroom with her. When she got back in bed, she fell into the kind of deep sleep that had eluded her all night. It was after nine by the time she woke up again.

She went downstairs and peered out through the glass panel alongside the front door. The sidewalk and street looked deserted.

On the kitchen counter, David had left their address book open to the page with Mr. Vlaskovic's new address and phone number. He'd scrawled *"3:00. Shower!"* on the top sheet of a pad of paper that was balanced on her favorite coffee mug.

Ivy dumped out the inch of coffee David had left in the brewer and dropped a slice of wheat bread into the toaster. The newspaper was on the kitchen table. There on the front page of the Metro section, above the fold, was Melinda's picture and the headline PREGNANT WOMAN MISSING FROM BRUSH HILLS.

Ivy scanned the column. Police had apparently made little progress in their search. At least there was no mention of Ivy or David.

The toast popped, and Ivy poured herself a glass of milk. She sat at the table and continued reading on the jump page. According to the article, Melinda lived in an apartment in Brush Hills. More than a year ago, she'd switched careers, quitting her job as a lab tech at Neponset Hospital and going to work for a real estate agency in South Boston.

Ivy took a bite of toast and forced herself to chew. Then she took a swallow of milk.

Neponset Hospital. That was where she and David attended childbirth classes and where she'd be headed when Sprout signaled her readiness to enter the world. It was also where Ivy had suffered her last miscarriage.

Summer, a year and a half ago. Week twenty, when all the books said the baby was officially viable and just when she'd let down her guard, she'd started cramping and spotting, then hemorrhaging. There had been so much pain, so much blood. David had stayed beside her, holding her hand, helpless and ashen-faced.

Ivy pushed away the newspaper.

That tiny baby had been in perfect health. Dr. Shapiro couldn't explain it. Just one of those "bad things that happen to good people," she'd said. Ivy knew that the platitude was meant to be comforting.

Afterward Ivy had clung to David, unable to stop crying. For months she'd felt hollowed out, as if her shadow were going to work and coming home, going through life's motions for her.

Then she'd gotten pregnant again. For

the past nine months, she'd felt as if she were walking along a precipice, sure that any moment she'd slip and fall into a gorge. She'd sworn David and Jody to secrecy and told no one else that she was pregnant until she could no longer button her coat, not really believing in it herself until her belly button popped out, like the timer on a roasting chicken.

This one would be different. It had to be. She looked down and touched her belly, firm and hard.

This baby girl was going to be born, full term and healthy.

It was nearly noon when Mr. Vlaskovic returned Ivy's call. He said he'd be happy to see her—was now convenient?

She had just enough time to pay him a visit and then get to Rose Gardens for the baby shower at three.

Ivy drove I-95 South, staying in the right-hand lane. About half the trees bordering the highway were bare; the remaining leaves had turned leathery brown with an occasional flash of red or yellow— reminders of what had been glorious fall foliage.

She glanced down at the passenger seat, where she'd set directions she'd printed from MapQuest. The exit was a few miles farther along.

She turned on the radio and switched to news, hoping to hear a bulletin, something like *Missing pregnant Brush Hills woman turns up alive and well in Albuquerque.* Instead she got an earful on another car bombing in Iraq and the struggling real estate market. When the commentator started a story on the latest DNA test for birth defects, she smacked the "off" button.

Ivy slowed behind a flatbed truck carrying a large, bright yellow forklift. It was the kind David used to move boulders. Sitting on the forklift's tines was a smaller forklift, large enough to haul around pallets of turf.

The smaller forklift rattled precariously, jumping whenever the truck hit a bump in the road. It looked as if any moment that wobbly little forklift would tip over, maybe even fall from the truck.

When Ivy pulled off the exit ramp, she was sobbing and laughing at the same time. Mama and baby forklifts? Pregnancy had addled her brain. What she was, she thought as she drove along the winding, tree-lined road, was a hormone-driven lunatic.

She felt a jab, upward into her diaphragm. Even the baby agreed.

She turned into a driveway marked by a large carved wooden plaque: OAK RIDGE ESTATES ASSISTED LIVING. Mr. Vlaskovic was waiting for her, sitting hunched in a massive wing chair in the lobby, the only man surrounded by a gaggle of women in pastel pantsuits who eyed Ivy with intense interest.

He pushed himself to his feet. Blue veins ran beneath the mottled, nearly transparent flesh on the back of the hand he offered Ivy. His dress shirt and khaki trousers were so stiffly pressed that they could have stood up on their own.

"My dear," he said, giving her hand a strong squeeze. He looked as if he'd once been quite a tall man. Now, in order to look her in the eye, he had to turn his head to the side like an inquisitive stork.

"Come," he said with a courtly bow, and offered Ivy his elbow. She took it, and they strolled off. He glanced back at the seated women, who were nudging one another and whispering, and then he winked at Ivy.

A woman shuffled toward them, pushing a walker, staring intently at her own knuckles. As she passed them, she looked up and her face opened in a smile. "Happy birthday, Paul. This is the big one."

Mr. Vlaskovic smiled and nodded. When they were out of earshot, he muttered, "Silly nonsense, birthdays. She thinks I'm turning eighty. It's really eighty-six. Getting older, *bah*." He held open a door, and Ivy moved past him into a sun-filled courtyard.

He eased himself onto a bench, much the way Ivy's grandmother used to set her prized porcelain teacup on a shelf in the china cabinet.

"I see you are expecting," he said, raising a thin gray eyebrow in the general direction of her stomach. "Any day, by the look of it."

She sat beside him. "I'm due on Thanksgiving," Ivy said, surprising herself by admitting her real due date. Why not? Mr. Vlaskovic wouldn't be pestering her as the time approached.

"Just three weeks." He pursed his lips and shook his head in wonder. "So? To what do I owe the pleasure of this unexpected visit? I distinctly remember selling the house to you *as is,* so I hope you have not come to ask me for a refund."

Ivy laughed. "Nothing like that. We love the house. It's about some things that were left in a wicker trunk that our neighbor had in her garage. She said they belonged to your family?"

"Wicker trunk," Mr. Vlaskovic said, the furrows in his forehead deepening. "I do remember an old trunk that my father's family brought over, but I have no idea what was inside. So now what? She wants to charge rent? You know, Mrs. Bindel drives a hard bargain."

"She certainly does," Ivy said. "Actually, she was going to throw it out, but there were a few things inside"—Ivy opened the bag she'd brought with her—"that I thought might have some sentimental value to you or to other family members." She took out the silver hairbrush, the mirror, the hair receiver, and the leather-bound diary and set them on the bench between them.

Mr. Vlaskovic's fingers hovered over the silver top of the hair receiver.

Ivy pulled out the photograph. She'd taped the halves back together.

"Oh," Mr. Vlaskovic said. He took it from her.

"Is that you?"

"On my father's lap?" He looked at Ivy and back at the photograph. "No, that's my older brother, Stefan. And this"—he poked a gnarled finger at the woman—"I can only presume, must be my mother."

"Presume?"

"We had no pictures of her. This would have been taken just before I was born. In fact, not long before . . ." His voice trailed off.

Ivy examined the photograph more carefully. She had found a dress like that in the wicker trunk. She remembered that it had had no waist, just a tie in the back. The somber woman could easily have been pregnant.

Mr. Vlaskovic barely nodded. "I was born, and then my mother—" He cleared his throat.

He picked up the diary, opened it, and lifted out the lock of hair tied with a blue ribbon. He read the first entry. Then he sat there, holding the lock of hair in his palm and staring into space.

"This dresser set must have been hers," Ivy said.

"That would appear to be the case," he said, though he seemed lost in thought.

"I thought you might want them back. Heirlooms, family history. Something to remember her by."

"Pfff." Mr. Vlaskovic exhaled, shaking himself out of his trance. "Memory is a much-overrated commodity. Spend any significant amount of time in a place like this and you'll see what I mean. Besides, heirlooms require heirs. Family. There is none. I'm the end." He chuckled. "Soon the *dead* end."

He tucked the photograph and the lock of hair into the diary and snapped the book shut. He began to give it back to Ivy, then withdrew his hand.

"Thank you. I think I will keep this." He gave her a thin smile. "With the rest, you're welcome to do whatever you wish."

Ivy returned the mirror and hairbrush and hair receiver to the bag.

Mr. Vlaskovic got to his feet and offered

her his arm. Together they walked back inside.

"By the way," Ivy said, "the other day I ran into someone who knew your family. Melinda White. She said her mother used to work for you?"

"White?" Mr. Vlaskovic slowed, mulling the name. "Can't say as I remember. . . . Or wait—there was a Mrs. White who used to clean for us. But that would have been a very long time ago, twenty-five years at least."

"That sounds about right," Ivy said.

"Twenty-five years." Mr. Vlaskovic worked his lips in and out. "Funny how these days that doesn't seem so very long."

When they reached the lobby, he dropped Ivy's arm and craned his neck to look up at her. "It was very kind of you to come all the way over here to see me. You could have just as easily thrown those things out."

"We did throw out some clothing that we assumed no one would want. And there was . . ." Ivy hesitated, uncertain whether to continue. "There was a straitjacket."

"Ah, yes. That." Mr. Vlaskovic's eyes turned watery. "Something else we never talked about," he said in a low voice that Ivy might not have heard if she hadn't been standing so close.

"Your brother?" Ivy asked, remembering the story the real estate agent had told them.

"Heavens, no. Whatever gave you that idea? More likely my mother. I remember so little, but she was . . . an invalid. Unhappy. Depressed, I suppose, would be the diagnosis today. Back then there was no treatment. Just custodial care, which, fortunately, my father could afford." He shook his head. "He did his best. Hired nurses. Tried to keep her from harming herself.

"And then one day she just vanished. That's how it was in those days. Illness, especially mental illness. Death. They thought it best to move on, not dwell on unpleasantness.

"But, you know, it's actually a very bad thing. My father—" He looked away, without completing the thought. "As a small boy, I was afraid to go up to the attic. I had nightmares about it. I thought she was still up there, waiting for me, waiting to gobble me up. It would have been so much better if they'd just told my brother and me what had happened to her."

He gave Ivy a piercing look. "Secrets can be toxic," he continued. "The truth is rarely as dreadful or as terrifying as what one imagines."

11

So their real estate agent had gotten it wrong, Ivy thought as she drove the winding road back to the highway. The attic bedroom had been finished for Paul Vlaskovic's mother, not his brother. Stories from the past, handed from person to person, often got twisted around like that. Emilia Vlaskovic had written those diary entries when she was pregnant with Stefan, her first child, at the start of what turned out to be a descent into a depression from which she never emerged.

Had she been carted off to an asylum

somewhere? Become ill and died? Committed suicide? Whatever had happened, was it any less dreadful or terrifying than what her young son Paul had imagined?

People didn't just disappear. Or did they? Ivy touched the hollow of her neck where her grandmother's silver amulet should have been hanging.

She swung the car onto the highway. The TV station with its giant satellite dishes mounted on a roof along the side of the road reminded her of the pert commentator who'd delivered her breathless report from their front lawn last night. *A local woman remains missing at this hour.* Ivy turned on the radio, hoping for a news update.

She was at the Brush Hills exit when she remembered the baby shower. Damn. It was already three o'clock. Guests would be arriving.

Ivy accelerated across town, slowing through the speed trap that Brush Hills cops set to snare commuters taking the back way through to the city. She turned onto a side street and into a neighborhood where the horsey set had lived for generations in gracious old homes.

The street sloped down to the broad mouth of the Neponset River. Lower, where there had once been marsh, then farmland, stood a dozen abandoned McMansions in various stages of unfinished. Unable to line up buyers, the developer had run out of money, and construction had come to a dead halt.

Ivy turned at the handsome carved sign with gold embossed letters: ROSE GARDENS AND LANDSCAPING. She continued down a tree-lined dirt road and onto one of the town's few remaining largely undeveloped parcels of land. Officially, David leased the land from his mother, whose family had farmed it back in the 1800s.

David's father had been apoplectic when David dropped out of Boston College in his junior year to start Rose Gardens. He'd done the unthinkable—walked away from a football scholarship. Varsity football had been Mr. Rose's all-consuming dream. Earning an M.B.A. and becoming a business executive were part of his father's vision of David's glorious destiny. What David wanted was to spend as much time as he could outside, working with his hands.

Rose men didn't rake and mow the lawn, his father had fumed. That's what "help" was for. David's parents' retirement and move to Park City, Utah, five years ago had been a relief—for both David and his dad. Now David's parents were on a cruise ship, somewhere far down the coast of South America.

In the beginning, David's office had been a one-room trailer, your basic ventilated tin can. The business specialized in creating environmentally friendly gardens with native, low-maintenance plants and spectacular hunks of granite from local quarries. His sales philosophy: *It's disrespectful to sell people something they don't want and can't maintain.*

Having said that, David hadn't fallen far from the family tree. "Your husband could sell shit to a zookeeper," Rose Gardens' office manager, Lillian Bailiss, had once told Ivy. From a one-man crew, David had grown the business to a staff of four full-timers and a half dozen regular day workers whom he kept busy three seasons a year.

Ivy pulled up to the log house that had a few years ago replaced the trailer. It was divided into an airy showroom with large plate-glass windows in the front and offices in back. A broad, welcoming porch, with wooden rocking chairs on it, stretched across the width of the building.

The parking area out front, bordered by a hitching rail, was full. Ivy recognized the black Camry that belonged to her boss and director of marketing at Mordant Technologies, Naresh Sharma. The red SUV belonged to her co-worker, Patty-Jo Linehan. The black Lexus was Theo's. The acid green VW belonged to Jody. David's truck and his employees' cars would be parked around back.

Ivy checked her face in the rearview mirror and ran her fingers through her hair. The showroom door opened, and David appeared, his hands open in a *Where the heck have you been?* gesture.

There was applause when she entered. Six or seven of her co-workers were there, all dressed for business, along with David's employees in jeans and work shirts. Jody waved from across the room. Moon-faced Riker was perched on her hip, waving a pretzel stick like he was conducting the crowd. Theo, the only one in the room in pinstripes, lounged against the wall.

The aroma of moist loam wafted into the generous, light-filled room from the adjacent greenhouse. Baby gifts were piled in a corner.

Ivy felt a rush of pleasure, seeing all their friends and colleagues, there to wish them both well, and pride at this beautiful space that David had created. Photos of "before and after" landscaping projects covered one wall, and another wall was hung thick with awards and certificates of appreciation from local organizations and charities that David supported.

Lillian Bailiss strode into the room. Tough and sinewy even into her late sixties, Lillian was a force of nature. David considered it the smartest business decision he'd ever made, coaxing her out of retirement. Since then *she'd* coaxed order from chaos, and the Rose Gardens balance sheet had moved steadily deeper into the black.

Lillian's eyes crinkled with pleasure. "Hi, hon." She put a cool hand on Ivy's cheek, and her expression clouded as she looked into Ivy's eyes. "You hanging in there?" Ivy knew she meant more than the pregnancy.

Ivy managed a nod.

A young woman Ivy didn't recognize came over, smiling. "So you're Ivy," she said. Her turned-up nose was sunburned, and her cheeks were the color of a ripe peach. "I've heard so much about you." Her ponytail bounced as she offered her hand. "I'm Cindy Goodwin."

She had a strong grip, and her palms were callused, the nails on her stubby fingers cut short. Work gloves sprouted from the hip pockets of Cindy's low-rise jeans.

"Cindy's our new assistant manager," Lillian said.

Ivy tried to hide her surprise. She knew that David had been looking to hire a second-in-command; she even recalled him telling her that he'd interviewed a woman for the job.

"I-eee!" The shriek got Ivy's attention. She turned to find Jody holding Riker, who was canted forward, reaching his chubby arms out to her.

"Hey, buddy," Ivy said, catching Riker in

her arms. At just a year old, he was a solid, exuberant cherub, all pink cheeks and dimples.

"Hi, sweetie," Jody said. With her tawny curls and plump curves, Jody had always been Ivy's polar opposite. A sprinter, Jody ran fast, short strides, her pumping legs a blur like the cartoon Road Runner. Ivy matched her speed with half as many loping strides. "So who's that?" Jody nodded in Cindy's wake.

"Rose Gardens' new assistant manager," Ivy said.

"Assistant manager? And here I pictured someone in bib overalls, not Cheerleader Barbie. Stomach's like a frickin' board, damn her," Jody said under her breath. Jody hadn't managed to shed the last twenty-five pounds she'd put on carrying Riker.

"What are you two whispering about?" David asked, slipping his arm around Ivy. Grinning like a fool and raising a bottle of champagne overhead, he announced, "To my beautiful wife!"

There was scattered applause.

David put his mouth to Ivy's ear. "Hey, Stretch. I do love you, you know. You and whoever it is that you've got hiding out inside you."

Emotion welled up, and Ivy sniffed back a tear. She handed Riker to Jody and hugged David.

Cindy appeared from an inner office carrying a bunch of pastel-colored helium balloons and a big cellophane-wrapped basket. Attached to the basket was a baby-size baseball cap with the Rose Gardens logo on it. Lillian carried in a sheet cake with white icing and yellow trim.

Theo wheeled over a desk chair, and Ivy sank into it, accepting a proffered glass of bubbly. She took a tiny sip—sparkling apple cider—and leaned back. She let go and allowed her brain to fog with the aromas of peat moss, bark mulch, and sugar frosting.

An hour later Ivy had consumed an embarrassing amount of cheese and crackers, gourmet potato chips, and cake. She opened the presents. The big package from her colleagues at Mordant was an Italian jogging stroller. The label trumpeted its "125-pound capacity." She imagined herself running along pushing Baby Huey.

"Watch out," Naresh said. Though he'd been her boss for four years, they'd collaborated as equals on the architecture of Mordant's Web site. "The kid will expect nothing short of a Porsche after riding around in this chariot." Usually a painfully formal individual, Naresh now wrapped Ivy in a stiff hug. He pulled away and fixed her with a long look, his eyes misting over. "So." She started to choke up, too.

"That stroller," Ivy managed to say. "It's the nicest present ever. Perfect. Who picked it out?"

Naresh beamed at her, then hit his fingertips lightly against his forehead. "Oh, yes. I have another little something for the new father." He fished in his pocket and came up with a small package. He handed it to David.

David held the box to his ear and shook. Whatever was inside rattled like dry beans. "Earplugs?"

"I know. A year's supply of Ambien," Ivy offered. From Naresh's shocked expression, she could tell that she'd guessed.

The room rocked with laughter, and David put up his hand for quiet. "Thank you all so much. You're the best friends—" he began. From outside came the sound of tires on gravel. A car door slammed. "—We could ever have wished for." Then another slam, and another. Heads turned. "And—"

Theo stepped to the window, then moved to the door just in time to intercept Detective Blanchard and three uniformed officers.

12

More cake, champagne, anyone?" Cindy asked. Her voice sounded artificially cheerful and naked in the awkward silence that filled the room as David and Theo talked to the police outside.

Jody stood beside Ivy, her hand on Ivy's arm while Riker whimpered, sensing the unease. Lillian Bailiss stood at the window, looking out. Everyone seemed to be avoiding Ivy's gaze.

Finally David and Theo returned. Detective Blanchard followed them in. He hung in the doorway, taking in the balloons, the mounds of wrinkled gift wrapping, and the remaining cake.

"Hey, everyone. I'm sorry about this," David said. His smile did little to mask the tension in his face. "Thanks to all of you for coming. For the good wishes. And for the wonderful gifts. If all my employees could stay here for a few moments after everyone else leaves, that would be great."

Moments later it felt as if two-thirds of the guests had simply evaporated. Cindy sat curled in a chair, chewing on her thumb and looking very much a little girl. Lillian tore a black garbage bag from a roll and shook it open with a snap. She made an efficient circuit, scooping up wrapping paper and ribbon, plates of half-eaten cake and plastic champagne glasses. The men, David's employees who worked in the nursery and managed crews, stood watching.

David cleared his throat and held up a piece of paper. "This is a search warrant, as I'm sure some of you guessed. The police are investigating the disappearance of a woman who was last seen at a yard sale at our house this weekend."

David gazed out the window for a long moment, a muscle working in his jaw. "I have no idea how long they're going to be. So, everyone, please take the rest of the day off." He held his hands open. "I'm as anxious as anyone else for them to find out what happened to this woman. We need to stay out of these guys' way. They're just doing their jobs."

Encroaching pine trees shadowed the parking area later as David and Theo loaded gifts into the trunk of Ivy's car. When they'd left the showroom, a police officer had been going through desk drawers in David's office. Another was in Lillian Bailiss's office. Ivy could hear the *thock . . . thock . . . thock* of a shovel hitting the pile of bark mulch by the barn.

"I'd really like to stay here," she said.

"It'll be better if you leave us to deal with this," Theo said.

"But this concerns me, too." She looked to David for support, but he was staring down at his feet and grinding a stone into the dirt with his heel.

"If you're not here," Theo said, "then they can't ask you questions and you won't have to refuse to answer. David needs to be here. Rose Gardens is his business."

His life and not hers?

David came around in front of her. He put his hands on her shoulders and pressed his lips against her forehead. "I know it's hard, but I'll be much calmer dealing with this alone, knowing you're somewhere safe."

Somewhere safe—and where exactly was that? Home felt like a fishbowl.

"How long do you think . . . ?" she started. It felt as if one of the stones from the driveway were lodged in the back of her throat.

"Until they're satisfied that there's nothing to find," Theo said.

"But—"

"But nothing," Theo said, opening her car door for her. "The best way you can help right now is by not being here."

Reluctantly, Ivy got into the car. She waved and backed out of the parking spot. Traffic crawled across town. All these people on their way home after a day of work, their major concern whether to eat in or get takeout.

It was dark by the time she pulled onto

Laurel Street. She parked in the driveway, under the porte cochere, and cut the engine. It hadn't occurred to her to leave any lights on. She checked the rearview mirror, the side mirrors, and glanced around uneasily, trying to penetrate the surrounding darkness. She felt watched, even though there were no media vans and no bicyclist with a camera phone waiting for her. The muscles in her back felt as if they were vibrating like violin strings.

She shouldn't have caved. She didn't want to be alone here, wondering what was happening and waiting for David to return.

She took out her cell phone, punched in Jody's number, and listened for the call to connect.

A rap at the glass alongside her head startled her, and it felt as if someone had reached down and pulled her heart into her throat.

At first all Ivy could see were two small beams of light, like sharp eyes staring at her. Then she realized that it was Mrs. Bindel wearing what looked like eyeglass frames with tiny lights mounted at the corners.

Ivy gave a weak wave. She turned off her cell phone and took some deep breaths to slow her heartbeat before she popped the trunk and got out of the car.

"Thought you might need some bucking up," said Mrs. Bindel, holding out a foil-covered plate. "This must be a difficult time." She looked at Ivy, sending the light beams directly into Ivy's face. Ivy shaded her eyes.

"Sorry," Mrs. Bindel said. "Reading lights. Nifty don't you think? I got them on the Internet." She touched a corner of the frames, and the lights switched off, making it seem even darker than before. "Wonderful thing, the Internet."

"It certainly is." Ivy laughed. So much for that old saw that people grew more inflexible with age.

She climbed the steps to the kitchen door and felt for the keyhole. She unlocked the door, opened it, reached in, and turned on the outside light.

"It's terrible. A woman disappears," Mrs. Bindel said in a voice that sounded like dry leaves. "Even in my day that story rarely had a happy ending. The police showed me her picture, but I told them I didn't recognize her."

Ivy returned to the car and pried the box containing the fancy stroller from the trunk. It weighed a ton. When she had one edge of the box on the lip of the trunk, she tugged it forward until the center of gravity shifted and it slid to the ground.

Mrs. Bindel set the plate on the step and helped Ivy drag the box over and prop it against the side of the house. "You'd better leave that for your husband to bring in for you," she said.

Ivy removed the gift basket and shopping bags loaded with other gifts from the trunk. Mrs. Bindel followed her to the kitchen door. Ivy dropped the basket and the bags onto the floor of the mudroom and turned back to Mrs. Bindel.

"You're so kind to bring this." She took the plate and lifted the aluminum foil. Banana smell. "Smells delicious. But you're right. It's a difficult time."

"I'd be glad to stay, if you'd like the company," Mrs. Bindel said.

Only minutes ago Ivy would have jumped at the offer. Now all she wanted was to go inside and be left alone. "Thanks. I appreciate that. I'll be all right. I'm just exhausted."

"If you're sure." Mrs. Bindel hesitated.

"I'm sure."

Mrs. Bindel was turning away when it occurred to Ivy to ask, "Are you absolutely certain that you didn't see the woman they're looking for? She was at the yard sale when you were there."

Mrs. Bindel turned back.

Ivy went on. "She was very pregnant. Talking to me. Holding a green glass swan and a bottle of water."

Mrs. Bindel seemed to grow an inch taller as she took this in. *"That's* the woman they're looking for?"

"The picture they've got is from high school. She's changed quite a bit."

Mrs. Bindel raised her eyebrows, and her wig shifted forward. "You can say that again. You're right, I did see her." Mrs. Bindel gave Ivy a close look that made her feel like an oyster being poked. "Didn't your husband take her inside?"

"He did. And then she left. You didn't happen to see her leaving, did you?"

"The police were particularly interested

in that, too." Mrs. Bindel pondered for a moment, her brow knitted. "Of course, now that I know who they're talking about . . . Still, I'm quite sure I didn't see her leave." She gave Ivy an earnest look. "I'm so sorry, my dear. I was preoccupied, thinking about all the things I needed to get rid of."

"Remember the next day you gave us that wicker trunk, and David put it out at the curb? Did you notice anyone out there, opening it up and looking inside?"

"The police asked me that, too. I told them that everyone and his brother seemed to be stopping by, hoping to find I don't know what—an unsigned van Gogh?"

"I thought *you* were out there at one point," Ivy said.

"I was so astonished. I went out to see if I'd missed something." Her expression was sour. "I hadn't. I thought I saw you out there, too, later that night."

"Me?"

"I happened to look up from my paper. It was dark, but I thought you were out at the curb. Folding and rearranging the things in the trunk."

Before Ivy could argue the point, Mrs.

Bindel touched the frames of her headgear and the lights came back on. "Good night, dear," she said, and started down the driveway and into the dark, until all Ivy could see were two receding beams of light that seemed to float and waver in midair. Then the lights swung around and pointed toward Ivy.

"Tsk, tsk. I couldn't imagine what you were doing out there, all alone in the dark." Mrs. Bindel's voice wafted up the driveway. "And why on earth were you wearing sunglasses in the middle of the night?"

13

Sunglasses! Mrs. Bindel had seen the same woman Ivy had seen. Ivy's moment of elation quickly evaporated. Unfortunately, Mrs. Bindel had taken her for Ivy and probably told the police as much. Now they had an eyewitness who could testify that Ivy had been outside that night, messing around with the contents of the trunk.

Ivy locked the side door and hung her key ring alongside the set of spare keys they kept on a hook in the mudroom. The answering machine on the kitchen counter blinked—more messages than she could count. Reluctantly, Ivy played the first one. "This is Steve Hamlin calling from the *South Shore Times*. . . ." She hit "skip."

She listened to the beginnings of the next three. More reporters. The fourth message began. "Hi—Ivy? It's Frannie Simon. I was so sorry to hear about what's happening—" The woman went on, and Ivy had no idea who she was until she said, "See you at the fitness center." Ivy cut the message off. Frannie Simon had never, ever called Ivy before.

Go away! Go away, everyone!

Ivy skipped quickly through the rest of the messages. More reporters. More acquaintances calling to get their curiosity satisfied. The Roses had turned into a sideshow, and knowing them would pass for social currency.

Just as she hit "skip" a final time, the phone rang. Ivy jumped back.

It rang, then rang again. Her answering machine picked up.

"Sorry no one can come to the phone," Ivy's recorded voice told the caller. "Leave a message, and we'll get right back to you." She cringed. She most certainly would not be getting back to any of them.

Beep.

She waited for the caller to say something. There was a click, and the machine turned off.

Ivy stared at the phone, daring it to ring again. When it didn't, she deleted all the messages and recorded a new greeting. In a brusque, formal voice, she announced, "There's no one here to take your call." And left it at that.

Satisfied, she hung up the phone.

Ivy walked through the dining room and continued to the entry hall, turning on lights as she went. Gazing up the grand staircase, she felt like Alice after she'd eaten the shrinking half of the mushroom, or perhaps it was the house that had expanded around her.

"What are you staring at?" Ivy asked the bronze statue, Bessie, who seemed to be eyeing her reproachfully from the newel post.

Ivy picked up the pile of mail that had come through the slot in the front door. She threw out business cards and handwritten notes from reporters, then carried the rest of the mail into the living room.

Yesterday's newspaper was on the

couch, along with the crossword puzzle David had been working on. She raised the lid of the window seat and tossed them inside.

She was cold again. She pulled the curtains closed and grabbed the crocheted afghan, wrapped it around her, and sat on the window seat, staring down at the unopened mail in her lap.

A wall of sound, that was what she needed. Ivy got up and switched on the stereo. She turned up the volume and let Radiohead's ethereal keyboard melodies, their fuzzes and hums of liquid percussion, fill her head.

Eight o'clock. David hadn't come home. She called his cell phone and got no answer. Voice mail picked up at Rose Gardens.

She went up to her office and checked the *Boston Globe* and Channel 7 Web sites for local breaking news. There was none. She opened her e-mail. Just a message from Jody. Had Ivy gotten home okay? Ivy e-mailed back that she had.

Ivy went downstairs to the kitchen and warmed a slice of leftover pizza. She ate it and tried not to think about what might be holding up David.

At nine o'clock she tried calling him again.

Ten o'clock. She found herself sitting on the edge of a chair in the kitchen, the crocheted afghan still wrapped around her, jittery and alert to the house's every sound. The whoosh of each car that drove by seemed to slither down her spine.

The baby poked what had to be a foot up into her ribs. Ivy put her fingers there and gently pressed back. *Hi there, Sprout. You stay right where you are. We'll get this all sorted out, don't you worry.*

At last Ivy heard the rumble of David's truck engine. She jumped to her feet. A minute later there was the sound of the key in the lock. The side door opened, and David came into the kitchen, carrying the box containing the fancy stroller. He dropped it in a corner.

"Where were you? I tried calling," Ivy said, and immediately wished she hadn't. It sounded like an accusation.

David didn't seem to notice. He un-zipped his jacket, shrugged it off, and threw it over a kitchen chair. He shucked his work boots and kicked them into a corner, then slid his wallet from his back pocket and flipped it onto the kitchen counter.

He smelled of whiskey. He'd probably helped himself to the bottle of Jack Daniel's he kept in his desk. She could hardly blame him. He opened the refrigerator, pulled out a beer.

"Hungry?" she asked. "There's another slice of pizza. Or we can order Chinese. Mrs. Bindel brought over banana bread."

David sank down on a stool. He twisted off the bottle cap, tipped back his head, and drank. He closed his eyes for a few moments, then opened them and stared off into space.

"So?" she asked. "What happened?"

"Paper bags." He smacked the beer bottle down on the counter. "They searched everywhere and took stuff away in goddamned paper grocery bags."

"What . . . stuff?"

"They didn't run that past me. Theo said they'll let him know and then he'll let me know."

"When?"

"Later."

"When later?"

"How the hell should I know?" David kneaded his fist in his hand. Finally he looked over at her. "Hey, I'm sorry. This is my first time being suspected of murder."

Murder? Tears stung at Ivy's eyes as she stared down at him.

Without a word David reached for her and drew her into his embrace, resting his head on her belly. She could feel him shaking, trying to stay in control.

"They think—" His voice broke off. He cleared his throat and looked up at her. "They think I had something to do with Melinda's disappearance."

"We both know that's ridiculous."

"What if they found something?"

"What's to find?"

"Hell, I don't know," David said. "We didn't think they'd find anything in that old trunk, and they did. And it's not as if the police paid much attention to following up on the people you saw out there who could have planted those clothes."

"David, you remember that woman I saw? Mrs. Bindel saw her, too. She thought it was me."

David pulled away. "That's what she told the police?" He groaned. "Great, now they think I have an accomplice—my own wife."

"Can they really think we'd be that stupid? Stash bloody clothing in a trunk and then set it out at the curb with a Help Yourself sign planted beside it? Brilliant plan. If I wanted to get rid of evidence like that, I'd burn it, or bury it, or bag it and dump it in a trash bin at a rest stop out on I-95. Or better yet wash and fold it away neatly in my bureau with my own clothes. I'd put it in that wicker trunk only if I . . ." The thought chilled her.

"Right," David said. "You'd only have done that if you *wanted* the police to find it."

14

The next morning, after David left for work, Ivy called a locksmith. She watched as the polite young man with tattoos, like translucent sleeves running up his arms, drilled holes in the hundred-year-old oak front door. The shiny brass around the new keyhole was a further desecration.

Dead bolts for the front and side doors? It was ridiculous. The locks they had were perfectly functional. But with her life spinning out of control, Ivy had to do something to shore up her borders.

The locksmith left her two keys. One she attached to her key ring, the duplicate she hung on the hook in the mudroom by the side door for David. She'd get one more copy made as a backup.

Keep busy. Try not to think. Those were pretty much the sum total of her plans for the day. As she locked up the house, the sounds of the new tumblers falling into place and the brass bolts sliding home were comforting.

First she headed to the grocery store to pick up milk, toilet paper, and the ingredients she needed to make batches of Thai chicken and chili. She'd freeze dinner-size servings for after the baby came.

At midday the store was quiet, not the rush she was used to after work or on the weekend. She was in and out in under a half hour. She stopped at the library to return a book on CD—a Ruth Rendell mystery that had accompanied her commute.

On the way home, she stopped in Brush Hills Square, a stretch of squat, granite-faced, two-story commercial buildings, to get a spare key made at Three Brothers Hardware. The store had changed hands but kept its name after the last of the original "three brothers" retired years ago. She hadn't been in there in eons, not since Home Depot had opened barely a mile away.

She parked at a meter and was pumping in a quarter when she noticed a police cruiser. It pulled up alongside her and crawled past. Ivy felt her cheeks grow warm. Was she being followed? Couldn't she run an errand without being harassed?

She hurried past the doorway to a defunct bowling alley in the basement of the building. A bell tinkled overhead as she entered the hardware store.

Through the store's plate-glass window, she saw where the cruiser had pulled in to the loading zone near the corner. Police monitored traffic all the time from there, she told herself, waiting for someone to run the light.

She dragged her attention away. The store, a throwback to the days when local hardware stores doubled as general stores, smelled of sawdust, sweat, and turpentine. There were narrow aisles with housewares—mixing bowls and kitchen utensils and dish towels—alongside weed whackers and paint supplies. Roofing nails, still sold by the pound, filled a barrel under a metal hanging scale.

A gray-haired man emerged from the back and settled himself on a stool behind a battered linoleum-topped counter. His face was pale and speckled, like the underside of a flounder. His gaze dropped to her belly.

Ivy offered the key. "Please, I need a copy of this."

He took it from her and examined it. "Was there a problem . . . ?" He looked up at her. Blinked. "Oh. Sorry. I thought . . ." He rubbed his grizzled chin, shook his head, and shrugged. "Sure thing. Take a minute."

Ivy was still pondering the clerk's apparent confusion later when she pulled out of her parking spot. The police cruiser was gone. She was halfway home when she noticed a large sedan with a tinted windshield that filled her rearview mirror.

She turned right. The sedan followed. Left. It was still on her tail. When she pulled into her own driveway, the sedan pulled in behind her. A car door slammed. In her side mirror, she saw Detective Blanchard striding toward her.

Ivy's heart raced as she sat gripping the steering wheel. She felt hemmed in, trapped as her thoughts spun forward. Was there a new development? Was he arresting her?

Thock. She engaged the automatic door lock. She got out her cell phone. Fingers trembling, she called David's office.

Lillian Bailiss answered. "Guess he's not here," she told Ivy after she checked David's office and then paged him. "He left for lunch at eleven-thirty. It's not like him to be gone for more than an hour without checking in. I'm sorry. I don't know what to tell you. You try his cell?"

Detective Blanchard stood at the driver's-side window, relaxed, a genial smile on his face. He stiffened when he saw Ivy talking on her phone.

Ivy called David's cell phone. After a single ring, her call went to voice mail. She left a short, semihysterical SOS.

Blanchard was now leaning against the hood of her car, whistling and picking his nails.

She called Theo. He wasn't in his office. Where the hell was everyone?

Theo's assistant gave her the number of his cell phone. Theo picked up after one ring.

"What does he want? He's not threatening you with anything, is he?" Theo asked.

"He hasn't said anything at all. He's just standing there, waiting for me to get out of the car. I don't know anything. How many different ways can I say that?" Ivy could hear hysteria rising in her voice.

Detective Blanchard watched her through the windshield. Ivy's heart pounded, and blood thrummed in her ears.

"Stay calm. You with me?" Theo said.

"I'm with you," Ivy whispered through gritted teeth.

"Take a deep breath," Theo said. "Get out of the car and hear what he has to say. Don't hang up, okay? Keep me on the line."

"Okay." Clutching the cell phone, Ivy opened the car door.

Blanchard sprang to attention and held the door open for her. Ivy peeled her sweat-drenched back from the seat and got out. She ignored the hand he offered.

"Mrs. Rose, I'm here to take you in for questioning," Blanchard said.

"Ask him if you're under arrest," Theo said in her ear.

"Am I under arrest?"

"Just want to ask a few questions. You don't mind coming with me, do you?"

"I heard that," Theo said. "Okay, go with him. But don't say anything unless I'm with you. Don't answer any questions. Remember, you've done nothing wrong. I'll meet you there."

Detective Blanchard let her unload the groceries, even offered to help. Waited while she locked up the house again.

Ivy rode to the police station in the back of the Crown Vic, buffered from the world by tinted glass. Through the square and on past blocks and blocks of suburban homes, she had the odd sensation that the car was stationary and that houses and trees were being pulled past like panoramas painted on sheets hung from a clothesline.

The car turned into the long driveway leading to the police station—a sprawling white-shingled building that looked like a country club. She'd often driven past but never gone inside.

Blanchard continued past a Do Not Enter sign and pulled up behind the building at a multi-bay attached garage, parked the car, and got out. Ivy groped for a door handle but found none. No window control either.

She willed herself to sit back as the garage door slid open to reveal a mundane interior, much larger but otherwise no different from the average garage. Blanchard got out. He stooped, his face close to the glass, and looked in at her.

This time when he opened the car door, he didn't offer her a hand. Didn't say a word.

Ivy got out and let herself be herded into the garage. A sign on the door to the building read CAUTION: DOOR LOCKS AUTOMATICALLY.

Blanchard pressed an intercom button. There was a whirring from overhead. Ivy glanced up. Two cameras swiveled toward them, and a moment later the door clicked open. Blanchard followed her in. With a thud, followed by a loud clank, the door closed behind them.

The first thing Ivy noticed was the smell—pine cleaner, sweat, and shit. She gagged and then swallowed bile that backed up in her throat. She could feel Detective Blanchard behind her, not pressing, allowing her to take in her surroundings.

There were no windows, just an anonymous, monochromatic space with whitewashed cinder-block walls and cement floors. Below a gray countertop, two pairs of handcuffs dangled from foot-long chains bolted to the wall. That had to be where they booked prisoners.

Ivy's vision seemed preternaturally clear, so much so that a pair of men's sneakers and a pair of muddy brown work boots in the corner seemed outlined, as if she could Photoshop them out of the scene.

Blanchard came around to the opposite side of the counter. "You have the right to remain silent and refuse to answer questions." He adjusted a video monitor at elbow level beside him. Her face was on the screen, the angle from above. She found the camera mounted on the wall, just over Blanchard's shoulder.

"Do you understand?"

"I thought you said you weren't arresting me?"

"I'm not."

"Then why—" she began. But Blanchard continued, intoning the familiar Miranda warning she'd heard a trillion times on TV and waiting for her to respond after each piece of it.

Remember, you've done nothing wrong—Theo's words and the knowledge that she was not under arrest did little to reassure her.

Finally: "Knowing and understanding your rights as I have explained them to you, are you willing to answer my questions without an attorney present?"

Ivy took a breath. "No."

"You'll wait for Mr. Spyridis?"

Ivy nodded.

"That's fine. He's already here. With your husband."

"With my . . . ?"

"We brought your husband in for questioning a few hours ago."

Ivy knees started to buckle. *Hours ago?* Why hadn't David called to tell her? Why hadn't Theo said he was with David at the police station?

Ivy glanced at the disembodied work boots. Those were David's. She slid over to an open doorway and peered in at what looked like a bank of holding cells. The two that she could see into were empty.

"You know, in my experience"— Blanchard had shifted to his "Uncle Bill" tone of voice—"it's not always wise for a husband and wife to share the same attorney. There can be a conflict of interest, if you know what I mean." He chewed his lower lip.

"Please just let Mr. Spyridis know I'm here," Ivy said, choosing her words carefully, making sure she spoke in a complete sentence and gave the impression at least that she wasn't the slightest bit freaked out by what was happening. "I'd like to get this over with as quickly as possible."

15

Ivy followed Detective Blanchard up a flight of stairs, down a hallway, and to a door at the end. She wondered if David was behind any of the closed doors they passed.

He opened the door and ushered her in.

Ivy had expected to find herself in some kind of an interrogation room, but this seemed to be Detective Blanchard's office—assuming that the pleasant-looking older woman whose framed photo was on the desk was his wife and the young man in a military uniform was his son.

Blanchard sat behind the desk. Ivy perched on the edge of a straight-backed wooden chair across from him. He glanced at the phone on his desk. Its red light was on.

The office was comfortably furnished, with a curtained window overlooking the parking lot. The desk blotter was bare. Bookshelves lined one wall, and on the opposite wall was a large mirror. Beside that was a framed diploma from Suffolk University, 1970. Albert—that was Blanchard's first name.

Sweat beaded on Ivy's upper lip and forehead. She took off her jacket and draped it over the back of her chair. It occurred to her that the warmth in the room might be deliberate.

"I thought you told me my attorney was here?" she said.

"He is. I'll go see what's holding him up."

He went out, leaving the door open behind him. Ivy heard his departing footsteps. Then, from down the hall, a knock.

"Where is she?" It was David's voice. "I want to see my wife."

Ivy stepped to the door and peered into

the hall just in time to see Blanchard disappear into the adjacent room. She could
hear voices, but the words were indistinct.

She hesitated for a moment. He hadn't
ordered her to stay put. She slipped into
the hallway. He'd left the door ajar to the
room he'd entered. She approached it.

"You bastards." David's voice again, hot
and angry. "Can they do this?"

She heard a low voice next, probably
Theo's. Then a woman's voice.

Through the door opening, Ivy could
see a room, approximately the same size
as the one she'd just left. It was dimly lit.
She pressed closer, taking in the details in
a rush: unadorned walls, a table covered
with papers and manila folders along with
a phone and a tape recorder, a half dozen
chairs.

The woman was young, wearing a dark
pantsuit. Not a uniform. David and Theo
were huddled together at the table, deep in
a heated discussion, unaware of Ivy's presence. Officer Fournier, the tall cop who'd
questioned them about the trunk outside
their house, leaned against the wall.

What brought her up short was the glass
panel on the wall—it was a window through

which she could see a desk and a chair with her jacket draped over the back. One-way glass.

The woman spoke. "Detective Blanchard is going to interrogate your wife with her attorney present. You're welcome to stay and watch. Or if you prefer, we can take you to a holding cell." Ivy realized she was probably the D.A.

They were going to observe her being questioned without telling her?

"David," Theo said in a low voice that Ivy was just able to make out, "I'd advise you, in the strongest possible terms, it's not in your best interest to stay. Let me take care of this. You have to trust me on this."

"It's not that I don't trust you. I need to be here for Ivy."

"But you won't be. You'll be in here where you can't do her any good. And I can't be in here advising you and in there advising her at the same time."

Ivy caught the eye roll Detective Blanchard directed at the woman.

Theo and David continued to argue, oblivious to her presence. Theo's exasperation grew as David became more and more adamant.

"Mrs. Rose," Blanchard said in a strong voice. "I thought I asked you to wait in my office."

David turned. When he saw her, his face filled with dismay. Then his look hardened as he shifted his gaze to Detective Blanchard. "You sons of bitches," he said.

Blanchard and the woman exchanged knowing looks, and Ivy realized that they'd intended to lure her from the office next door, wanted her to overhear David facing this difficult choice. They'd wanted her to discover that she'd be watched while she was questioned. They were taking advantage of the fact that she and David shared the same attorney, and Ivy had played right into their hands.

Divide and conquer, pit husband against wife—it was a tried-and-true winning strategy.

Feeling like a passenger on a runaway train, Ivy let Blanchard propel her back to the office next door. She sat at the desk, her fingers knitted together, kneading one thumb over the other.

A minute later Theo entered the room. He'd recovered his usual patina of confidence.

"The speakerphone," Theo said, indicating the phone on the desk. He turned to Blanchard. "Could you turn it off, please, while I confer with my client?"

Blanchard punched a button, and the red light went out.

"Five minutes," Blanchard said, and left the room.

Ivy felt sick. This couldn't be happening. "David?" she asked.

Theo tipped his head in the direction of the room next door. "He's there. Watching. I couldn't convince him not to."

Ivy stood and looked at her own reflection in the mirror. She walked around the desk and put her face close to the glass, pressing her palms hard against it. She hoped David was on the other side, doing the same.

"Ivy." Theo's voice was low and sharp. "We need to talk."

He turned her chair so her back would be to the mirror. She sat, and he pulled another chair beside her.

He covered his mouth with his hand. "It's very important that you take your cues from me. Understood?" Ivy forced herself to nod. "These guys don't have a clue what happened to Melinda White," Theo went on, his voice a harsh whisper. "Right now all they have is some clothing and blood evidence. If they had a case, they'd be going for an indictment. They're not. They're fishing."

"Fishing." Ivy repeated the word.

"You haven't been arrested, and neither has David. But if they find the smallest chink, believe me, they'll exploit it. They're going to try to manipulate you, to manipulate the facts. It's not going to be easy. These guys are smart. They know just where to stick it and how to twist it."

Ivy felt numb. She had to force herself to concentrate on Theo's words.

"They're going to ask you questions. They'll tape-record what you say, and the D.A. is going to be on the other side of the one-way glass, listening and observing along with David. Whatever happens, check with me before you say anything. Then stick to the facts. Don't speculate. Don't offer information that hasn't been asked for. Understood?"

"I think so."

"I need you to be sure." He reached over and squeezed her hand. "Can you do this?"

Ivy nodded.

A few moments later, there was a tap at the door, and Blanchard returned. He sat in the desk chair and pressed a button on the phone. The red light came back on. Next he opened a drawer, pulled out a small tape recorder. He clicked in a fresh tape and turned on the machine.

He began, "Detective Sergeant Albert Blanchard, Brush Hills Police, Wednesday, November fifth . . ."

The first questions were innocuous enough. Ivy's name. Her age. Where had she grown up? How long had she and David been married? How long had they lived in the house? As Ivy provided the answers, it felt as if none if this were real, as if the room were a stage set and Ivy were reading lines that Theo had composed for her.

Were there problems in their marriage? Theo nodded to answer that one, too. Ivy gave a firm "None."

Blanchard moved on to Ivy and David's

relationship with their neighbors. Finally, how well had she known Melinda White?

Ivy told him they'd grown up in the same town, gone to school together but never been friendly.

"So when had you seen her last, before your yard sale?"

Theo's look gave her permission to answer. "I honestly don't remember seeing her, not since we graduated high school."

"Melinda White didn't graduate," Blanchard said. "She dropped out in her senior year."

"I didn't know that," Ivy said.

"Completed her final semester and got a GED a year later," Blanchard said, throwing out the information as if it were inconsequential.

He went on. "Mrs. Rose, could you tell me what happened Saturday, the first of November, and your interactions that morning with the vic—with Melinda White?"

Theo hesitated, then nodded. Ivy told, in as much detail as she could muster. Blanchard took an occasional note but didn't seem to be listening.

"We've questioned your neighbors and

quite a few others who were at your yard sale, and although we can find people who say they saw Ms. White go into your home with your husband, not a single person has come forward who saw her come out. Can you explain that?"

Ivy was about to answer when she caught Theo's head shake. *Don't speculate.*

Blanchard continued. "If we could find even a single person to corroborate your story that Melinda left your house that morning, then we'd be pursuing other avenues. So I guess it boils down to your word . . . against everyone else's."

Ivy couldn't stop herself. "She arrived. She left. That's all I know."

Blanchard shrugged. Then he started in on the wicker trunk. Ivy told him that it had come from Mrs. Bindel's garage. She enumerated what they'd found inside.

"Before you left the trunk out at the curb, did you or your husband put anything into it that hadn't been there when you opened it up?"

Ivy didn't wait for Theo's nod. "No. We just put things back."

"*After* you put the trunk out at the curb, did you put anything more into it?"

"No!"

Theo cleared his throat, a subtle rebuke. *Stay calm.*

Blanchard leaned back and contemplated Ivy. "Mrs. Rose, we have a reliable witness who saw you outside later that night, alone, placing something in that trunk."

There it was. Ivy had known that it would be coming, but still she felt blind-sided. "That wasn't me. You're making it sound—"

Theo's emphatic "Ivy!" shut her up.

Blanchard went on. "This witness will testify that you and your husband dragged the trunk out to the curb Sunday after-noon. That you left it there. And that, at around ten o'clock that night, you went outside, opened that trunk, and—"

"That's enough," Theo said, cutting him off. "Mrs. Rose has answered your ques-tion. Move on to something else."

Blanchard reached into his desk drawer and brought out a manila folder. "It doesn't matter, really. We have an overwhelming amount of evidence."

He pulled out a photograph and set it on the desk in front of Ivy. It was a picture of the blue and yellow flowered maternity blouse and a pair of denim jeans. "This top and these pants were found in the trunk in front of your home. Those stains are human blood, and the blood type matches Melinda White's."

Ivy didn't need Theo's frown to know not to respond.

Blanchard set down another photo—the glass swan head. "You know about this. We found more glass fragments in a vacuum-cleaner bag in your garbage. I wonder what the jury will say when we tell them you were vacuuming your attic *after* the victim disappeared. Or that we found the vacuum-cleaner bag slit open and the insides picked through."

Theo was acting relaxed, unimpressed, as if all this circumstantial evidence proved nothing. But Ivy's heart raced as Blanchard droned on, outlining the evidence the way a prosecuting attorney would to a jury. She could see how damaging it all sounded.

"You know what we found yesterday when we searched the premises of your husband's business?" He flipped over another photograph. It was a white canvas bag, just like the one Melinda White had been carrying at the yard sale. Sitting on top of it was a wood-handled knife with a long, straight-edged blade that tapered to a point. Ivy winced and looked away.

"Recognize these items? We found them in a Dumpster behind the barn at Rose Gardens. What if I told you that the fingerprints on the handle are yours?"

Ivy's gaze was drawn back to the photograph. She had a set of knives in a wooden block on her kitchen counter. One of them was just like that one in the picture. If the knife in the picture were hers, from her kitchen, then it stood to reason that her prints would be on the handle. David's, too.

"Would it surprise you that we found traces of human blood on this knife?" Blanchard's mouth was set in a grim, satisfied line. "We also found traces of blood in your husband's truck. What would you say if I told you that the DNA from this blood evidence matches the DNA from the toothbrush we collected from Ms. White's apartment?"

DNA evidence? Now she knew he was lying. The knife had been collected only yesterday afternoon. There hadn't been time to do a DNA analysis. And if Melinda's blood were on it, then someone else had put it there and then hidden the knife at Rose Gardens, where they knew the police would go looking.

"Who suggested that you conduct that search?" Ivy said. "That's who you should be questioning. That's who planted all this so-called evidence for you to find."

"So-called evidence?" Blanchard gave her a pitying look. "We also found a few interesting items when we searched Ms. White's apartment." He dropped an evidence bag on the table. "Recognize him?"

Through the plastic, Ivy could see a candid snapshot, a close-up of David.

"We found this, stuck to the door of her refrigerator. It's the same photograph Melinda's co-workers at Neponset Hospital say Melinda showed them last year, before she quit her job there. She showed this same picture to colleagues at SoBo Realty. She told them all that this was her fiancé."

No. It was just a photograph. Ivy dug

her thumbnail into her palm. Could have
been taken by anyone. There'd been no
relationship. There couldn't have been.

"When did you realize that your husband was having an affair?" Blanchard
asked, his eyes drilling into hers.

He pushed the photograph closer to Ivy
and lowered his voice. "Melinda White has
a sister. She has a mother. You can imagine how painful it is for them, not knowing
what happened to her."

Ivy didn't feel it coming in time to stop
the sob as her insides wrenched.

"Imagine how you'd feel in their place if
your child, the one you're carrying, were to
disappear. Vanish into thin air." Blanchard
kept at it, relentless. "If you know anything
that will help them come to terms with this,
please, now is the time to speak up."

Ivy hunched her shoulders and turned
away from the one-way glass. She didn't
want David to see her anguish.

Blanchard tapped a pencil on the table
and waited.

"Oh, and we do have one more thing."
He reached into his desk drawer and
pulled out another cassette recorder. He
set it on the table between them. "This is

the message we found on Melinda White's answering machine in her apartment. I think you'll find it interesting. We did."

He clicked it on. An electronic voice announced, "Saturday, November first, 6:05 P.M." A beep. Then, "Melin—Mindy? Are you there?" It was David's voice. "Please, pick up if you're there." There was a long pause. "Shit. You're not there. We need to talk. I'm sorry about what happened. Really I am. I didn't realize. . . . I didn't remember. . . . I know that must seem insane to you, but . . . Can we at least talk? I don't want to leave things like this."

The phone on the desk rang. A single ring, then silence. It resonated in the air like the round-ending bell of a prizefight.

Blanchard let it ring once more before he picked up the receiver. He listened, poker-faced, then hung up, got to his feet, and fixed Theo with a placid look. "I believe your *other* client has a confession to make."

16

Ivy watched in stunned silence as Theo jumped to his feet and left the room with Blanchard hard on his heels. Ivy stumbled after them and hung in the doorway, watching them argue in the hall.

"None of this will hold up in court," Theo said. "What you're doing here amounts to coercion. Without access to counsel. There's no excuse for—"

"Spare me," Blanchard shot back. "It was Mr. Rose's choice to stay and watch."

"Choice? Bullshit. Whatever he's said, it's inadmissible in court. Any judge would agree. It's my job to protect my clients, and you've made that impossible—"

"If you'd been doing your job, Counselor, you'd have advised your clients to get separate attorneys. There's an inherent conflict of interest here, and you know it."

Ivy pushed past them and into the room next door. David sat, his head in his hands. She knelt on the floor beside him.

"What are you doing?" she asked.

He looked at her, exhausted and drained. "I'm sorry. It was a mistake. I—"

"David!" Theo said from the doorway. "Stop talking."

"I can't do that," David said. "I keep quiet and they make my wife look like a murderer. I'm going to tell the truth, and to hell with it. It's all I've got." David squeezed Ivy's hand. "I'm so sorry," he whispered.

Ivy felt herself go cold.

David straightened and addressed Detective Blanchard. "Yes, I put the canvas bag and the knife in the Dumpster. I found them in the back of my truck yesterday when I got to work. I swear, I didn't put them there."

"In your truck," Blanchard said.

"In the back, under a plastic tarp."

Blanchard got up and exchanged a few words with Officer Fournier. Fournier left the room.

"I know that it sounds insane," David went on, "but I can't help it. I recognized the bag. I realized that my having it made it look like I had something to do with Melinda's disappearance. I didn't know there was a knife inside, because I didn't open it up to look. I just wanted to get rid of it."

"David," Theo said, shaking his head, his shoulders sagging in surrender.

"I know, I know, I should have called the police. But I panicked. I just wanted to make it all go away. And the truth is, I have no idea when Melinda left our house," David said, his voice flat, his face expressionless. "That's because I never saw her leave."

The woman D.A. shot Blanchard a surprised look.

"I took her inside," David went on, "showed her the house, just like I said. But when we got to the attic, she started going on about how unhappy she'd been as a kid. It was as if being there, in that house again, flipped a switch, and she lost it. She smashed the glass swan, threw it against the wall.

"I just watched. There was nothing else I could do. She asked me if I'd leave her alone, give her some privacy and some time to calm down. When I went back later, she was gone."

"How much later?" Blanchard asked.

"Maybe ten minutes. I just assumed she'd let herself out. That's why I called her, later that night. I wanted to check that she was all right."

"So you're saying Melinda White let *herself* out?" Blanchard said, his voice ringing with skepticism. "That the last time you saw her, she was in your attic, alive and well?"

"And distraught. But yes, alive and well. That's the truth. Why would I call and leave her a message if I knew she'd disappeared?"

"Good question," Blanchard said. "Here's what I think. I think you called her and left that message because you wanted to make it look as if you believed she was still alive when you knew full well that she was not."

"David Rose, you're under arrest for tampering with physical evidence. . . ." The words still rang in Ivy's head as Theo drove her home. They'd left the police station by the back exit and slipped away unnoticed through media vans assembled for a hastily called press conference.

In the moment that the police gave them before taking David away, he'd kissed Ivy hard on the mouth. "I don't know what I'd do if I lost you." He pressed his face into her hair. "I didn't hurt her. I didn't touch her. I didn't even know her. Ivy, you have to believe me."

Believe you? With each version of what happened, more of what Ivy believed had eroded.

Theo drove fast, tailgating slower drivers, accelerating through yellow lights, barely slowing at stop signs. Tires squealed as he rounded a corner, and a small silver cross swung erratically from a chain that had been looped around the rearview mirror. There were Greek letters on it—she recognized the circle with a line through it, phi.

"There'll be a hearing tomorrow morning. We'll post bail. Don't worry, David will be home by tomorrow afternoon." Arrogant. Reassuring. It was what Ivy wanted to hear.

She reached out and steadied herself against the dashboard as the car jerked to a halt at a stoplight.

"I'll call you as soon as I know anything," he said, then went on to admonish her against talking to reporters, or neighbors, or even to friends about the details of what was going on.

Ivy nodded as if she were listening, his words sliding by like quicksilver.

The light changed, and Theo sped off. "As your attorney . . ." he droned on. Ivy watched Theo as he talked, smacking the heel of his hand against the steering wheel for emphasis and swerving through traffic.

Maybe she'd been too quick to dismiss Detective Blanchard's suggestion that she retain her own lawyer. The bond of friendship was between Theo and David, forged over decades of shared adventures. Then again, was it a good thing to have such a close friend as your attorney? Maybe *David* needed someone else, someone with more emotional distance and more experience in criminal law to represent him.

It was nearly dark when Theo turned the corner onto Laurel Street.

"Uh-oh," he said.

Ivy felt sick to her stomach when she saw the vehicles parked up and down the block. A camera crew was setting up on the sidewalk out front.

"Don't pull up in front of the house," she said. "There'll be a feeding frenzy. I'll get out here."

Theo stopped the car. The chain and cross suspended from the rearview mirror ticked back and forth like a metronome. Ivy watched her hand reach for the door.

"Hang in there." Theo touched her shoulder. "Remember, they have no murder victim, no body, and no witnesses. You and David both have spotless records. No history with Melinda White. There are plenty of alternative scenarios."

Was he trying to convince her or himself?

Theo went on. "You guys are the victims here. Everything they've found can be explained. We won't have any difficulty creating reasonable doubt in the minds of a jury."

A jury? But David had been arrested only for evidence tampering.

"It's rotten luck that your house happens to be where this woman is last seen before she vanishes. Or maybe it's not about luck at all. What I want you to think about is who's holding a grudge? Who's got it in for you and David? Because evidence like this doesn't just pile up by itself.

"But here's what I don't get. If someone's trying to frame David, then why hide the body? Why not give the police what they need to charge him with murder?"

17

Ivy walked up the block to her house in the half-light of dusk. It was hard to be invisible when you were nine months pregnant, but she managed to slip up the side of Mrs. Bindel's house and cut through the backyards without being spotted.

In the shadow of the porte cochere, it took a few tries to insert the new key. She'd just managed to get the door open when the side of the house was bathed with an instant of hot, white light. Then a second blinding flash. Ivy felt herself rushed from behind.

"Mrs. Rose, what's your reaction to your

husband's being arrested for murder?" a man shouted.

Microphones thrust forward.

"What can you tell us about the evidence investigators recovered from Rose Gardens?" A woman's voice.

"Were you friends with Melinda White?"

Ivy managed to wedge herself through the door, slam it shut, and lock it from the inside. She stood in the shadowy mudroom, panting and trembling. She could still hear the voices outside. These people were trying to burrow in through the walls of her home, into the pores of her skin.

This was *her* home, where she was supposed to feel safe, where she was supposed to be able to walk around stark naked if she wanted to, or yell like a shrew and break dishes with impunity.

There was a sharp rap at the door, and the doorbell chimed. Ivy clapped her hands over her ears and ran through the kitchen. She moved through the downstairs as rapidly as she could, pulling the curtains and blinds or shades in every window.

She returned to the kitchen. There was David's favorite coffee mug, still on the kitchen table. She picked it up and started to carry it to the sink. That's when she noticed that the knife block had been pulled forward from its usual spot at the back of the kitchen counter. She didn't remember leaving it there.

The carving knife—the one that looked like the one the police had found in the white canvas bag in the Dumpster at Rose Gardens—was missing.

From outside came a woman's voice: ". . . missing since Saturday . . ."

Ivy hurled David's cup against the wall. It shattered, leaving a brown splatter. She backed up until she hit the wall. Her feet seemed to go out from under her, and she slid to the floor, landing hard.

The baby!

The phone rang. Let it.

Ivy couldn't risk hurting the baby. Not now. She put her hands on her belly, ignoring the pain that reverberated from her tailbone up her spine. Her water hadn't broken. She wasn't bleeding.

The phone rang again. The baby's sharp kick, upward into her lowest rib, was reassuring.

The phone rang a third time. Probably

one of those vultures outside. Or it could
be Theo, checking that she'd gotten inside
in one piece.

Ivy got to her knees. The answering machine clicked on, and there was her own
voice, telling the world to go away. *Beep.*

"Phooey. Where the hell are you?"
Jody's voice echoed from the machine.

Ivy struggled to her feet and grabbed
the receiver. "Jody!"

"Thank God," Jody said. "I've been leaving you messages all day. You were supposed to call me. Remember? I stopped
by, and your neighbor told me you'd been
arrested." In the background Ivy could hear
Riker squealing.

"Not arrested. They took me in for questioning. David's the one who's been arrested."

"For what?"

"Tampering with evidence."

"You're home alone?"

"Alone? I wish. There are a million reporters outside."

"Do you want to come here? Of course
you do. I'll come get you."

Out of pure reflex, Ivy started to say, *I'm
okay.* But Jody got in first with, "Pack a

bag. Now. I'll be there in fifteen minutes, max. I'll call from the corner." The line went dead.

Ivy stared at the receiver. Jody was exactly what she needed. Thank heavens one of them was still sane.

Ivy called Theo and left a message that she was going to stay with Jody and that she'd have her cell with her. Ten minutes later she was sitting at her kitchen table, coiled to spring. She'd thrown a toothbrush, a nightgown, and a change of clothes into a shopping bag.

When the phone rang, Ivy grabbed it.

"I just came through the square," Jody said. "Now I'm coming up Elm Street." There was a long pause. "There's Laurel Street." Another pause. "Okay, now I'm turning your corner. Cripes, where'd all those people come from?"

"Don't stop in front. They'll barrage you with—"

Jody cut her off. "Who said anything about stopping? Listen to me. . . . Here's what I want you to do. You listening?"

"Go on."

"You're in the kitchen?"

"Uh-huh."

"Turn out the lights and check whether anyone's at the side door."

Ivy did. "No one's there."

"Good. Hang up and let yourself out. I'll count to twenty and swoop by. You run out and jump in."

Run? Jump? Yeah, right.

"It'll be just like old times," Jody went on. "Girls rock!" It sounded pretty lame, but that had been their war cry, shouted as the girls' varsity relay team broke from their huddle before each race.

"Okay, now start counting with me. One, two . . ." Jody said.

"Three, four," Ivy joined in and disconnected the call.

Five, six . . . She looked down at her stomach. This girl wasn't going to be rocking so much as lumbering. *Eight, nine* . . . She grabbed her purse and the shopping bag, let herself out the side door, and locked it. She crept to the edge of the porte cochere.

From what she could see of the people milling in front of the house, no one had spotted her yet. Down the block she could make out only headlights, but she knew that it was Jody's Beetle, idling at the corner.

When she got to twenty, she held the bag in front of her face and bolted out the driveway to the sidewalk, then to the curb, surprised that she could move that fast.

"Mrs. Rose!" a voice shouted.

But already Jody's car was there, a streak of yellow-green, the door swinging open. Ivy clambered in. There was a squeal of rubber as Jody accelerated, and the door slammed shut.

"Wahoo! Fasten your seat belt," Jody said as she skidded around the corner.

The exhilaration lasted about ten seconds.

"So David's arraignment's in the morning?" Jody said later as she bounced Riker in her lap at the kitchen table of her fifties ranch-style house. Chinese take-out containers with dregs of shrimp lo mein, kung pao chicken, and moo shoo pork remained on the table.

"David's arraignment"—those were two words Ivy never imagined that she'd hear together in a sentence.

"Theo says he'll be out on bail by tomorrow afternoon." Ivy reached into her pocket
and felt for her cell phone. She checked
that it was on. No messages.

Jody removed Riker's sippy cup and a
wad of crumpled napkin from his high-
chair tray and deposited them on the
counter. The top of her loose-fitting navy
blue sweats was streaked with what might
have been oatmeal.

It felt good to be in this chaotic household
with dirty dishes in the sink, toys all over the
floor, and Cheerios crunching underfoot.
Riker was rubbing his ear and fussing.

Jody's husband, Zach, came into the
room. He wore dusty jeans and a
maroon sweatshirt with raveled cuffs, and
he smelled of sawdust, varnish, and ciga-
rettes. He was a finish carpenter—which
explained, Jody liked to joke, why their
house was a mass of unfinished projects.
There was a half-completed wall of bookshelves in the den and a trough in the
kitchen floor where he'd ripped out a wall
to what had once been a mudroom. He'd
get started on a project during a lull, then
drop it when paid work came along. With

Jody still on leave from teaching, they needed every cent he could bring in.

"Hey, Ivy." His look was sober. "Jody told me about what's been happening. What a nightmare. You know you're welcome to stay here. You and David both. Whenever, and for however long you need."

Riker held out his chubby arms to Zach.

"C'mere, stinky," Zach said, and scooped Riker off Jody's lap. He held him up overhead, just managing to dodge a gob of drool as Riker giggled. "Bedtime for you, buddy."

Tucking Riker under his arm like a squirmy football, he left the room.

"Know what I was remembering?" Jody said, picking an errant rock shrimp from the lo mein noodles and popping it into her mouth. "How Melinda had a thing about you. You and David both."

"A thing?"

"An obsession."

"She didn't."

"She so did."

"The police found a photograph of David in her apartment on her refrigerator. Apparently she's been showing it to friends for more than a year, telling them David's her boyfriend."

"Right. And I'm goin' out with Brad Pitt." Jody wiped her hands on a dish towel. "Hang on a sec."

Jody left the room and returned a few moments later with her copy of the high-school yearbook from their senior year. She flipped through the pages. "Damn, where is it?" Flipped through some more. "There!"

She dropped the yearbook open onto the table and stabbed her finger at a photo of kids at a pep rally. Some football players were grinning in their jerseys and holding their helmets under their arms. There was David, with the number 7 across his chest—that was the same number worn by Doug Flutie, David's hero and the main reason he'd gone to Boston College.

"That's you, isn't it?" Jody pointed to a girl, her back to the camera, waving at the team. "I remember that silly jacket you used to wear all the time."

Sure enough, there she was in David's football jacket, the body made of thick red wool, the arms white leather, not yet turned a dusky yellow with age.

"It's true, I loved that jacket," Ivy said.

"You were *in* love, and your brain was addled. And look who's here." Jody pointed to a girl standing alone to the side, set apart from the crowd. Her hair frizzed around her head, and she had on glasses. "See how she's watching you?"

Ivy looked more closely. It was Melinda. She had on a baggy sweater over a dress over loose-fitting pants—or maybe they were leg warmers. And she did seem to be staring at Ivy.

"Jesus, where did she find those outfits?" Jody asked. "She looked like Afghan refugees were sending her their clothes."

"Play nice," Ivy told her. "We're grownups now."

"Remember her house? It was on one of those little streets off the square. Wait a minute—"

Jody slid her chair over to her makeshift desk—a piece of Formica countertop resting on a pair of sawhorses. She typed at the computer, and Ivy watched over her shoulder as Jody pulled up an online directory and typed in "White" and "Brush Hills, MA."

"Melinda. On Gannett Street," Jody said. "That's way over, the other side of town."

"That's probably her apartment, where she's living now," Ivy said.

Jody scrolled through the list.

"You're not going to find it," Ivy said. "Melinda told me her mother sold the house and moved to Florida."

Jody continued scrolling. "You're right. I hate it when that happens." She closed the browser and sat back for a moment. "Maybe . . ." She jumped up and opened a low kitchen cabinet. Inside was a stack of phone books. "Here!" She pulled one out. It was dated 2004. "Zach never throws anything away, and every once in a while—" She flipped to the W's in the back. "White, White, White . . . Belcher Street. That sounds right. Gereda White. Could be her mother." Jody tore out the page and handed it to Ivy.

There it was, Gereda White, 6 Belcher Street. It was just the other side of the square.

"Hey, maybe Melinda parked at your house and walked over to the house where she grew up," Jody said.

"Then what?"

"I don't know. Got hit by a bus? Fell in a hole and broke both legs? Spontaneously combusted?" Jody gave Ivy a speculative look. "We could go over there and—"

"Down, girl," Ivy said. "Don't even think about it."

"Hey, where's your sense of adventure?"

"Jody, David is in jail. This isn't some kind of game."

Eagerness faded from Jody's face. "Sorry. I wasn't thinking."

"Besides, this could be totally bogus. Are you sure they lived on Belcher Street? Knowing you, that's probably the wrong house. Remember that time . . . ?"

Jody flushed. In high school they'd toilet-papered a house Jody was sure belonged to Coach Reiner. Turned out it belonged to a Korean family, recently moved to Brush Hills. The police thought it was a racial slur until the girls came forward and confessed.

"Definitely not bogus this time," Jody said, her eyes narrowing. "Belcher Street. I think I was there once. Melinda's birthday party in maybe fourth grade. Odd, the things you remember. There were these dark green shades in the living room, and one of them was torn. The place smelled funky, like they never opened any windows. And Melinda had this tiny bedroom in kind of a winterized sunporch. I remember that the walls were pink. Emphatically pink. And she had a lamp with a ceramic base that looked like Kate Winslet in a Cinderella dress. You'd have loved it."

"*Now* I'd love it. Then I'd have hated it."

"The hedges out front were big and scary."

Belcher Street? Big scary hedges? "You know, I think I went trick-or-treating at a house like that. Sixth grade. We were a little too old to still be doing it. Jan Zylstra dared us to ring the bell. And then Randy— remember him?"

"Sure. 'Do Anything on a Dare' Disterman?"

"Randy crept up and rang the bell. Then beat it. It must have been Melinda's mother who came to the door holding a bowl of candy. Randy pelted the house with eggs. Mrs. White dropped the bowl and screamed at us." Ivy closed her eyes and shuddered at the memory of egg yolk dripping down the poor woman's face. "What were we thinking?"

"Kids are monsters," Jody said. "It's amazing any of us survives adolescence without being permanently bent."

18

Ivy kept her cell phone close by the bed as she slept in Jody's guest room—or tried to sleep. She tossed and turned, reporters' voices ringing in her head. *Were you friends with Melinda White? What's your reaction to your husband's being arrested for murder?*

David hadn't been arrested for murder, damn it. And what the hell did they *think* her reaction was?

Ivy pressed her face into the pillow. It had been so stupid for David to tell the police that he'd seen Melinda leave the house when he hadn't. Why lie? On top of that, he'd called Melinda and left a voice message. It sounded innocent when he explained, but the police didn't seem to be listening. He'd compounded it by trying to get rid of the knife and the canvas bag that he'd found in his truck.

She could see the photograph of the knife and the bloodstained canvas bag, and in the back of her throat she tasted blood. She could hear Detective Blanchard's smug voice: *We have an overwhelming amount of evidence.* First the police had twisted the facts to implicate her, then they'd twisted them to implicate David. All of it could easily have been planted.

Ivy felt a single vibration in her belly. She wanted desperately to set the clock back to Before. There was another vibration, sharp and quick. She put her hand there, and a minute later she felt another twitch. Could babies hiccup in the womb? The thought made her smile.

In an old house . . . She ran the opening lines from *Madeline* like a satin ribbon through her mind, trying to calm her inner turmoil with the rhyming verses. One day she'd hold her daughter in her lap and share with her the story of the girl in the funny hat and pinafore, brave little Madeline who was not afraid of anything.

Ivy was still awake when Riker started fussing at three in the morning. She heard Zach muttering to himself as he shuffled down the hall. Then she must have finally fallen asleep, because the next thing she knew, the front door slammed and she smelled coffee and breakfast sausages. It was seven, and her pillow was damp.

She remembered where she was. And why. An ache in her butt and lower back as she leaned off the bed to scoop up her cell phone reminded her how she'd landed on her tailbone.

No messages.

Feeling jet-lagged and shaky, she got up and dressed. She wanted to be able to leave, straightaway, as soon as Theo called to tell her when and where they were holding the bail hearing.

She went into the kitchen. Jody was reading the newspaper at the table. She glanced up, folded over the paper, and put her coffee cup on top of it.

"Hey! Good morning. Sleep okay?" Her smile seemed a little too bright. "What can I get you? Coffee? Eggs? Sausages? English muffin? How about all of the above?" She got up and went to the counter.

Ivy moved Jody's cup. Before she could open the newspaper, Jody swooped past and took it from her. "I was just reading an article about why pregnant women don't tip over," Jody said. "The researcher was a woman, of course. Turns out it's something about the curvature of a woman's spine, a lower center of gravity. . . ."

Ivy peeled Jody's fingers from the newspaper and spread it open on the table. There, in the middle of the page, was a photograph of Ivy and David looking young and very happy. It was the snapshot they'd sent to the newspaper years ago with their engagement announcement. Ivy remembered how giddy they'd been that day as they set the camera on a tripod with a time delay, raced to the couch, and posed grinning with their arms around each other's shoulders. David had on the dress shirt and tie his mother had coerced him into wearing for the photo— what you couldn't see were the torn blue jeans he had on, too.

Ivy read the headline:

**Missing Brush Hills Woman
Believed Murdered**

The lead read: *"Brush Hills landscaper David Rose is being held in the disappearance of Melinda White."*

Ivy dropped into a chair. She scanned the rest of the article. *"According to a police source, Rose is considered a person of interest in what may soon turn into a murder investigation."*

"Stop," Jody said, gently prying away the newspaper. "Trust me. You don't want to read what they're saying. It's total garbage."

Ivy's cell phone rang. She snatched it from her pocket.

"Get any sleep?" Theo asked.

"Some," Ivy said. "When's the hearing?"

"Can you bring David a change of clothes?" Theo said.

"Sure, but . . . you said there'd be a bail hearing today."

There was a pause on Theo's end. "There's been a delay."

Ivy's stomach clenched. "A delay?" She could feel Jody watching her.

"Nothing to worry about. It'll give us the weekend to—"

"The weekend?" Ivy cupped a hand over the receiver. "But today's only Thursday."

Jody crossed the kitchen to the sink, turned on the faucet, and started washing dishes.

"We just need to get some issues straightened out," Theo said.

"What issues?"

"Yeah, well, that's the thing." There was a longer silence.

Ivy moved into the living room. "Theo, what in the hell is going on?"

"Nothing's going on. I just don't know if I should—"

"For God's sake, would you just tell me? I'm pregnant, not an invalid."

"See, the whole thing about bail is whether the judge thinks someone is a flight risk."

"How can they think David's a flight risk? We're going to have a baby any day now. Where the hell's he going to go?"

"It's a little complicated. You're sure . . . ?"

"Yes, damn it! Tell me." But even as she said it, she knew she didn't want to hear his explanation.

"The D.A. has been monitoring activity

on your credit cards. A single one-way ticket to the Cayman Islands in David's name was booked Tuesday."

Single? One-way? Never in a million years would David disappear on her. Abandon her and the baby? That was insane.

"The ticket was for a flight leaving last night," Theo continued. "Obviously, David wasn't on it."

"You're telling me that the day before yesterday David booked himself a ticket to the Cayman Islands?"

"No. I'm not. He's as surprised as anyone."

"Then who . . . ?"

"I don't know. All I know is it was done over the Internet, and whoever booked it used your MasterCard."

19

Sure you're okay?" Jody asked as she pulled her car up in front of Ivy's house. No reporters in sight.

Ivy was so sick and tired of being asked that same stupid question, and she was so not okay.

"All right, all right. I'll shut up," Jody said. "But you know I could stay with you for a while. Zach's home with Riker."

A leathery oak leaf splatted against the windshield.

"I don't know why you're so hell-bent on going home right away," Jody continued.

"You could at least have let me make you something more than toast for breakfast. In fact, I wish you'd just stay with us until this is over."

Ivy had told Jody about the delayed bail hearing, that she had to take some clean clothes to David in jail, but she couldn't bring herself to talk about David's one-way ticket to the Cayman Islands. She couldn't face the pity in her friend's face when she heard this latest revelation.

Ivy forced a smile. "You're the best friend I could ever hope for, and you know I love you. And it's great to know that you're here for me when I need you to be. But right now I need some space. I just want to be home. But I'll take a rain check."

"Rain check." Jody made a face, like the idea had a bad taste. "But you listen to me. It's no imposition. Not in the slightest. You change your mind, just holler."

"I will." Ivy got her bag and climbed out of the car. "Promise." She shut the car door and started for the house. A dog was barking.

Jody rolled down the passenger-side window. "And if you start having contractions . . ." she called to Ivy.

Ivy smiled and turned back. "I'm not having any contractions! I'm not due for weeks."

"I do not want you going through labor alone," Jody said. "Do you understand me? When it's showtime . . ."

"Yeah, yeah, yeah. When it's showtime, you'll be the first to know. But this baby's on strict instructions to stay where she is until—"

"Right, and we all know how obedient little children do exactly what their parents tell them," Jody shot back. "All the same, I'll wait until you're inside, just in case your water breaks."

At the front door, Ivy groped about in her purse for her key ring. She jammed the key into the lock, but it would go only partway in. She cursed and tried to force it before she realized—she was using the key to the old lock. Beside it on the ring was the shiny new one. Old life, new.

The key slipped in easily. Ivy stepped inside, over the pile of mail that had come in through the slot. She waved to Jody and closed the door. She dropped the paper bag and her purse on the hall table and started up the stairs, determined to find out if a ticket to the Cayman Islands had been booked from their computer.

A scuffling sound and a muffled thump halted her halfway up. She spun around, expecting to find someone standing at the foot of the stairs or in the doorway to the living room. No one was there.

Ivy leaned her shoulder against the wall and rested her hands on her pregnant belly. She closed her eyes, willing her breathing to slow, her heart to stop banging against her rib cage.

Get a grip. She'd changed the locks. She was the only one with copies of the new key. If she'd be going it alone, she'd better toughen up. Judges might be able to delay bail hearings, but no one could delay this baby's birth. When her little one finally came roaring down the birth canal, she was going to need a mother who wasn't cowering in some corner, afraid of her own shadow.

Ivy opened her eyes. Bessie, the bronze statue at the foot of the stairs, was turned backward, facing her.

Then Ivy registered the smell. Sandal-wood and spicy clove. Opium perfume. Ivy gagged as the smell morphed into a disgusting stench of cotton candy and patchouli, and a blind panic welled up inside her.

She tore down the stairs and across the hall, feeling as if an invisible hand were thrusting her forward from behind. She threw open the front door.

Jody's VW was still there, idling at the curb. Thank God! A second later Jody was out of her car and running up the walk.

"What happened?" she demanded. "You're white as a sheet. I knew it wasn't a good idea to leave you alone."

"Nothing happened," Ivy said, panting. "I just . . . I just got spooked. I thought I heard something. And there was this smell."

"What smell?"

"Like perfume. And the statue at the base of the stairs is turned cockeyed."

"You're coming home with me." Jody grabbed Ivy's arm.

"No!"

"Okay, then I'm coming in with you." Jody marched past Ivy and up the porch steps. She stood in front of the doorway, her arms folded, tapping her toe. "Come on in." When Ivy hesitated, Jody added,

"I'm not leaving, and you can't make me."

Jody came halfway down the steps toward Ivy. "Please? Come on, Ivy, humor me. We'll check the place, top to bottom. Then maybe I'll let you talk me into going home."

As she and Jody entered, the house seemed to loom over them, the arched window like a single hooded eye peering down from inside the roof peak.

"Do you smell that?" Ivy asked.

Jody raised her head and sniffed. "No." She sniffed again. "Maybe. I'm not sure."

Jody pulled open the door of the hall closet. "Might as well start right here." She shoved the coats aside and pulled out suitcase after suitcase that were stored in back. "Nada."

Ivy followed her into the living room. The blinds were open. Ivy picked up the newspaper with David's unfinished crossword puzzle that sat on the coffee table. "I thought . . ." she started.

"You thought what?" Jody said.

"Nothing," Ivy said. Jody glared at her. "It's just that I was sure I'd closed the blinds in here. And thrown the paper into the window seat."

"When?"

"Yesterday."

"Maybe David took them out again," Jody said.

"Maybe," Ivy said. She followed Jody's gaze to the closed window seat. It was easily roomy enough inside to hide someone. "Sure. That's probably what happened."

"Uh-huh." Jody edged closer to the window seat. "I'm sure you're right." She and Ivy exchanged a look.

An arm's length from the window seat, Jody darted her hand out and threw open the lid. They both peered in. Empty.

Ivy tossed the newspaper inside, and Jody let the lid drop shut.

They checked the den and the dining room, then the kitchen and the mudroom, making sure that no one was hiding among the coats hanging on hooks by the side door.

"Nothing up this sleeve," Jody said.

On the way back through, Jody kicked open all the base kitchen cabinets. She raised the dumbwaiter's bottom panel.

Just watching Jody nonchalantly poke her head into the opening and look up and down the shaft made Ivy's stomach lurch.

Ivy forced herself to look in, too. Nothing there but the cable. An oil smell from the basement furnace wafted up. She slid the panel shut and wiped a skim of sweat from her forehead with the back of her hand.

"On to the basement," Jody said. She turned on the light at the top of the stairs and started down. Ivy followed.

The basement floor was packed dirt. A feeble amount of gray light made it through narrow, ceiling-high windows. Pipes and electrical conduits crisscrossed overhead, and lightbulbs dangled from black wires.

Jody yanked light cords as she went, and, one after another, bare bulbs came on like connect-the-dots. Overhead sagged fiberglass insulation that David had tacked between the beams to keep cold and damp from seeping into the house. Lally columns marked the location of the house's load-bearing walls.

Jody marched the perimeter of the space,

and Ivy's back ached from tension as she followed—down one side, past the oil tank, a metal drum on legs that was about the size of Jody's Volkswagen; across the back, past the toolbox Ivy and David had bought at Sears, a shiny red metal cabinet on casters with five drawers and CRAFTSMAN emblazoned in silver letter blocks near the top. With all the junk they'd cleared out for the yard sale, there were no longer so many places to hide.

Up the opposite wall. Jody pushed aside pieces of old paneling that leaned against the opening to the base of the dumbwaiter's chimneylike shaft. There was the dumbwaiter, nothing more than an open cube, sitting idle where it had probably rested for decades.

Across the front of the house was solid wall. Any windows would have looked out under the front porch.

Back upstairs they went. In the front hall, Ivy turned Bessie so the statue was once again facing forward. Then she followed Jody to the second floor.

They checked the baby's room and its narrow closet. The little twin-masted sailboats Ivy had stenciled on the wall seemed to bob serenely against the yellow background.

Ivy looked out the window. The wing chair in Mrs. Bindel's living-room window was empty. Outside, she heard birds, the muted roar of someone's leaf blower, and a dog barking.

She followed Jody across the landing to the guest bedroom. It looked untouched. Her parents' mahogany bedroom set and the pink and yellow patchwork quilt from the thirties that Ivy had picked up at a yard sale were reassuringly familiar. The other spare bedroom had nothing in it but a disassembled crib and changing table, boxes of Pampers, and bags of baby clothing and toys. Enough for triplets.

In the bathroom the sink was dry to the touch, one towel was neatly folded, and a second one lay crumpled on the hamper where David had left it.

Ivy stood beside Jody in the doorway to the master bedroom and looked in. The pillows were arranged artfully on the bed— did she ever leave them like that? At least the shades were still drawn.

"Now I smell it," Jody said, wrinkling her nose. "Perfume."

Ivy turned on the overhead light and watched Jody enter the bedroom, watched her pick up the bottle of Opium perfume from the dresser and remove the stopper. "This is it," Jody said, waving the stopper in Ivy's direction. "Definitely."

A shot of scent wafted over to Ivy.

Jody stoppered the bottle. She checked under the bed, then opened each closet and rooted around inside.

Back out on the second-floor landing, the house felt quiet. Too quiet, Ivy thought as she followed Jody up the attic stairs.

"Row, row, row your boat . . ." Ivy began to sing.

Jody stomped up the steps ahead of her and joined in, singing and clapping, turning on lights as she went, and filling the big attic bedroom with sound as she checked under the bed and in the closet. *"Merrily, merrily, merrily, merrily . . ."*

"Row, row, row . . ." Ivy started over at the top of her lungs.

When they got to the unfinished part of the attic, Ivy hollered, "Ollie ollie oxen free, free, free!" The space looked just as Ivy remembered it when she'd been up there last, vacuuming.

"That's it," Jody said. She turned to face Ivy, placing her hands on her hips. "I think we've done it. No big hairy monsters."

Ivy felt giddy with relief as Jody high-fived her. Before heading down the stairs, she took one last look around. Her gaze snagged on the box of books sitting on the landing.

Hadn't David told her that a buyer at the yard sale was interested in the last box of books? Wasn't that his excuse for having to go into the house anyway, so giving Melinda a quick tour was no problem?

Then why was a box of books still there?

20

Ivy came down the stairs in a daze.

David said he'd brought those books out for a buyer, but obviously he hadn't. He said he'd seen Melinda leave the house, but he didn't. He said he hadn't booked himself a ticket to the Cayman Islands. . . .

"What? You look like you're in pain," Jody said, waiting for her at the foot of the stairs.

Ivy rested her hand on her belly. "Just another Braxton Hicks. Surprised me, is all."

"You're sure it's false labor?"

"Positive."

"So how about some lunch or—" Jody started.

Ivy cut her off. "Listen, you've been great. Thank you. Seriously, thank you so much. I feel much better now. I feel safe, and I'm definitely not in labor. I'm fine."

"Fine." Jody raised her eyebrows.

"Or at least as fine as I'm going to get."

"And you want me to leave."

"And I want you to leave. I love you, but—"

"I'll get you back for this," Jody said as she walked to the door and pulled it open. She turned back.

Ivy gave her a thumbs-up and waved. "Go."

"E-mail me. And don't forget to eat something," Jody said, and headed out to her car.

Ivy stood in the open door and watched the VW take off. The same woman Ivy had seen Sunday morning from her porch was once again plugging along on the opposite sidewalk, pushing her double stroller. Looking so normal in her jeans, baggy white T-shirt, and red bandanna worn Indian style over her forehead, the woman stopped and gave Ivy a frankly curious and not particularly friendly stare.

Ivy shivered and shut the door, double-locking it with the key.

The floor of the front hall was littered with suitcases Jody had hauled from the closet. There was David's duffel bag. Ivy pulled it aside and returned the rest of the luggage to the closet.

Last was Ivy's overnight bag, the one she'd packed a few weeks earlier. She'd followed, to the letter, their childbirth teacher's strict instructions. Inside were a nightgown that buttoned down the front, a toothbrush, some red lollipops to suck on between contractions, and a nursing bra. Their plan had been for her to call David the minute her water broke or when she started having regular contractions. She'd counted on having him there with her, keeping track of her labor pains, calling the doctor, driving her to the hospital, holding Ivy's hand through the whole ordeal and encouraging her to relax, to focus, and to remember to breathe. Counted on having David playing the role of father to her mother of their little girl.

She and David . . .

Ivy wiped away a tear with the back of her hand. She threw her overnight bag back into the closet and yanked the coats together on the rod. She was about to slam the door when she noticed David's high-school football jacket, hanging from the rod. The once-supple leather arms were flaking, and the satin lining had nearly disintegrated, but Ivy had refused to let him throw it away.

She pulled it from the hanger and held it in her arms, inhaling deeply the smell that she so associated with the person she'd fallen in love with. She'd worn that jacket to so many football games. Sat with it draped around her bare shoulders after the first time they'd made love.

She could picture herself in six months, the baby sucking on a binkie and Ivy dragging that red and white jacket around like a security blanket.

She hung the jacket back up and then carried David's duffel bag up the stairs and dropped it on the landing. In her office she sat at her computer and jiggled the mouse. With a static crackle, the screen came to life.

She opened the browser and clicked

HISTORY. A window opened on the side of the screen showing recently visited Web pages. She clicked TUESDAY and scrolled through the list. Gmail. Google. The *Boston Globe*. Weather. Sites she visited just about daily. MapQuest—she'd gone there to get directions to visit Mr. Vlaskovic.

Then she saw it. Ivy sat there trying to catch her breath, trying to make herself accept evidence that was staring her in the face. There, right in the middle of the listing, was what she'd hoped she wouldn't find—Caymanislands.com. And right after that, Travelocity.

Ivy shut the browser window and pushed away from the desk. From this very computer, David had booked himself a ticket out of this nightmare. He hadn't even bothered to cover his tracks.

If it had been her, she'd have booked tickets for two.

Barely able to see through a veil of tears, Ivy returned to her bedroom, ignoring the phantom smell of perfume. She threw David's duffel bag onto the bed, unzipped it, and tossed in clean underwear, socks, a pair of pants, and a pullover. She went into the bathroom for his toothbrush.

Choking back sobs, Ivy put her hand over her mouth. Who was this man whom she'd loved unconditionally since high school? She searched for clues from the past and could find none. *This one's a keeper*—that had been Grandma Fay's assessment of David.

Could they both have been so wrong?

Damn him. What did he think anyway? That he could abandon the baby and leave her behind to deal with the consequences? The despair and confusion that swirled inside her coalesced into a hard lump as she threw David's razor and toothbrush into his shaving kit, dropped them into the duffel bag, and zipped it shut.

Quickly, she changed into fresh clothes, washed her face, and brushed her hair hard, until her scalp stung. The face staring back at her from the mirror looked tense and determined.

She carried the bag into the hall and dropped it over the railing. It landed with a thud in the middle of the downstairs hall.

And don't forget to eat something—she remembered Jody's parting words. She'd need all the strength she could muster to get through the rest of what this day had in store for her.

She went into the kitchen and knocked back some orange juice. Like medicine, it left a bitter taste in her mouth. She chased it with a handful of nuts.

Then she checked that the front door was double-locked and let herself out the side door. She threw the duffel bag into the backseat and was about to get in the front when the sound of screeching tires startled her.

There was frantic barking, then howling. A car horn blared.

A week earlier those sounds would have sent her hurtling onto the street to see what was wrong. Instead now she fought the urge to flee into the house. She made herself creep forward to the edge of the porte cochere.

There was Mrs. Bindel's dog, Phoebe, sitting back on her haunches in the middle of the street, growling and snapping, teeth bared, ears flat and low on her head, staring into the maw of a black Range Rover. The driver's-side window rolled down, and Ivy knew from the man's angry expression and Yankees cap—wearing one in Red Sox territory was an invitation to a fight—that the guy wasn't leaning out to pat the dog on the head and give her a cookie.

The minute the man saw Ivy, he started to bellow. "That damned deranged dog of yours is going to get itself killed. What the hell is the matter with you people?"

"She's not my dog. And you don't need to shout," Ivy said.

She approached Phoebe cautiously. A few feet away, she bent over—in her present state, crouching wasn't an option—and extended a hand. "Shh, it's okay, I'm a friend. Remember me?"

Ivy had no idea if this was the correct way to approach a frightened dog, but it seemed to be working. Phoebe's ears lifted slightly—a result of confusion, perhaps, now that there were two targets.

"Good dog. Good puppy," Ivy said, inching closer. The dog yipped and whined and backed up, tail between her legs.

Ivy held out her hand. "Come on, Phoebe." At the sound of her name, the dog lowered her posture a bit and the ears came up more. "That's a good girl."

Phoebe inched toward Ivy and sniffed, then licked her hand. Then she seemed to let go and collapse, legs going out from under her.

Ivy grabbed for the dog's collar and started to haul her from the middle of the street.

Phoebe yelped and mewled. The dog had to weigh at least forty pounds, and the poor thing trembled. Her fur bunched in distress over expressive brown eyes, and she huffed hot doggy breath in Ivy's face.

"Idiot!" the man said, shaking his head in disgust. "Get a leash." Tires screeched as he took off.

"Get yourself a leash," Ivy muttered. "Or better yet a muzzle."

Ivy patted Phoebe's head and tried to calm the dog's trembling. She couldn't remember ever seeing Phoebe alone outside. Where was Mrs. Bindel?

She pulled Phoebe to Mrs. Bindel's front door, rang the bell, and waited. No answer. She knocked. Still nothing.

Maybe Mrs. Bindel was in the backyard. Ivy carried the dog off the front porch. They were halfway around the house when the dog barked, squirmed free, and took off yelping.

Ivy followed. Behind the house Mrs. Bindel's forsythia, quince, and rhododendron bushes were clipped into tight spheres. Ivy ducked under the old-fashioned clothesline strung across mown grass from which no dandelion would dare rear its head.

Phoebe grunt-snorted to the poured-concrete steps by Mrs. Bindel's back door and sank down in the grass, snuffling. Mrs. Bindel lay there on the lawn, looking small and fragile, her head resting on the bottom step.

Ivy rushed over to the stricken figure. She wavered, and vertigo overtook her as she registered the grotesque angle of Mrs. Bindel's head, like a doll's head that has been twisted backward.

She made herself bend forward and press her fingertips to Mrs. Bindel's neck. The papery flesh was cool, not cold. Mrs. Bindel's face was damp, even though the misty rain had stopped. There was definitely a pulse.

Relief coursed through Ivy when she realized that Mrs. Bindel's head wasn't really twisted. It was just that her wig was slewed sideways, covering part of her face.

Gingerly, Ivy lifted the wig. Just a few strands of white hair sprouted from Mrs. Bindel's scalp, and there was an angry purple contusion. Her pale face looked almost like a baby's in repose.

Ivy adjusted the wig properly. Her neighbor would have been mortified if complete strangers, even if they were ambulance attendants, saw her without it.

She had to call an ambulance. Her cell phone was in the car. As Ivy stood, Phoebe yipped and got up, too.

"Phoebe, sit!" To her surprise, the dog did. "Good girl. You wait here."

Phoebe snorted and lay down, head on her paws beside her mistress.

That's when Ivy noticed that smell. Again. Sandalwood and spice.

She leaned forward and lifted one of Mrs. Bindel's inert hands. The scent seemed to be coming from Mrs. Bindel's fingers.

21

A police cruiser and an ambulance arrived within minutes of Ivy's 911 call. Paramedics quickly checked Mrs. Bindel and strapped an oxygen mask over her pale face. She seemed so small and insubstantial, as if a stiff breeze could whisk her away.

"Is she going to be all right?" Ivy asked one of the uniformed EMTs.

"You a relative?" he asked.

"I live next door. I found her and called it in."

"She's got a steady pulse." He didn't

look as if he'd convinced himself. "But she's pretty old."

But she's pretty tough, Ivy wanted to shoot back.

The man and his partner started to carry the stretcher from the yard.

Ivy sat cross-legged on the grass beside Phoebe, watching as Mrs. Bindel was loaded into the back of the ambulance. The dog looked up at Ivy, anxiety radiating from big dark eyes, then set a paw on Ivy's knee. Ivy scratched Phoebe behind the ears.

Detective Blanchard pulled up in his gold Crown Vic just before the EMTs closed the ambulance doors. He got out, nodded in Ivy's direction, then conferred with one of the attendants. The EMT pointed to the back steps, then to the top of his own head, the spot where Mrs. Bindel had been bruised.

Blanchard approached Ivy, taking out his pad and pen. "So what brought you out here?"

"I live next door, remember?" Ivy could hear the hostility in her tone, but she didn't care. "I was getting into my car when—"

"Going where?" Blanchard interrupted.

None of your damned business. "To see my husband. As far as I know, there's no law against that."

"I see," he said, returning Ivy's challenge with a bland façade. "It appears that your neighbor was quite badly hurt."

"I know. I found her." Ivy watched the ambulance drive away, siren wailing.

Blanchard waited for Ivy to continue, pen poised.

"I heard a commotion on the street," she said. "Some guy in an SUV was leaning on his horn, and Phoebe—the dog—was barking at him. Phoebe never goes out alone without Mrs. Bindel—I knew that something was off."

Phoebe's snout was now wedged into Ivy's lap.

"Did anyone else see him?"

"I don't know. I don't think so."

"Did you see anyone or anything else unusual? Then? Or perhaps earlier in the day?"

Ivy tried to remember. The street had been deserted when Jody dropped her off. She told Blanchard about the woman who'd been pushing a stroller across the street. "She's the only other person I noticed, and I see her out all the time."

Blanchard asked for the woman's name, and Ivy admitted that she didn't know. Didn't even know where she lived.

"But she didn't see the man in the Range Rover," he said.

"He had on a Yankees cap," Ivy said.

"Brave soul." Blanchard took a note and then squinted down at her. "I don't suppose you got a license plate?"

"Why would I? And why would he—" Ivy was about to ask why someone who'd attacked Mrs. Bindel would hang around afterward, honking his horn and drawing attention to himself. Then she realized that Detective Blanchard didn't believe her. He thought she was fabricating the man in the Range Rover, just like he thought she'd made up the woman standing out at the curb by the wicker trunk.

"You can't think I . . . ?" Ivy started. What—attacked Mrs. Bindel? "There was a man. I didn't make him up."

"The skid marks out on the street are genuine enough," Blanchard said. "And they're wider than the tires on your car.

Maybe this man saw something that will help us discover what happened to your neighbor."

Reasonable enough. "Well, I didn't get the license plate. I wasn't thinking about that, because I had to get Phoebe out of the street." The dog's head came up. "I assumed that Mrs. Bindel was in the house or in her yard."

"So you say your neighbor doesn't normally let the dog out alone?"

"Never."

The crow's-feet at the corners of Blanchard's eyes deepened as he gazed at the spot where Mrs. Bindel had fallen. "So when did you first notice the dog barking?"

"When I was getting into my car, right before—" Ivy broke off. "No, I heard barking about twenty minutes earlier." She stopped again. "Actually, there might even have been a dog barking when I got home. In fact, I'm pretty sure there was."

Blanchard looked annoyed. "How long before you found your next-door neighbor unconscious are you *pretty sure* that you heard barking?"

"An hour, maybe hour and a half. My

friend was with me. She might have noticed the barking, too."

"Your friend?"

"She parked in front of the house for a
while. Then she came in."

Now Blanchard looked thoroughly ex-
asperated. "And she drives what?"

"A VW Bug. You can ask her what she
saw."

Detective Blanchard wrote down Jody's
name and her phone number.

"So where exactly did you find your
neighbor?" he asked.

Ivy indicated the spot and described
Mrs. Bindel's position. Blanchard went
over and crouched there. He swept his
hand in an arc through the surrounding
grass. He stood and walked slowly in ever-
widening circles. When he was out about
eight feet from the center, he stopped. He
reached into his pocket for a handkerchief
and used it to pick up a fist-size rock. A
speculative look crossed his face.

"You don't think this was an accident,
do you?" Ivy said.

"You mean, did your neighbor trip and
fall and bang her head on the edge of a

step? What do you think?" He tilted his head and ran his hand back and forth over his mouth, waiting for her reply.

Mrs. Bindel had been lying on her side, her head resting on the bottom step. "I don't know, but I don't see how she could have ended up in that position if she'd tripped on a step."

"I agree." Blanchard's mouth tightened in a grim line. "I think your neighbor was very fortunate. Her wig saved her from much more serious injury."

Ivy put her cheek to Phoebe's head. She couldn't imagine why anyone would want to hurt Mrs. Bindel.

"Is there anything else you remember?" Blanchard asked.

What would he say if she told him about Bessie turned sideways, or that there was a perfumy smell in her house? Worst case, he'd write her off as a demented pregnant woman.

"It's probably unimportant—" she started.

"Let me be the judge of that."

She told him.

"I haven't used that perfume for months,"

she added. "And when I found Mrs. Bindel, I thought she had that same smell on her hand."

She waited for him to dismiss the observation. Instead his face turned somber. "You lock all your doors when you leave the house?"

"Always."

"And you did so when you left this morning?"

"Yes."

Detective Blanchard gazed in the direction of her house. "Perhaps you gave your neighbor a key to use in case of emergency? Or maybe the previous owner gave her a house key?" Ivy shook her head. "Or you keep an extra set hidden outside? A lot of people do."

"I just had the locks changed, and no one has a copy of the new key except us."

Blanchard wrote a final note in his book, flipped the pad closed, and put it in his pocket. "Here's what I think," he said. "We don't have a lot of crime in Brush Hills. Mostly it's drunk driving and burglary. Occasionally vandalism. A woman disappears? That's unusual. Right next door another woman gets attacked in her backyard? That's unusual, too. Put them together and you've got yourself a coincidence. My gut says they're probably related. So I look for a common thread."

"Common . . ." Ivy felt her mouth drop open. "You can't possibly think that I . . . ?"

"Help me here." Blanchard gave her his benign Uncle Bill face. "Give me something else to go with."

22

After Detective Blanchard left, Ivy was furious with herself for failing to challenge him. Unfortunately, she could see his point. It made sense that there was some connection between Melinda's disappearance and the attack on Mrs. Bindel.

A chill passed through Ivy. Hit in the head with a rock the size of a tennis ball. Had Mrs. Bindel seen her attacker? Would she be able to identify that person when she regained consciousness? *If* she regained consciousness. Ivy was encouraged by Detective Blanchard's remark that her injury could have been much worse.

Ivy found a length of rope and tethered Phoebe to Mrs. Bindel's clothesline. The dog submitted with a baleful look. Then Ivy filled a plastic tub with water and brought it over. Later she'd pick up dog food.

She returned to her car and got in. David's duffel bag sat crumpled on the passenger seat. She hit the automatic door lock and backed out of the driveway. As she drove, she rehearsed what she'd say to David. He had to give her some straight answers.

By the time she arrived at the police station, her jaw ached from grinding her teeth. She parked in a visitor spot and got out of the car.

As she pulled the duffel bag off the seat, she felt a tightening across her abdomen, not painful or even uncomfortable. And she felt queasy. She put a hand on her belly, closed her eyes.

One, two, three . . . When she got to ten, the tightness had passed. Another Braxton Hicks.

A police officer whom Ivy had never met before led her to a barren basement room with cinder-block walls. A damp smell pervaded the space, furnished with a few card tables and flimsy molded-plastic chairs. A young woman was already sitting at one of the tables with a man in a suit, perhaps her lawyer. The schoolhouse clock on the wall said it was ten past one.

Ivy took a seat and waited, her arms and legs crossed, her foot jiggling. Minutes later another officer appeared, escorting David.

"Hey, Stretch," David said. He looked pale and tired—not a villain, just David with his blood and energy leached out.

Ivy gripped the arms of her chair, trying to stay in control. Her eyes filled with tears, and anger threatened to uncoil within her. All the speeches she'd prepared flew out of her head. She wanted to throw herself at him, to beat his chest and scream, to demand how in the hell he could have gotten them into this mess. Didn't he realize what was at stake?

"You hanging in there?" David asked, barely looking at her. "Feeling okay?" He dropped into a chair, leaned forward, and put his hand on her belly. "Hey, Sprout. Miss me?"

Ivy didn't trust herself to speak. She'd come to face him down, to make him tell her what in the hell was going on. But he looked so deflated that it would be like pummeling Jell-O.

He lifted his head and met her gaze. "What?"

Ivy felt her lower lip quivering. Where to start? She held her hands out in a gesture of helplessness. "The phone message, the knife, the plane ticket . . ."

"Ivy, please . . . you can't think—"

"That plane ticket was booked on our computer."

"What?" The word exploded as David's eyes lit up and his face flushed.

"The browser history lists a Cayman Islands Web site and then a visit to Travelocity."

"No . . . way. . . ." The words came out like air from a slow leak. David's eyes shifted from side to side. "That's impossible. When?"

"Tuesday. And in the attic," Ivy continued, lowering her voice to a harsh whisper, "there's a box of books that you supposedly went inside to get."

David's expression clouded. "What books?"

"Good question. There was no buyer

at the yard sale asking for books, was there?" Words rushed out before Ivy could stop them. "You made that up as an excuse to get Melinda inside."

Heat lightning pulsed behind David's eyes. "*Get her inside?* Get her inside and what?"

"And . . ." Ivy's voice trailed off.

"Listen to me." David leaned close and squeezed Ivy's arm.

"Stop, you're hurting me," she said.

He loosened his grip. "I did not purchase any ticket to the Cayman Islands," he said, his voice low and urgent. "I don't even know where the damn things are, and outside of crossword puzzles I'd never heard of them until the cops told me about the plane ticket. I never, *ever* touched Melinda White, during or after the yard sale, and I can't even believe I have to tell you that. Suppose, just suppose, that I *was* going to run away from all this mess. Don't you think I'd take you with me . . . ?" His voice broke on the final words.

Ivy tried to swallow. In the silence she could hear the fluorescent lights buzzing overhead.

"I want to believe you," she said. "But it

seems like there's been one lie after another after another. I'm feeling so beaten
down. And now . . ."

"Something else happened?" David
said. "What?"

David looked increasingly alarmed as
she told him how she'd found Mrs. Bindel
unconscious in her backyard. "Melinda's
disappearance. Now Mrs. Bindel getting
attacked. What in the hell is going on?"

Ivy wrapped her arms around her stomach. She said, "Look for a common thread.
That's what Detective Blanchard said—
only he thinks the thread is me."

"The guy's an idiot." David sat back.
"There has to be another answer, some
rational explanation for all the crazy things
that are happening. Okay, what do we
know for sure?"

He held up his index finger. "Melinda
came to our yard sale. I left her in the
attic—distraught, but alive and whole."
He raised a second finger. "Unfortunately,
no one saw her leave. But that doesn't
mean she didn't. And yes, she freaked
me out. And yes, I guess I forgot about
the goddamned books."

"The bloodstained blouse," Ivy said.

"And pants." David held up a third finger.
"That neither of us put in the wicker trunk.
Then we have the canvas bag with the
knife." David raised a fourth finger. "Had to
have been placed in my truck Monday
after I got home from work."

"The ticket to the Cayman Islands,
booked from our home computer," Ivy
added.

David balled his hand into a fist. "Try to
figure that one out. The only thing clear
to me is that someone wanted to get rid of
Melinda White and make it look as if I
killed her. And now, on top of everything
else, our neighbor gets bashed in the
head. I'd like to see them try to blame me
for that."

"Who got bashed in the head?" It was
Theo's voice.

David's gaze shifted upward. Ivy turned
around. Theo looked glum.

"Our neighbor," Ivy said. "This afternoon
someone attacked her in her backyard.
Hit her with a rock. The police think it has
something to do with Melinda's disappearance."

The plastic chair scraped across the
floor as Theo pulled it over. He sat, leaned

forward, and rested his forearms on the table. He spoke in a low voice. "They got preliminary test results on the blood on the maternity blouse and the canvas bag—it's Melinda White's blood type. And there's more." His face lengthened. "They found fetal tissue."

The news crashed into Ivy as a cramp worked its way around from her back. She closed her eyes, then forced them open as images of what might have happened to Melinda and her baby flashed through her brain.

"They have to do more testing," Theo continued. "They've got Melinda's DNA, and they've subpoenaed a DNA sample from you, David."

"The sooner the better," David said. "Then they'll start looking for that baby's father. And high time, too."

23

Mrs. Rose," Detective Blanchard said later as he escorted her back to the lobby. "Do you have a sister?"

"I—" Ivy tripped on a step.

Blanchard caught her by the elbow. "Melinda's sister, Ruth, calls me every day to find out if there's been a break in the case, and every day I have to tell her we're still investigating. Did you know that she and Melinda were best friends? That they talk on the phone every day? Share what's going on in their lives?"

They were at the entrance now. "What's excruciating for her is the waiting," he said, holding the door shut, "and not knowing what happened to her sister."

Ivy wheeled on him. "I'm sure she desperately wants you to find her sister. So do I. Why don't you get out of my face, stop wasting time, and get out there and find out what happened to her?"

"I think we know what happened to her. Soon we'll have an indictment."

Ivy pushed the door open and brushed past him.

"There's plenty of evidence, and all of it implicates your husband. How much will it take before you stop protecting him?" he called after her.

Blinded by tears, Ivy stumbled to her car. *Son of a bitch.* Her heels thudded on the concrete walk. Dense afternoon cloud cover made it feel like dusk, and there was a biting chill in the air.

She got into the car, slammed the door, and gripped the steering wheel until her knuckles turned white. Then she jammed the key into the ignition and started the engine. The radio came on, and she bashed it into silence.

Tires squealed as she pulled in to the street. When Ivy realized she was whipping past a soccer field, going more than fifty, she braked and pulled over. She sank back in the seat and tried to slow her breathing.

Arrogant bastard. The worst thing was, Blanchard was right. As evidence against David mounted, the possibility that Melinda was merely misplaced had diminished to zero.

Fetal tissue . . . Ivy's stomach clenched, and she rolled down the window, taking great gulps of moist, cold air. It was too horrifying to imagine what might have happened. But David was right: Paternity-test results would at least give the police another lead to pursue.

Ivy forced herself to get moving. She shifted into gear and started driving again. Like an automaton, she went to the supermarket and bought dog food. By the drive home, rush hour was in full swing, and she was wishing she'd put the ten-pound bag of kibble in the trunk. She was feeling increasingly nauseous, and the smell didn't help.

She kept the window open as she sat stuck in traffic just blocks from home. Every time the bus in front of her inched forward, it spewed exhaust fumes. An airline ad across the back announced, "You are now free to move about the country." If only.

The noise of a jackhammer from road work on the block ahead filled the car. A horn honked, and Ivy accelerated, closing the five-foot gap that had opened up in front of her.

Traffic crept forward a few more feet, and she pulled even with a side street. The sign said BELCHER ST. That was the street where Melinda's mother lived, where Melinda had grown up. She'd probably walked to the square, bought candy at the convenience store, bowled at the now-defunct Kezey's Good Time Lanes.

Melinda is dead. Why was that so hard to accept?

Ivy touched the spot on her belly where Melinda had pressed her hand. It had made Ivy recoil at the uninvited intimacy. But then Melinda had always been odd, her social interactions off-key and just this side of inappropriate. Ivy remembered that other kids rolled their eyes whenever they saw Mrs. White marching Melinda to school.

Ivy had been on the yearbook council,

but it hadn't been her idea to nominate Melinda for Friendliest as a hilarious goof on the girl everyone called "the leech." Still, Ivy could have done something to stop it from happening, but that possibility had never occurred to her. In truth, she'd never thought one way or another about Melinda or her feelings. She'd been every bit as callow and mean as her classmates, just more passive about it.

And yet Melinda had survived. She'd finished high school. Had jobs in a hospital and in a real estate office. Transformed herself. Ivy remembered her standing in their driveway, her fingers curled around the neck of that green glass swan. Talking about how her mother used to work for Mr. Vlaskovic. About how important it was for "us" to eat healthy, and waxing nostalgic for Doc Martens and stirrup pants—Doc Martens and stirrup pants that Melinda had never had.

The car behind Ivy honked again. *Jerk!* A pedestrian on the sidewalk stared at her. Ivy cringed, realizing she'd said the word aloud.

On impulse she turned onto Belcher Street.

She drove down the quiet, vaguely familiar block. It was lined, one after the other, with modest bungalow houses, built close together and set back just a few yards from the sidewalk, the silhouette of each like a cardboard cutout of the next. One was painted yellow, another mint green, another tan with bottle green trim. Most had some perfunctory foundation planting, yew bushes or rhododendrons.

None had the wildly overgrown hedgerow, separating front lawn from sidewalk, that Ivy remembered from the night she'd been on this street trick-or-treating. She could still see Mrs. White standing backlit in the doorway, egg dripping down her face. The memory brought with it a flash of horror and shame—Ivy might not have tossed a single egg, but she'd brought the eggs and joined in with her friends, hooting laughter in the dark.

She slowed in front of a gray house in the middle of the block. It had the center entrance like the one she remembered. The number 15 was tacked beside the front door. She hadn't saved the page that Jody had torn from the old phonebook, but she remembered that the name Gereda

White had been listed at number 6—or was it 9? Definitely not 15.

She continued along the blocks, the numbers going down. The house at 9 Belcher had a side entrance. That couldn't be it.

A house on the opposite side of the street had a center entrance and a row of waist-high, neatly trimmed hedges out front. Yew bushes on either side of the front entrance were overgrown, the branches a dense tangle of tentacles reaching across a door that looked as if it hadn't been used for years. There was a garbage can out front with a white 6 painted on it.

Ivy let the car roll past and stopped at the house next door. She adjusted her sideview mirror.

There was a small room, like a winter-ized sunporch, hanging off the side of 6 Belcher Street. Jody had said that Melinda's bedroom was in a room like that.

Ivy's hands tightened around the steering wheel, and the revving of the car's engine grew to a roar. It took her a moment to register that her foot was pressing down on the gas pedal. She eased up and turned off the engine.

Before she realized she'd decided do it, Ivy found herself getting out of the car. She started back along the sidewalk toward the house.

She lifted the lid of the garbage can. It was empty. That seemed odd. Most of the trash barrels and recycling bins in front of other houses on the street were overflowing.

The more she looked, the more convinced she became that this had been Melinda's house. The sun was low in the sky, and curls of peeling paint cast dark shadows like gashes in its walls. Plants sprouted from the roof gutters. Had this been a scary place to grow up, or just profoundly sad?

A gust of wind whipped her hair about her face, and Ivy pulled her jacket around her. She noticed that a shade in a window of what she'd decided had been Melinda's bedroom was raised a few inches, and a light was on inside.

Ivy glanced about. She'd come this far. Just a quick peek—what could it hurt?

She hurried across the lawn, squeezed behind a prickly quince bush, hunkered down, and peered in.

Ivy's breath caught in her throat. The color of the walls. *Emphatically pink,* Jody had called it. Just beneath the window, inches from where Ivy stood, a narrow bed with a maple headboard was neatly made up with a pink and white gingham spread. The light in the room was coming from a lamp on a small desk against the opposite wall. The base was a woman in a swirling yellow ball gown—Kate Winslet in a Cinderella dress.

It was Melinda's room, just as Jody had described it. Hadn't Mrs. White sold the house and moved away?

The surface of the desk was cluttered with half-burned candles. Ivy shivered and brushed away an insect crawling on her neck.

Stuck to the wall over the candles was a dense collage of photographs and newspaper clippings. They were too far away and too jumbled to see clearly, but one jumped out at her. It looked like a clipping with a photograph of a football player, pedaling backward, arm raised, about to throw a pass. The white number 7 on the dark football jersey was clear as could be.

Seven. That had been David's number.

"Bitch." The voice that seemed to come out of nowhere was her own.

Ivy wanted to reach through the glass and tear David's photo from the wall. Search the room for other pictures of him and God knew what other mementos Melinda had saved—more evidence the police would say linked David to Melinda. She knew the reasoning: Women were killed by lovers, not casual acquaintances.

If she could just get inside long enough to destroy what she knew, beyond any shadow of a doubt, had to be evidence of an obsession, not a relationship . . . Ivy felt Jody's presence, like a devilish sprite perched on one shoulder and urging her on.

She tested the window, but it was locked shut. Good thing, too, because climbing wasn't remotely possible, given her current state. Walking in through a door seemed the more prudent option. Assuming that no one was home.

Ivy crossed in front of the house, picking her way across uneven ground, the lawn a mess of crabgrass, weeds, and bald patches. Shades were drawn in all the other windows. No cars were parked in the driveway.

She scanned the street. No traffic. No neighbors looking out through the windows of nearby houses.

She climbed the crumbling brick front steps. Behind the branches of the encroaching yew bushes, thick layers of white paint coated the door—icing on gingerbread. *The witch's house,* that's what the kids used to call the place. A mail slot was duct-taped over, as was a doorbell. She peered in through the small pane of glass in the door. She could barely make out a dark entrance hall with a doorway leading back to another shadowy room. Who was living here, and why were Melinda's things still there, preserved as if in a time capsule?

Ivy knocked. Seconds ticked by as she stood shivering in the murky gloom. No lights came on. No footsteps. She knocked again, harder. Waited. Then pulled the end of her sleeve down over her hand and reached for the doorknob. She turned it and tried to push the door open. It wouldn't budge.

There had to be a side or a back entrance, maybe both.

Ivy crossed back in front of the house and moved quickly up the driveway. Past a ragtag herb garden—some mint, a scraggly chive plant, and a patch of yellow flowers like button-size chrysanthemums—was a door.

Ivy climbed two concrete steps. A few envelopes and a large cardboard mailer, its side starting to split open, were wedged inside a storm door. That seemed reassuring. Anyone who'd recently returned to the house would have taken in the mail.

Ivy bent down. She could just make out the addressee, "Elaine Gallagher." If Elaine Gallagher had bought the house from Mrs. White, then why did that little bedroom look as if Melinda White were still living in it?

Ivy wrapped the end of her sleeve over her hand again and pulled open the storm door. The mail toppled out onto the top step. Through a small panel of glass in the door, she could see a dark kitchen.

She reached for the knob, fully expecting the door to be locked. But it wasn't. When the door opened, Ivy gasped and slammed it shut, yanking her hand away as if it had been scalded. The bang seemed to rattle the windows and echo up and down the street. The storm door crashed shut in its wake.

Backing away, Ivy tripped over a pile of nested plastic tubs that had been stacked by the door and sent them rolling into the grass.

Were those footsteps from inside? Heart pounding, Ivy waited for lights to come on.

Car headlights lit the street, and a dark sedan drove past. Thank God, not a gold Crown Vic. But what on earth had she been thinking? She knew that the police were keeping tabs on her. Her presence would only draw attention to the house.

Ivy scrambled to gather the plastic tubs. They turned out to be empty five-gallon drums of Ice Melt—probably a ten-year supply for this modest driveway and front walk. She restacked the containers and returned them to the back step.

She started to pick up the mail that had scattered. The split in the side of the over-size mailer had expanded, and some of the contents spilled out. Envelopes. Mail within mail? Maybe these were letters forwarded to Elaine Gallagher from her previous residence.

A bank statement. A credit-card bill. What looked like a check from the Social Security Administration. As Ivy stuffed them back into the mailer, her eye snagged on the addressee—Gereda White, P.O. Box 519, Naples, Florida.

If Mrs. White lived in Florida with Melinda's sister, Ruth, then why were her credit-card bill and her bank statement and her pension check being forwarded to her here?

Ivy turned over the cardboard mailer. Who the hell was Elaine Gallagher?

24

Ivy steeled herself and pushed open the door. A sour, almost-rancid smell greeted her. Taking shallow breaths, she stepped into a dark kitchen. Shades were pulled in the windows, and the house was silent and cold. Empty countertops and closed cabinets greeted her. Through a half-open doorway, she caught a glimpse of a back bedroom.

She fought the impulse to run, to get the hell out of there as fast as she could. No one was home, she assured herself. The noise she'd made banging the door shut would have wakened the dead. It would take only a minute or two to get rid of that photo and anything else that had to do with David.

She forced herself across the kitchen, through a small dining room, and into the front hall. She hurried on, through the living room. Dust coated a maple cobbler's bench loaded with Hummel figurines in front of a brown and black plaid sofa. In no way did this feel like a house that someone had bought and moved into a year ago—it felt like a house that no one had lived in for years.

She stood in the doorway of the sunporch that had been Melinda's bedroom. To her right was a tall, narrow bookcase. Beside it was the desk she'd seen through the window.

Ivy stepped inside. Her scalp prickled as she examined the wall over the desk. There was the football photo she'd seen through the window. Around it were snapshots of Melinda and her mother, taken before Melinda had lost all that weight and transformed herself. Among them were more pictures of David.

There was his graduation picture, the one that had been reprinted in the *Brush*

Hills Times annual issue where they ran all the high-school seniors' photos. There was a newspaper clipping of David standing proudly alongside the brand-new sign for Rose Gardens. There were unposed snapshots, too. One of David in front of their house. Another of him getting out of the pickup truck he'd sold two years ago. David sitting on their front porch, wearing the sweatshirt Ivy had given him last Christmas. In every one, David seemed unaware of the camera.

Ivy steadied herself on the edge of the desk as nausea bloomed and filled her like a noxious cloud. She sat in the chair and lowered her head. She tried to keep breathing. A bellows heaved in her skull, and the room seemed to shift and twist like a carnival ride. She grabbed the trash can from under the desk, sure she was going to throw up.

Mercifully, the queasiness passed. Ivy sat up, took a deep breath, and stood.

She reached for the clipping of David throwing the football and stopped. Fingerprints. She pulled her jacket sleeves over her hands like mitts and rubbed the edge of the desk she'd been holding. She tore down the clippings and snapshots and put them into her pants pockets.

She paused at two strips of photo-booth head shots tacked side by side. She took them down. One strip looked like Melinda in high school, maybe fifteen or sixteen years old, with frizzy hair and glasses. The other strip seemed more recent, more like Melinda at the yard sale. Older and slimmer, but with the same eyes, broad forehead, and round face as in the earlier photo strip.

Damn you. Ivy crumpled the two strips together and jammed them in her pocket as well.

Beneath the layer of photographs was a half sheet of paper. A bowling score sheet. It was dated March 9, 1992, and handstamped at the top: KEZEY'S GOOD TIME LANES. That was the bowling alley that had been in the basement of the hardware store in Brush Hills Square.

Ivy was about to leave the score sheet on the bulletin board when she noticed some of the names of the bowlers, printed in the left-hand column in careful, childlike block letters. EDDIE. DAVID. JAKE. THEO.

Eddie Walsh and Jake O'Connor had

been on the football team with David and Theo. This must have been a souvenir from one of the many times when they'd played at Kezey's.

Ivy took the score sheet and stuffed it into her bulging pocket.

She jerked open a desk drawer and rifled through it, then another, looking for anything else that might connect Melinda to David. She checked the bookcase for scrapbooks or diaries. The top shelves were filled with textbooks. *Basic Medical Laboratory Techniques. Fundamentals of Urine and Body Fluid Analysis.* A book on prepping for the Massachusetts real estate exam and one called *How to Buy and Sell Houses Fast.*

Three middle shelves were paperbacks, mostly romance novels. The bottom shelf held videotapes with handwritten labels—*Sex and the City, Extreme Makeover, The Swan*. The final title reminded her of the glass swans Melinda had said her mother collected. Ivy hadn't seen any in the house.

Ivy picked through a small bureau filled with women's clothing reeking of mothballs. In the bottom of the last drawer, she found another clipping. Curled and yellowed with age, it was Ivy and David's wedding announcement, the same photo that had run in the newspaper that morning. Only alongside David, where Ivy's head should have been, was a neat hole.

She had a thing about you. You and David both.

Jody had been wrong. It hadn't been both of them—David had been the object of Melinda's obsession. Ivy was the one she wanted cut from the frame.

Ivy jammed the mutilated clipping into her pocket. She ran her hand across the desk, sweeping away the ridiculous votive candles.

She was about to look in the closet when she heard a scuffling overhead. Her heart leaped, and instinctively she ducked her head. There was a thump.

Ivy took off. She ran from the room, through the living room.

There couldn't be anyone upstairs, she told herself—there was only roof over Melinda's bedroom and barely room for a crawl space above the rest of the house. But reason didn't slow her down. Through the front hall she ran.

The sounds she heard had to be squirrels or birds or wind blowing debris across the room's flat roof. Still she ran. She wanted out, into the cold, clear night, as far away as she could get from this house with its noxious smells and moist, clammy interior.

When she got to the kitchen door, queasiness overtook her. She gasped, unable to breathe as it grew, like a churning wave of swamp water. Gas pain doubled her over. Beads of sweat popped on her forehead and upper lip. She needed a toilet. *Now!*

Ivy staggered into the shadowy bedroom. Pushed past the bed and double windows that must have overlooked the backyard.

A door was partway open and, in the dark room beyond, a tile floor. In three steps she was there. She'd never been so happy to see anything as she was to see that toilet seat with its matted furry cover. She made it, not a second to spare.

There was nothing to do but surrender and let her body take charge. She sat on the toilet, doubled over. Was it something she'd eaten? She'd had only orange juice and nuts. She'd turned down the sausages, eggs, and coffee that Jody had offered, and the mere thought of them now made her want to puke.

That was all she needed, to be erupting at both ends.

Ivy closed her eyes. The last time she'd felt sick like this, it had been in the airport in Mexico City. All she'd wanted then was to be home, in her own bathroom with her own clean-smelling towels, her bed and fresh sheets to crawl into.

Now it was as if that safe place had ceased to exist.

Ivy waited. And waited. And waited. Finally it stopped. At least there was toilet paper on the roll.

Afterward, her shirt glued to her back, she could just make out her face in the mirror in the dark bathroom as she washed her hands, using a cracked bar of soap. Her skin was pasty and her bangs stuck to her forehead. She splashed water on her sweat-slicked face.

A hand towel hung over the edge of the tub. She touched it and recoiled. It was stiff, almost like cardboard. Ivy wiped her forehead with the back of her arm.

Her stomach clenched again. *Please,*

no more. She bent over and grasped the edge of the tub as the nausea built and finally, slowly receded.

That's when she noticed, just beyond the edge of a pale green plastic shower curtain, that the tub was filled to the brim. With what? Beach sand? The surface was smooth and flat.

Ivy reached for the shower curtain. It crackled as she pushed it aside. Whatever filled the tub was white and crystalline. At the near end, there was something sticking up out of it.

She turned on the light switch. A fluorescent tube over the mirror *tinked* and fluttered to life. Ivy winced away the bright light, but even after her eyes adjusted, it took her a moment to identify what she was looking at.

Just visible, above the white sand that filled the tub, were toes with pink polish on the nails.

25

Ivy screamed and screamed and screamed. Then she just stood there with her hands over her face, fingers splayed and her mouth open, no sound coming out.

She backed out of the bathroom. *Get out of here!*

She ran from the bedroom and through the kitchen. The storm door screeched and slapped shut behind her. The mail she'd left stacked on the steps and the empty tubs of Ice Melt she'd restacked went flying into the grass.

She ran out the driveway and across

the sidewalk to her car. Hand shaking, she managed to get the key inserted in the ignition.

Not sand. The bathtub had been filled to the top with white crystals. Ice Melt. A desiccant, she remembered from high-school chemistry, some version of coarse salt. Used to cure meats, like ham. Her stomach clenched as she got into the car.

Pink toenails. The image plowed through her head. The body—it might be Elaine Gallagher, the woman whose mail was being delivered there. But that nail polish said otherwise. Melinda's fingernails had been polished that same iridescent pink.

Call the police. Ivy picked up her cell phone from the passenger seat and flipped it open. She knew full well that if she used it, the police could easily trace the call. They'd come looking for her, wanting to know what she'd been doing in that house.

She closed the cell phone.

But she couldn't *not* call. If it was Melinda, then the mystery of where she'd gone would be solved and the police could turn their attention to figuring out what had really happened. They'd have to release David, wouldn't they?

But she couldn't possibly go back into that house and make the call. There had to be another way. Maybe she could use a neighbor's phone. There were lights on in the living-room window of the house next door. That was no good either. She'd be too easily identified.

There was a gas station just a few blocks from here. Gas stations always had pay phones. She'd make the call, short and sweet and anonymous. *I'd like to report a dead body.*

As she turned the key in the ignition, an aching started, deep in her lower back and the pit of her stomach. *Please, not again.* She gagged as nausea built.

She closed her eyes and leaned her head back. Her belly had gone rock solid. *Breathe. Focus.* Ivy counted, *One, two,* trying to stay in control. *Seven, eight.*

She got to twenty before the pain began to abate. When it had passed, she took a deep inhale, exhale, and opened her eyes.

Nausea. Diarrhea. Cramping. Coming in waves. She didn't have food poisoning. She wasn't getting the flu. Though her miscarriages had felt nothing like this, she knew she was in labor.

How long . . . ? She tried to think. She'd been feeling sick, off and on, ever since leaving the house, three hours ago.

She remembered Dr. Shapiro's instructions: When the contractions were regular and lasting thirty seconds or longer, wrangle David and get to the hospital. That time was now.

Don't panic. Sarah had told them that over and over in childbirth class. First labors lasted six to twenty hours. Worst case, she was three hours in.

Ivy started the car. She was taking no chances with this baby. The hospital was barely a twenty-minute drive.

Clutching the wheel like a life preserver, Ivy threaded her way back to the main street. The traffic jam that had clogged Brush Hills Square had eased out. After a brief wait at the light, she was moving.

She drove another mile, and another. She pictured the sign for Neponset Hospital's emergency entrance growing closer and closer.

When a miasma of discomfort started to take hold, she pulled over. Already the pains had a familiar shape, beginning in her lower back, almost like a menstrual cramp, nausea rising. Ivy gasped as her muscles contracted.

Find a focal point to enhance your relaxation. She touched her throat. Her grandmother's amulet—that's what she'd intended to use. They'd practiced this. She'd rub the charm's smooth, rounded stone between her thumb and forefinger as she breathed, in through the nose and out through the mouth, while David counted and held her hand. Breathing turned out to be a whole lot easier when the contraction was imaginary.

As this very real contraction loosened its hold, a tear leaked from her eye. How the hell was she going to get through this without David?

She picked up her cell phone and dialed Jody's number. *Please, be there.*

After a single ring, Jody picked up. "Finally." Jody started right in. "The police were here, asking about your neighbor. I've been trying—"

"Jody."

"—to call you and—"

"Jody! Stop!"

There was silence on the other end.

"Listen, I'm on my way to the hospital. I'm in labor."

"You're . . ." In the empty beats, Ivy could hear Jody's intake of breath. "Who's driving?"

"I am."

"Ivy, that's nuts. Wait right there. I'll come get you. Where are you?"

"I'm not far from the hospital. I'll be fine. Just meet me there. But first there's something important that I need you to do."

"Ivy, you shouldn't be driving."

"Shut up and listen to me." Ivy heard the panic in her voice. "Find a pay phone, like at a gas station or something. Call the Brush Hills Police. Tell them there's a dead body in the bathroom at 6 Belcher Street."

"Isn't that—"

"Then hang up."

"How do you—"

"Do not tell them who you are. Just tell them where to find the body. Please, Jody. I'll explain everything at the hospital." She disconnected the call and turned off the phone.

Minutes later Ivy turned the car in to the emergency entrance at Neponset Hospital.

"I'm in labor," she told the man in scrubs who emerged from the sliding doors and approached her car. No, she wasn't bleeding and her water hadn't broken. She gave him a rundown of her symptoms as if she were delivering the weather report.

Ivy peeled her fingers off the steering wheel. An orderly brought around a wheelchair and helped ease her from the car. She was pushed through the brightly lit, cheerful waiting area and over to an admitting desk in a cubicle, buffered from the quiet hum of the ER. An older woman with orangey hair and a pin on her blouse that read ASK ME smiled at her and started her paperwork as another contraction came and went. The woman's ID badge said that her name was Patricia Kennedy, and in the photo she was a brunette.

There should have been something calming about being here, getting sucked in and carried along on the conveyor belt of hospital protocol and administrative procedures. But comfort was not what Ivy felt as she was pushed down the corridor and into the elevator. She remembered the last time she was here.

It had been the middle of a hot July night, a year and a half ago. She was twenty weeks pregnant, finally starting to believe that the pregnancy was going to hold, when the cramping and spotting started. By the time she and David arrived at the emergency entrance, blood was dripping down her legs. She'd been rushed in on a gurney and immediately hooked up to an IV and a fetal monitor.

The doctors had done what they could to stop her contractions, but night had turned to morning, and the painful cramping had continued.

She remembered how Dr. Shapiro's brow had creased as she pressed a stethoscope to Ivy's belly. The flat line on the fetal monitor told the story.

She'd never even made it out of the ER. Her whole body had been shaking as one of the attending nurses scooped up the remains of her dead child, the same nurse with kind eyes over her surgical mask who'd explained that the "fetus"—

such an ugly word—would have to be sent to pathology.

David had been there, holding her hand through the ordeal. Melinda had probably been working there as a technician—she might even have been on duty that night when Ivy's dead baby was taken to the hospital lab.

Today everything was different, Ivy thought as the elevator doors opened on the maternity floor. She'd gone virtually full term, thirty-seven weeks.

Amulet or no amulet, David or no David, she was giving birth to a healthy baby girl.

26

Ivy was in a bed with both ends cranked up. She wore a hospital gown, and she'd been hooked up to a fetal monitor. The nurse had left a blood-pressure cuff loosely wrapped around her arm.

Ivy lay there, her hands on her belly, waiting for the next contraction. Two bright green lines surged and blipped across the monitor screen. She heard a woman in labor moaning in the room next door.

A light tap at the door, and there stood Jody. She ran in and hugged Ivy.

"So?" Jody pulled back, Ivy's hand sandwiched between her own warm palms.

"You okay?" Jody's eyes brimmed with tears.

Ivy managed a nod. "We're both just peachy keen."

"So it's showtime," Jody said with a tense smile. "You doing your breathing like a good girl?"

"Trying to."

"When was your last contraction?"

"It's been a while," Ivy said. "Twenty minutes. Maybe a little longer, even."

"And before that?"

"Seemed like every ten minutes. I had three just on the drive over."

"Remember they sent me home from the hospital twice when I went into labor with Riker?"

"You think they'll send me home?"

"Don't listen to me. What do I know? As my grandmother would say, it's Doris Day time. *Qué será será.*"

Jody pulled the easy chair over closer to the bed and sat.

"You made the call?" Ivy asked.

Jody nodded.

"What did they say?"

Jody looked around as if someone might overhear her. "I didn't give them a chance to say. I told the operator there was a dead body, gave the information, and hung up."

Ivy could picture the police arriving at the house. Knocking. Finding the side door open, as Ivy had. Going inside. Raising Melinda's body from its bath of salt crystals. At last searching for evidence that they should have searched for days ago, evidence that would either exonerate David or prove, even to her, that he was a murderer.

"You think it's Melinda?" Jody asked.

"Seems likely."

"So tell me what happened," Jody said.

Ivy explained how she'd taken a spontaneous detour down the street where Melinda used to live. "There was a traffic jam in the square. Otherwise I'd never have turned off."

She told Jody about the mailer addressed to Elaine Gallagher but packed with mail for Melinda's mother. About Melinda's old bedroom. "Jody, it's still just the way you described it. Pink walls. That funky lamp. What look like her clothes in the drawers, her books on the shelves—just like she was still living there. And she

had pictures of David. She had our engagement picture from the newspaper,
only she'd cut—" Ivy sobbed. "She'd cut
my face out of it."

The whisper of soft-soled shoes and the
clatter of a metal cart drifted in from the
corridor. Jody got up and closed the door.

"All I wanted to do was destroy the pictures of David and get out as fast as I
could." Ivy told her how she'd taken the
photographs and then started to feel sick.
How she'd just made it to the bathroom in
time.

"That's where I found her," Ivy said. She
told Jody about the salt-filled bathtub, the
painted toenails.

They sat for a few moments in silence.

"I hate pink," Jody said.

"The police are probably there now."

"On the drive over, I passed a couple of
police cars with their sirens going," Jody
said. "What did you do with those pictures?"

"They're in"—as Ivy said the words, she
felt her stomach harden—"my pants pockets." Finally another contraction.

Jody got up and opened the narrow
closet. She pulled Ivy's pants from a shelf

inside where they were folded and emp-
tied the pictures from one of the pockets.

"I told you she had a thing about you
guys. But do you believe me?"

"I believe you"—Ivy gritted her teeth as
the pain built—"now." She could barely
squeeze the word out.

Jody dropped the pants and rushed to
Ivy's side. "Here we go." She stroked Ivy's
forehead. "Relax. Breathe. Let your muscles do the work for you. Don't fight it."

Ivy focused on Jody's soft touch. On
the sound of her voice as the pain grew.

"Good, good. You're doing great. Hang
in there."

This one didn't seem nearly as bad—or
maybe it was just that it was easier to bear
with Jody there. Already the contraction
began to ease.

"Fifteen seconds at least," Jody said.

Ivy took a deep breath and blew out.

A nurse pushed open the door and entered the room. She was young, with long
straight hair, even darker than Ivy's, tied at
the nape of her neck. She examined the
monitor screen and checked Ivy's blood
pressure.

Before the nurse left, she wrapped the

cord of the emergency call buzzer so it dangled from the bed railing. "You need anything, you just press this."

Jody picked up Ivy's pants and the photos from the floor where she'd dropped them. She dug the remaining pieces of paper from the pockets and spread everything out at the foot of the bed.

"Looks like this one's pretty recent," Jody said, smoothing out the photograph of David in front of Rose Gardens. "She's been taking pictures of him. Stalking him. David didn't suspect? You had no idea?"

"Not a clue."

"Scary." Jody picked out the bowling score sheet. "Kezey's. Good God, do you remember that place? Just say the name and I can smell the smell. Sweaty socks and"—she wrinkled her nose—"crayon wax and stale cigarette smoke. And remember Old Man Kezey?"

Ivy did. The place was run by a greasy-haired man who carded kids who came without a grown-up—anyone who couldn't pull out a driver's license that showed he or she was eighteen had to pay a dollar surcharge to bowl. Still, Kezey's was the only show in town—the only place to hang out where kids could get to without a car.

"Melinda used to work at Kezey's," Jody said. "I remember seeing her there after school. And . . . cripes, here she is." Jody held up the older of the photo-booth strips.

"There's another strip of photos there, too," Ivy said.

Jody found the other strip and held the two side by side. "What do you think? Is this Melinda's sister, Ruth?"

"Her sister?" Ivy let the words out slowly. That was a possibility she hadn't considered.

Jody picked up the engagement picture with Ivy's face cut out of it. "Sick. This is really sick."

"You're telling me."

"What do you want to do with all these?" Jody gathered the photos and clippings into a pile at the foot of the bed.

"Burn them."

"Sounds like a plan." Jody settled back in her chair. "So Melinda White really is dead. And here I kept thinking that any minute she was going to turn up. I wonder if there's anything on the news yet." She picked up a remote control from the windowsill and pointed it at the TV mounted on a rack hanging from the ceiling. "You mind?"

"Go ahead," Ivy said.

Jody turned on the TV and flipped until she found a late news broadcast. There was a fire in a triple-decker in Southie. An attempted carjacking on the Pike. A volleyball left in a paper bag had shut down security in the Delta Air Lines terminal at Logan.

Nothing about the body of a missing woman found in a Brush Hills home.

Ivy felt a wave of exhaustion. She could barely lift her head. A commercial came on, a white butterfly flitting through a landscape to the music of harp strings. She closed her eyes and let the sound wash over her. She laced her fingers over her belly and wondered how long it would be before it hardened again.

She didn't even realize she'd fallen asleep until she awoke with a start. Dr. Shapiro was standing over her. Jody, who looked like she'd been snoozing in her chair, yawned and stretched. The TV was turned off, and it was after midnight.

Dr. Shapiro drew the curtain around the bed and examined Ivy. Afterward she pulled the monitor screen closer to the bed.

"This line is monitoring your contractions," Dr. Shapiro said, indicating a top line that was lazing along. "And this"—she indicated the bottom line that rose and fell, rose and fell—"is your baby. See? Looking good, just not ready to come out yet and greet the world."

"So I'm not in labor?"

"Happens all the time, especially with a first baby."

"The pains, diarrhea—I thought for sure . . ."

"You were having good, strong contractions when you were admitted. But for the last hour, nothing. If your labor doesn't heat up by morning, we'll release you. You'll be more comfortable sitting this out at home. Babies have their own timetables. Eventually they all come out."

"You don't have to stay," Ivy told Jody after Dr. Shapiro had left. "Looks like a false alarm."

"I'll leave in a bit. Then I can come back in the morning and drive you home."

"But my car—"

"Oh. I forgot. Your car's here," Jody said.

"I can always drive myself."

"Would you stop? Don't even think about it. I'll get someone to drive me, and one of us will drive your car home for you. I'll take care of it." Jody folded her arms and stared Ivy down. "Go back to sleep."

It had been a long day since waking at Jody's. Returning home to that perfumy smell. Jody staying with her to search the house and finding nothing—nothing except for that box of books that testified to another of David's lies. Her computer with its record of visits to travel Web sites—another lie.

Then finding Mrs. Bindel. The ambulance had probably taken her neighbor to the closest hospital. In the morning, if her labor hadn't kicked in again, Ivy would see if she could find her. Maybe Mrs. Bindel remembered what had happened when she and her dog—

The dog! Poor Phoebe. She would still be tethered to the clothesline, forlorn, waiting for Ivy to return.

"Jody, one other thing . . ." Ivy started.

But Jody was curled up in the chair, already fast asleep.

Outside, Ivy heard a wailing siren grow louder and louder, then fall silent as it pulled into the hospital's emergency entrance. She imagined the crime-scene tape that would be cordoning off the bungalow house on Belcher Street. The media vans, once camped out in front of her house, would be parked up and down the street. Police investigators would be inside collecting evidence and dusting for fingerprints.

Ivy hoped that she hadn't left behind evidence of her presence. She'd had her hands covered when she was in Melinda's bedroom. But had she remembered to do that in the bathroom? Had she touched the side of the tub? Too late now to do anything about it.

She shuddered, remembering those painted toenails. How long after the yard sale had Melinda been killed? Where did it happen, and when had her body been moved to the tub? Those same questions would at long last propel the police investigation in new directions.

Ivy turned on her side and watched the

fetal monitor. Her contractions had flat-lined, but the baby's heartbeat pulsed along. *Blip. Blip. Blip. Blip. . . .* She let her eyes close.

Ivy lurched awake. She'd just caught sight of a nurse wearing purple scrubs leaving her room. Her ponytail swung as she disappeared into the corridor. Reminded Ivy of Cindy Goodwin, David's new assistant manager and Jody's Cheerleader Barbie. The chair where Jody had been sleeping was empty and the light in the room turned off.

The top line on the fetal monitor—the baby's line—still pulsed, regular and reassuring. It cast a pale green reflection on the walls and ceiling.

Ivy closed her eyes and pictured herself stepping through the pen-and-ink illustrations of *Madeline* as she mentally recited the rhyming verses.

She had no idea how much later it was when she felt a hand on her abdomen. A shadowy figure loomed at the end of the bed. "We know you were there." She recognized Detective Blanchard's raspy voice.

What was he doing here in the hospital in the middle of the night? Why couldn't she see his face? How could he reach her from where he was standing? And yet she felt his hand. She tried to move, to dislodge it, but she was paralyzed.

This isn't real, she told herself.

She forced herself awake, gasping as if she'd just come to the surface after being knocked over and pummeled by an ocean wave. A woman in pink scrubs stood by the bed. She had a surgical mask over her face. Her hand rested on Ivy's belly as she stared at the fetal monitor. Not Detective Blanchard.

Ivy's head fell back on the pillow. Just a nurse. The ID badge that swung from the breast pocket of her scrubs flashed green reflections of the light from the fetal monitor.

"Everything is fine. Perfectly fine. Relax," the nurse said. "I'm just checking on the baby."

Then, without another word, she left. The only trace of her presence was the lingering smell of latex rubber and a faint whiff of Opium perfume.

27

Unable to get the smells out of her head, Ivy slept fitfully through what was left of the night. Seemed like just about every half hour a different nurse came in and checked on her. By seven-thirty the next morning, Dr. Shapiro had been in, disconnected her from the fetal monitor, and proclaimed her fit for discharge.

"Don't go far," she'd warned Ivy.

No worries there. When Ivy got home, she planned to go straight up to bed.

Jody called. Theo would drive over with her at ten. Ivy checked the morning news programs. None were reporting a body in a suburban Brush Hills home.

Ivy took a scalding-hot shower, letting the water beat against her sore back. She changed into yesterday's clothes again. The photos and papers she'd taken from Melinda's bedroom were gone. Ivy hoped Jody had incinerated them.

She checked the TV news again. Still nothing.

Restless, Ivy picked up the hospital phone. "Corinne Bindel. B-I-N-D-E-L." She spelled the name to the operator.

Yes, Mrs. Bindel was a patient at the hospital. Her condition had been upgraded from serious to fair. That was all the operator could tell her.

Ivy hung up and nibbled at the last of a piece of toast on her breakfast tray, resisting the urge to check the TV again.

Her hair still damp, she left the room. A floor plan and directory hung on the wall alongside the elevators. Ivy didn't know where Mrs. Bindel was, but the hospital wasn't that big—not like those downtown medical complexes that were small cities unto themselves.

Ivy scanned down the list of departments. Admissions and Administration were on the first floor. Intensive Care was on 3 East. Maternity, 2 West. That was where she was now. Medical/Surgical, 2 East—that seemed a likely possibility.

Ivy followed a sign for 2 East that pointed past the elevators. She continued down a corridor, through double doors, and left through another set of double doors. She came to a large nurses' station. A doctor was there, talking on the phone. Ivy hurried past, trying to look as if she had a clear destination.

Each of the patient rooms in the unit had a card by the door with names lettered in bold black marker. Ivy made her way down one side of the long corridor and was halfway up the other side before she found the room she was looking for.

Through the open door, Ivy could see Mrs. Bindel lying in the nearest bed. Ivy entered the room. The woman in the neighboring bed glanced over at Ivy and then rolled over to face the window.

Mrs. Bindel lay on her back, her head swathed in bandages, her eyes closed. Her lips were dry and cracked. Ivy pulled a chair close to the bed and sat. She

picked up Mrs. Bindel's hand. An IV nee-
dle was taped to her arm, and the tube
snaked off the bed. Her chest rose and
lowered. *Fair condition.* What did that
mean anyway?

As Ivy sat there, she remembered her
last visit to Grandma Fay. It had been a
few months after she and David were married. That afternoon she'd arrived and
found her grandmother slumped in her
easy chair, the newspaper still in her lap.
Without her vivid personality to animate
her, her grandmother seemed so diminished by death, nothing more than a bag
of skin and birdlike bones.

Ivy had been her grandmother's official
health-care proxy, but, as usual, Grandma
Fay had made her own decision about how
and when to go. One day she was walking
to the supermarket with her wheelie cart,
bossing everyone around. Then a twinge
of indigestion, some chest pain, and a few
hours later she was gone. It was a perfect
death for someone who always said she
"didn't want to be a bother."

"If only people had an 'off' button,"
Grandma Fay had once said to Ivy. "Or in

my case we should label it 'enough already.'"

Ivy was startled back into the present
when Mrs. Bindel's hand moved. Her eyelids fluttered open, and her gaze wandered
about the room, finally fastening on Ivy.
Her look of recognition turned to confusion. She put her hand to her bandaged
head.

"Yes," Ivy said, "you hurt your head. Do
you remember?"

"I . . ." Mrs. Bindel's eyes turned bright
and anxious. "You . . . ?"

"Yes, I found you. I called the ambulance."

"Phoebe?"

"Oh, she's fine." Ivy felt a pang of guilt.
The minute she got home, she'd take
Phoebe inside and feed the poor dog. At
least she'd left water. "Mrs. Bindel, do you
remember what happened?"

"Garden," Mrs. Bindel said, her eyes unfocused. "Daylilies."

"Your daylilies were beautiful this year,"
Ivy said. "Were you dividing them in the
garden?"

Mrs. Bindel stared at Ivy.

"That's where I found you, outside, lying in the grass near your back steps. Did you see someone out there?" Ivy asked. "Did someone hurt you?"

Mrs. Bindel's gaze shifted over Ivy's shoulder. Her eyes widened, and with surprising strength she pulled her hand from Ivy's grasp.

"Did—" Ivy's question was cut off by a sharp rap at the door.

She turned to face Detective Blanchard.

"Mrs. Rose—what are you doing here?" He entered the room.

Ivy swallowed the urge to retort, *None of your damned business.* "I was admitted to the hospital last night. In labor."

His gaze dropped to her belly.

"It stopped," Ivy added.

"You've been here overnight?"

"I'm being released this morning."

"So you don't know?"

Ivy's heart lurched into high gear. "Don't know what?"

He indicated for her to follow him out into the corridor. "There's been a development in the case." As he talked, Ivy could feel him watching her closely.

She tried to look surprised. She savored

the vindication she'd be able to finally show when Blanchard revealed that all this time Melinda's body had been in the house where she grew up.

"We found the body of Gereda White. Melinda White's mother," Blanchard said.

Melinda's *mother*? Ivy was too stunned to speak.

"In a house that she once owned. Looks as if Mrs. White has been dead for quite some time."

"I . . . I don't know what to say. How . . . ?"

"We won't know cause of death until the body is autopsied."

"But . . . ?" Ivy started. How to phrase her question without giving herself away? "I thought Mrs. White was living in Florida with Melinda's sister, Ruth."

Blanchard looked appropriately cha-grined. "So did we. But apparently all of us were wrong. The Naples police went to Ruth White's apartment and found no one living there. Neighbors haven't seen any-one coming or going for weeks." He looked down at his shoes. "We're analyzing rec-ords from Ruth White's cell phone to pin-point her location, the times when she called us. It's a Florida number, but she could have been calling from anywhere."

"Does Melinda even *have* a sister named Ruth?" Ivy asked.

"Of course. That we did check." Detective Blanchard's scowl deepened. "We're still investigating. The rest of the facts remain unaltered."

"But—"

He held up his hand. "I've told you more than I should have. Trust me, the investigation is progressing."

"Trust you?" Ivy said, incredulous. "So when are you going to release my husband?"

28

I hate to admit it, but the guy's got a point,"
Theo said as he drove Ivy home from the
hospital. The interior of his Lexus smelled
of leather and cigar smoke. "Discovering
Mrs. White's body doesn't alter the fact
that a woman who disappeared was last
seen going into your house. She and David argued. The cops found blood evidence and a knife that David admits he
tried to hide. And there's still that one-way
ticket to the Cayman Islands. At a bare
minimum, they've still got the goods to
hold David on evidence tampering."

Theo's words blared at Ivy as if from

dense fog. Condensation had misted the windshield, and the overcast sky made it feel more like late afternoon than mid-morning.

"So how are you?" Theo asked, his eyes avoiding Ivy's belly.

"Physically?" Ivy fastened the seat belt below the bulge. "Fine."

Theo started the wipers and drove slowly out the hospital access road. In the distance Ivy spotted Jody walking through the hospital parking lot, searching for Ivy's car.

"It's so infuriating." Theo looked both ways before turning onto a divided road-way. "They won't tell us anything about how they found Mrs. White or the circum-stances of her death."

The wipers thunked back and forth.

"The detective told me that Mrs. White had been dead for quite some time," Ivy said.

"Quite some time?" Theo shot her a sideways glance.

"I know. What does that mean? And where's the woman who's supposed to be living in that house? Didn't Mrs. White sell it to someone?"

"The house *was* sold," Theo said. "About eight months ago. We found the sale in the town records. The new owner is a woman, Elaine Gallagher. I've got a detective trying to find out who and where she is. I wonder how they knew to search that house. Must have gotten a tip from someone."

"Must have," Ivy said. She stared out the window. She was not about to tell Theo she'd been in the Belcher Street house, that she'd found the bathtub filled with Ice Melt. That Jody had been the anonymous tipster. And she certainly wasn't going to tell him about the photographs of David that she'd found in what had once been Melinda's bedroom. She was just glad they'd been taken care of.

Theo hit the steering wheel with the heel of his hand. "So where the hell is this woman Ruth White who is supposed to be taking care of the demented but actually dead Mrs. White?"

"Obviously, David had nothing to do with murdering their mother," Ivy said.

"Obviously. And we don't know that she was killed. Besides, David isn't under arrest for murder." Ivy heard the unsaid *not yet.* "Right now we need to keep our heads down and focus on Monday's bail hearing." Theo's silver cross swung back and forth, back and forth from the rearview mirror. "We've still got to come up with an explanation for that ticket to the Cayman Islands. David didn't book it, so someone else did."

"What if it turns out that the ticket was booked from our computer?" Ivy asked.

Theo's foot came off the accelerator. "Was it?"

"I don't know. But if it was?"

The car cruised a stretch of winding road and then came to a stop at a light. "If it was, then someone had to have had access to your house to do it," Theo said. "Who? And how could we prove that it wasn't you or David? It's not like there are surveillance cameras inside the house."

"Maybe there's a witness who saw someone trying to get into the house."

"Who hasn't come forward?"

"Who hasn't been able to come forward. My neighbor. Maybe Mrs. Bindel saw someone trying to use the old key after I'd changed the locks. Maybe that's why she was knocked unconscious. Right now she doesn't remember. But maybe she will."

Ivy recalled Mrs. Bindel's expression when she'd woken up in the hospital and seen Ivy at her bedside. Initial confusion had turned to something else. Fear? Ivy hadn't been able to ask, because that was when Detective Blanchard arrived.

"The police were in our house searching," she said. "Maybe they copied the key. Maybe one of them came back later when no one was home. One of the people I saw rummaging through the wicker trunk was a man." Ivy tried to remember, but all she could conjure was a silhouette. Tall. Thin.

"A police conspiracy? That'll give the judge a laugh. And hope it's not the case, because that's next to impossible to prove."

The light turned green. The tires spun before they got traction. Theo drove through the square, past the Three Brothers Hardware store and Kezey's Good Time Lanes. The bowling score sheet she'd found in Melinda's bedroom had been from there.

"Remember the old bowling alley?" Ivy said.

"Sure." Theo glanced over. "Wonder if they'll ever take down that sign."

"You guys used to hang out there. After football practice. You and David?"

Theo nodded as he turned off the main street.

"And Eddie and Jake?"

Theo shot her a surprised look. "Yeah. The whole team did." He turned onto Laurel Street.

"Melinda White worked there after school," Ivy said.

The car rolled to a halt in front of the house. There was a long beat before Theo spoke. "Maybe. I don't really remember."

"Like you said, the team used to play there."

Theo's grip tightened on the steering wheel. "Ivy, did you mention this to the police?"

"This what?"

He turned to face her. "Kezey's. Bowling."

"Why would I?"

His eyes searched hers. "Good question. Why would you?"

Ivy didn't answer.

"Well, don't mention it to anyone. Please don't."

Dread burrowed into the pit of Ivy's stomach. "What happened?"

"It's ancient history."

Not ancient enough if he didn't want her so much as mentioning the bowling alley to anyone.

Theo pulled the hand brake. "I'm telling you, nothing"—he swiveled in his seat to face her—"happened."

Ivy held his gaze. "Theo. Obviously, something did."

"Ivy—"

"What happened?"

Theo groaned. "This is so irrelevant."

"Theo!"

"Okay, okay. She . . . Melinda . . . thought David . . ." He paused for a moment, as if picking his words. "We were there after practice one day, and she thought David came on to her."

Ivy stared at the silver cross as it swung from the rearview mirror. *Came on to her.* What was that supposed to mean?

"I'm sure she believed he did," Theo went on. "That he had a thing for her. But of course he didn't."

"How do you know?"

"How do I—Because I was there."

The cooling engine ticked. "That's not what I meant. How do you know what *Melinda thought* happened?" Ivy said.

"I . . . shit." Theo looked away. His jaw twitched. "David told me. That's why he took Melinda into the house during the yard sale. She started rehashing what had happened at the bowling alley. Years and years ago. Her version. He thought it was better to talk about it . . . in private."

Theo pulled the key from the ignition. "But I'm telling you, she was delusional."

"How bad is the 'what she thought happened' version?" Ivy asked.

"He . . . she . . ." Theo licked his lips. "Crap, do you really need to know this? I mean, it was no big deal."

Ivy reached out to stop the silver cross from swinging and waited.

"It was after practice, fall of our senior year," Theo said. "We went down there. To bowl. The place was empty. Mr. Kezey was out, so someone got a case of beer, and we started to drink and bowl and . . . you know, fool around."

"Fool around?"

"We got sloshed. All of us. Pretty much

trashed the place." He smirked. "I admit, things got a little out of control."

"A little?"

"A lot, I guess."

"And Melinda?"

"She was drinking, too. Having a grand old time. Then . . ." Theo ran his tongue over his lips again.

"Then what?" Ivy said.

"You mean did we . . . ? Was there . . . ? No way. But not because of her. Because, believe me, she was asking for it."

Ivy winced. His smug tone turned her stomach. Melinda had probably never gotten drunk before. Boys were paying attention to her for what had to be the first time ever. No big deal for a bunch of football jocks, but for Melinda it had to have been a very big deal.

Theo exhaled sharply. "It was obvious that Melinda had the hots for David. He was *nice* to her, for God's sake. Big mistake."

"So you're saying that at the yard sale David took Melinda inside because she wanted to talk to him about something that happened back in high school?"

"Exactly. Is that insane or what? Only . . . nothing happened."

Theo sat forward and looked at himself in the rearview mirror. He ran his palm against the hair on the side of his head, then looked over his shoulder as Jody pulled Ivy's car into the driveway.

He turned to Ivy. "Ivy, David said she was acting crazy. Out of control. He told you all about it, how she got all little-girlie. Smashed that glass. She was furious when he told her that she was . . . mistaken about what had happened. Which is pretty funny, actually, because he got so drunk he passed out. I practically had to carry him home. And she was so drunk that . . ." He chuckled. "Anyway, I'm surprised either of them remembers anything at all, other than the hangover they had when they woke up. Must have been a corker."

Theo let himself out of the car. Ivy waited while he came around to the passenger side, feeling as if she'd been slugged in the back with a sandbag. Yes, David had told her about Melinda's meltdown in the attic, but he certainly hadn't told her everything. He'd glossed over Melinda's accusations, just as Theo was glossing over them now.

Theo opened the car door for her. The rain had stopped.

"Know what I thought when I first heard they'd found a body?" he said. Ivy bit back the repulsion she felt as she took Theo's offered hand and heaved herself from the car. "That it was Melinda, and she'd committed suicide. And I'll tell you something else. I just hope she *is* dead. Because if she's not, she's gone over the edge, and that's big trouble."

For whom? What if Melinda turned up alive and well and eager to tell the police what had happened at Kezey's? Tell them her version, that is. Even if some statute of limitations had expired and it was too late to press charges, the story would come out. David would find himself at the center of a scandal. There would be questions about Theo's role. The would-be state senator could have his reputation sullied by innuendo that he might never be able to disprove. His political career would be DOA.

Jody walked down the driveway toward Ivy. "I opened the side door for you. Left your keys in the kitchen. You okay? No more labor pains?"

"Not a twinge," Ivy said. "I'm fine."

"You don't look fine to me. You want us to come in for a bit before Theo drives me home?"

Ivy held up her hands to ward off any more offers. "No. Thanks." She might have welcomed Jody's company, but the last thing she wanted was to spend another minute with Theo. "Really. All I want to do is go inside and get some sleep."

She started up the driveway.

"I'll have my cell turned on." Jody's voice followed her.

Ivy was about to climb the steps to the side door when the sound of barking from behind Mrs. Bindel's house brought her to a halt. Crap. Once again she'd forgotten all about the damn dog.

"Jody!" she called out, turning back.

Jody trotted halfway up the drive. "Tuck you in?"

"Could you do me a big favor and carry in that big bag of dog food that's in my car? Leave it for me in the kitchen. I promised I'd look after Phoebe, Mrs. Bindel's dog."

Ivy crossed into the neighboring yard.

Phoebe's barking turned to pitiful mewling yelps as she approached. The dog had gotten herself tangled in the rope that tethered her to the clothesline. Phoebe couldn't even reach the plastic tub of water Ivy had left there.

Ivy untied the rope from the clothesline. She lowered herself and sat cross-legged in the damp grass near the tub of water and waited for the dog to come over.

Phoebe's stumpy tail wagged so hard that her entire rear end rumbaed. She licked Ivy's face, lapped up some water, and licked Ivy's face some more. Ivy untangled the rope, then put her arms around Phoebe and buried her face in the dog's warm, moist coat. Dogs were great for comic relief.

Ivy rolled onto her knees, then stood. Phoebe tried to pull her toward Mrs. Bindel's house. After a brief tug-of-war, the dog surrendered and let Ivy lead her to her house. Inside, Ivy untied the rope from Phoebe's collar and left it coiled around a doorknob in the mudroom. She dropped her purse onto the kitchen counter, beside where Jody had left her keys. The bag of dog food was on the floor.

While Phoebe sniffed her way around the kitchen, Ivy slit open the bag and scooped some pellets into a bowl. She had no idea whether she should add some water, but she did, mixed it around, and set the bowl on the floor.

Phoebe came over and immediately started to eat. After a few moments, she gave Ivy an anxious look, rolls of velvety flesh bunched up over her eyes, and then went back to eating.

Ivy returned to the mudroom. *Click, click, click.* The sound of claws on the floor as the dog followed her. She double-locked the side door, then leaned down and scratched Phoebe behind the ears.

The truth was, she was glad not to be alone. Equally glad to have a companion who didn't require conversation.

Ivy poured herself a glass of orange juice and drank while Phoebe ate. She'd drunk half when she registered the bitter-tasting edge. She dumped out the rest, rinsed the glass, and put it in the sink.

With Phoebe trailing behind, she walked through the downstairs. In the front hall, Bessie was facing forward, as she should be. The front door was double-locked. The living-room shades were drawn and the room in perfect order. Couch cushions were plumped and arranged. No newspapers or magazines had been left on the floor or coffee table.

Ivy yawned. She really was bone tired.

Upstairs, Ivy poked her head into each of the bedrooms. Then she stripped off the clothes she'd had on yesterday, too, and put on fresh underwear and sweats. She brushed her teeth, scrubbing away a nasty aftertaste that lingered in her mouth from the orange juice.

Bed beckoned. But she knew she wouldn't be able to sleep. She'd be churning, rehashing Theo's words: *Nothing happened.* The bald truth was, she didn't believe him. Theo was a spinner, a consummate politician even when he wasn't running for office—someone who liked to neatly tuck in the ragged edges of messy reality.

In any event, she'd caught David in yet another evasion. *How much more will it take before you stop protecting him?* Maybe Detective Blanchard was right.

Sure, physical evidence could easily have been planted by someone trying to implicate David, but over and over, David had lied. He'd finally admitted that he'd hidden the bag with the knife in it. Fetal tissue—it made Ivy nauseous just thinking about it.

What if the paternal DNA turned out to be David's? David and Melinda? Impossible—that's what Ivy would have said a few days ago. Even now, at her core, beyond reason, beyond that growing body of physical evidence, she was convinced that David was not a murderer. If one piece could be disproved, the rest would crumble.

That ticket to the Cayman Islands—she'd seen the evidence with her own eyes that it had been booked from their computer. Or had she? Visits to a couple of travel Web sites hardly seemed conclusive.

Ivy went into her office and settled in at her desk. She jiggled the mouse, and the screen lit up. Phoebe wormed her way underneath and lay at Ivy's feet. Ivy yawned and opened the browser window.

She clicked the HISTORY button. Clicked TUESDAY. Again she saw the list of sites visited, in reverse chronological order.

Caymanislands.com was followed by Travelocity.com. They were sandwiched between MapQuest before and the Channel 7 Web site after.

That was three days ago. She tried to remember. She'd slept late, not getting up until after David had left for work. The visit to MapQuest had been for driving directions to Mr. Vlaskovic's. And she was nearly certain that she hadn't checked the TV-news Web site until after she returned to the house following the baby shower.

She touched her fingers to the screen, excitement stirring. Travelocity and the Cayman Islands Web site had been visited Tuesday when David was at work. It had been the same day that preparations were under way for the baby shower—his co-workers could vouch for him.

Elated, Ivy hit PRINT SCREEN. A moment later the printer hummed into action. She grabbed the paper as it slid out. She'd take the printout to Theo, who'd show it to the judge at Monday's bail hearing. Or even better, maybe he could request an emergency hearing before then.

She had it, proof that David was no flight risk. Proof that someone had come into this office on Tuesday and used her laptop to purchase a plane ticket in David's name. Proof that someone had gotten into the house, come and gone without either her or David's realizing.

Thank God that the next day she'd had the locks changed.

29

Ivy called Theo with the good news. When he didn't pick up, she left a message. As she finished the call, a wave of exhaustion rolled over her. She needed to sleep. But first she wanted to check whether there was news.

The local news site came up with a red banner: BREAKING NEWS! And beneath that: GRISLY DISCOVERY IN BRUSH HILLS.

A photograph of Melinda White overlapped a larger picture showing the front of the gray bungalow, both filling the left side of the screen. Anticipation turned to queasiness as Ivy remembered the sour smell inside the home and the salt-filled tub.

She read: *"Last night police discovered the body of Gereda White, an elderly Brush Hills woman. . . ."* She scanned down. *"Police said that an anonymous tip led them to the house, which Mrs. White once owned."*

A sidebar read, *"Mystery deepens around the disappearance of Mrs. White's pregnant daughter, 33-year-old Melinda White."*

Damn right it did. Ivy stared at the inset photo of Melinda. She looked as she had in one of the black-and-white photo-booth strips that Ivy had found in her bedroom. Jody had speculated that the second, more recent set might be of Melinda's sister, Ruth. Ruth, who'd reported Melinda missing. Ruth, who had a rented apartment in Florida that she hadn't been to in weeks, and who obviously was not taking care of Mom.

Was it Ruth who'd come to their yard sale and introduced herself as Melinda? Who'd manipulated David into taking her inside and leaving her there alone? And what if by then, like her mother, Melinda was already dead?

It made Ivy's head hurt just thinking about it. She shut the laptop, went into her bedroom, and crawled into the unmade bed. Phoebe stood, her snout resting on the bed. The dog gave a pitiful whine. Then a yelp. The sounds perfectly expressed how Ivy felt, too.

What the heck. Phoebe wasn't hers for keeps, so there'd be no bad habits to break. She reached over and hauled the dog up onto the bed beside her. Phoebe circled twice before settling.

When Ivy closed her eyes, she focused on the sliver of good news she had for David. She hoped the revelation would give those reporters something else to spin— which reminded her. She reached over and turned off the ringer on the bedside phone.

As she drifted into sleep, she could feel Phoebe's body, warm against her side.

Ivy came to with a start. A steady rain thrummed at the window. She propped herself on an elbow and checked the clock. It was nearly four. She'd slept for hours and wanted nothing more than to turn over and go back to sleep, but Phoebe had other ideas. The dog stood in the doorway, whining. At least she was well housebroken.

Ivy rolled out of bed and shoved her feet into a pair of old running shoes. Phoebe led the way downstairs. Between the rain and having all the shades pulled, it was dark in the house. Still groggy, Ivy got the rope from the side door and tied it to Phoebe's collar. She grabbed a rain slicker from the mudroom and used the spare key hanging alongside the door to let herself out.

Light pulsed in the sky. Ivy counted to twenty before the distant groan of thunder followed. The overcast sky provided welcome cover as she and Phoebe walked the edges of her own and Mrs. Bindel's yards. Drizzle hit her face like tiny needles as she waited for Phoebe to do her business.

On the way back, Ivy paused for a moment at the spot where she'd found Mrs. Bindel's inert body. She remembered that angry, livid bruise on her neighbor's pale scalp and the good-size rock that Detective Blanchard had found nearby.

She shivered and hurried back inside.

Ivy toweled off the dog in the mudroom, locked the door, and hung the spare key back on its hook. She was halfway through the dark kitchen when she stopped. Turned back.

Something was off.

She flipped on the switch, and the overhead fixture flooded the room with light. Her purse was not on the kitchen counter, where she was sure she'd left it. Her keys were gone, too.

Instead, on the counter sat one of her grandmother's red glass dessert plates. On it lay the newspaper clipping of Ivy and David's engagement announcement.

A siren went off in Ivy's head. Someone was in the house. She had to get out of here. But she couldn't take her eyes off the clipping. Yellow and curled, it looked like the copy she'd found in Melinda's bedroom at her mother's house.

But how could it be? Hadn't Jody gathered up all that material from Ivy's hospital bed and burned it?

Ivy stepped closer. Where her own face had been cut out, another face now filled the hole. She turned the clipping over and ripped away the photograph that had been taped onto the back.

It took her a moment to process what she was seeing—the face was in a frame from one of the photo-booth strips she'd found in Melinda's old bedroom.

A low growl sent a chill rippling across Ivy's back. Phoebe stood in the doorway to the mudroom, teeth bared and snarling, staring past Ivy toward the dining room.

Ivy turned. A figure emerged from the shadows. The woman who'd been at their yard sale stood there, staring at Ivy. Was this Melinda? Ruth?

Raw terror clawed its way up Ivy's throat. "Get out of my house."

The woman stepped into the bright kitchen. She was not pregnant.

"Keep away from me!"

The woman took a step closer.

"Why are you doing this?"

The woman's gaze dropped to Ivy's belly. "Because that's my baby."

Ivy backed up fast, banging against the

kitchen counter. She grabbed one of the knives from the block and held it out in front of her, the tip wavering, the blade catching the light.

"Stay away!" Ivy screamed.

She registered the pink scrubs that the woman had on—just like that nurse who'd come to check on her in the middle of the night, the nurse who'd worn a surgical mask over her face and left behind her the scent of latex and Opium perfume. She hadn't been there to check on Ivy. She'd been looking for Ivy's baby.

The woman snagged a dish towel that was hanging on the stove.

Phoebe growled and scrabbled back into the mudroom. Before Ivy realized what had happened, the woman snapped the dish towel at her. Her hand stung, and the knife skittered across the floor. Ivy plunged after it.

The woman grabbed Ivy from behind and kicked the knife, sending it spinning across the room.

Ivy kicked and screamed, but she was held tight. They stood there, locked to-gether. The cloying scent of Opium seemed to pulse off the woman in waves.

Ivy gagged and retched. Bile backed up in her throat.

The phone rang. Then it rang again.

"That's my friend." Ivy somehow managed to squeeze out the words. "Checking on me. If I don't answer—" The phone rang a third time. The woman tightened her grip. "—She'll know something's wrong." Ivy could barely breathe.

The phone rang once more, and the answering machine picked up. Ivy's surly message played: "There's no one here to take your call." The beep sounded.

"Mrs. Rose?" Ivy didn't recognize the formal woman's voice. "This is Phyllis Stone from the Norfolk County Crime Lab. I understand you've agreed to come in and give a DNA sample? A detective from the Brush Hills Police Department asked me to call you and schedule an appointment."

That bastard Blanchard—was this his idea? A new way to harass her?

The voice continued. "Call me and let me know when you want to come. It'll only take a minute. We're open nine to five. And be sure to bring a photo ID."

If Ivy could just get to the phone, knock it off the hook. Scream.

Ivy tried to buck, to heave the woman off her, barely registering the caller giving an address and a phone number. She jabbed an elbow into the woman's stomach and twisted free. The woman shrieked and staggered sideways.

Ivy grabbed for the phone, but it was too late. Dial tone buzzed in her ear. She started to punch in 911, but the woman unplugged the phone cable from the wall.

Ivy dropped the receiver, grabbed the teakettle from the stove, and brought it down as hard she could on the woman's head. Then she raced into the mudroom. The spare key was there, hanging from the hook by the door.

She felt movement behind her. *Hurry!*

She jammed the key in the lock, turned it. She had the door barely open when the woman's forearm clamped around her neck. Before Ivy could resist, she was shoved hard against the door, slamming it shut. The sound seemed to explode in her skull.

Something stuck into Ivy's side—the knifepoint, she realized, pricking through the sweatshirt and into her skin. She tried to pull away. Winded and breathing heavily, the woman wrapped her arm more tightly around Ivy's neck and twisted the knife tip against Ivy's ribs.

Ivy's head throbbed, and patterns of yellow and black kaleidoscoped in front of her tightly shut eyes.

"Lock the door and give me the key," the woman said, her voice low.

Ivy hunched her back, struggling to make a safe hollow for the baby. She screamed as the knife cut into her skin. She tried to angle her body to keep the baby from being crushed inside her, trying to ease the pressure of the knifepoint. Phoebe cowered in the corner of the mudroom, mewling.

"Why are you doing this?" Ivy cried.

"Lock it."

"I can't move. Not with you pressing against me so hard."

The woman eased up.

"Then what are you going to do?" As she talked, Ivy turned the key right and immediately back to the left. "Kill me—like you killed your own mother?" She pulled the key from the lock.

The woman had turned still. "I didn't . . .

kill . . . my mother," she said, biting off the words.

"That's not what the police believe."

She snatched the key from Ivy. "You think I care? Just as long as they think I'm dead."

30

Did you kill your sister, Ruth, too?" Ivy asked as she climbed the stairs, with the woman she now knew was Melinda right behind her.

"Shut up," Melinda said. "Keep moving."

Step after step after step to the second floor, Ivy could feel the knifepoint pressed against her back. Melinda had her hand wrapped so tightly around Ivy's hair that her scalp stung and smarted as she climbed each tread.

"My friends are checking on me," Ivy said. "If I don't answer the phone—"

"They're not going to worry."

"There's a bail hearing Monday. If I'm not there—"

"Monday?" Melinda laughed. "This will all be over long before then."

Over?

"Keep going." Melinda yanked Ivy's head.

Another flight up. Ivy's sneakers tracked through sawdust that coated the attic landing. The door stood open—a sliding metal bolt had been screwed into it and a hole drilled into the doorjamb. Melinda released her hair, pushed her into the bedroom and down onto the bed.

Ivy looked frantically about the room. The lamp was gone. The bed had been stripped. Even the wastebasket that had been in the corner had been removed. On the floor was a crumpled piece of yellowed canvas. Ivy's heart lurched when she realized what it was—the straitjacket from the wicker trunk.

Melinda picked it up and shook it out. "Wasn't it just perfect, finding this in that old trunk? Talk about a sign from the Almighty. Like that swan at your yard sale. That's what my mother always said she wanted me to do with her money after she died—turn myself into a swan."

Melinda held the straitjacket by the shoulders and lifted one of the sleeves. It tapered to a point, ending in a dangling leather strap. "Whether I have to use this is up to you."

Ivy gave an involuntary shudder. She held very still, but her mind was racing. She had to get out of here. The open bedroom door—Ivy shifted forward until she was perched at the edge of the bed.

Melinda dropped the straitjacket onto the floor and backed up, slamming the door shut behind her. She leaned against it.

"You're not leaving." She jerked her chin toward the bed. "Sit back. Relax."

Ivy slid back. "Why are you doing this to me? What do you want?"

"I told you." There was a manic gleam in Melinda's eyes. "I want the baby David owes me."

"Owes you? *Owes you?*" Ivy voice was shrill. "That's—"

"Crazy?" Melinda gave Ivy a long look. "So David never told you about us?"

Us? In all those photos from Melinda's

bedroom, there hadn't been a single one of Melinda and David together. Any "us" had to have been in Melinda's fantasy world. But that didn't make it any less real to her.

"David liked you," Ivy said.

"He told you that?" Melinda's eyes widened with hope, and for a moment the new, slimmed-down version of Melinda with her straightened teeth and frosted hair merged with the pudgy, pudding-faced girl who'd worn white, frilly-edged ankle socks in fourth grade.

Then her look hardened. "You're lying." She tightened her grip on the knife and held it out in front of her. "I'm not a complete idiot. David didn't even know who I was when he saw me at the yard sale. Not at first." She smiled. "Not until I reminded him about what happened."

"What happened?" The words leaked out before Ivy could stop them.

"Right. Like you don't know. Like you weren't laughing your heads off—you and the rest of the popular kids."

Popular? Ivy was genuinely astonished. She'd had no illusions that she'd ever been part of the popular crowd. But envy was all about perspective, and Melinda had been the ultimate outsider.

"The day after it happened, all the kids were talking about it. Not even whispering. Not bothering to hide their stares and snickers." Melinda's mouth twisted into an ugly sneer. *"Fat, pathetic Melinda White went down on the football team.* Only that's not what happened. But it didn't matter, because everyone wanted to believe that it did. You remember that, don't you?"

"I . . ." Ivy didn't know what to say. She did remember some talk, but she'd had no idea that Melinda was *that* girl, or which boys had been involved. It had been before she and David had started seeing each other, back in the days when she seemed as likely to get abducted by aliens as she was to date Brush Hills High's star quarterback.

"Later, when they voted me Friendliest?" Melinda said. "Like I wouldn't get the joke."

Ivy remembered the kids on the yearbook committee laughing and winking at one another when the vote came in.

"They thought if you were homely, you

were stupid, too." A tear squeezed from the corner of Melinda's eye, and she lowered the knife. But just for a moment. "They didn't know what really happened."

"The truth never came out, did it?" Ivy said, her words dropping into an anguished silence. "You're the only one who knows." She realized that Melinda wanted to tell, needed to tell. She shifted forward, bit by bit, until her feet touched the floor.

"You want to hear exactly what your precious husband and his friends did to me?" Melinda raised the knife and pointed it at Ivy. "I've thought of it every day of every week of every year. When I'm awake. It's even in my dreams. I remember every detail. I can still hear them, thumping down the stairs, hollering." She stood very still, her eyes unfocused, for the moment rooted in the past. "Strutting and preening in their football jackets. Coming in all at once, the way they always did."

What Ivy wanted to do was hum, barricade herself from these lies. These crazy lies. They had to be lies.

Melinda's gaze floated to the ceiling. "Aretha. That's who was playing on that ra-

dio station Mr. Kezey liked. David was singing along, off-key. Moonwalking." Melinda
smiled at the memory. "He comes over and
leans across the counter. 'Hey, pretty girl,
whatchoo want?'" Melinda's cheeks flushed.
"'Pretty girl.' That's what he called me. And
he wants to know, where is everybody?
Because the only other people there are
getting ready to leave.

"He goes, 'So where's the Bowling
Nazi?'

"I know he's joking around, but I pretend
I don't. I pick up the phone and ask if he
wants me to call Mr. Kezey. He goes—"
Melinda leaned forward and put her hand
over her mouth. "'*Neg-a-tive.*' Like he's all
cool.

"I set them up in a couple of lanes. Then
David comes back over with his friend.
Moussed hair. Dark eyes. Thinks he's God's
gift. And I see that they've got open beer
bottles. If Kezey'd been there, he'd have
been apoplectic.

"His friend, the lounge lizard, slides his
tongue between his lips, like that's supposed to turn me on. 'I want a . . . pair.
Size elevens.'" Melinda raised her hand

and smoothed the side of her head with her palm, a perfect imitation of Theo's characteristic gesture.

"And I remember. This guy's a world-class jerk. He's one of those dudes who sit on a table at the entrance to the cafeteria every day, rating girls. They even hold up scorecards. But when I go by, it's like I'm not there.

"So I tell them, 'You're not supposed to bring your own beverages.'

"His friend moves in real close and drags the bottom of his beer bottle along the inside of my arm. And he says something like, 'But you're cool with it, right?' And he offers me a drink.

"And I don't know why"—Melinda put out her hand for the phantom bottle, her eyes unfocused again—"but I take it. I drink. It's not bad. Not nearly as nasty-tasting as I expect it to be. I take another drink, and I'm handing it back when I realize that the rest of the guys aren't bowling. They're watching me and cracking up. One of them holds up his arms and screams, 'SCORE!'"

Tears crawled down Melinda's face. "I feel like such a complete fool. David says,

'Don't pay any attention to those assholes.' He gives me his beer and takes my hand and leads me over to the scorekeeper's chair.

"I finish that beer, then another. They're bowling. A spare. A gutter ball. A strike. Another strike," Melinda said, her voice a singsong. Ivy could almost feel the bowling balls thundering down the lanes, hear the clatter of the pins getting cleared. "And they're high-fiving me.

"Then David's friend lifts me up out of the chair and gives me a ball. I tell him I don't know how to bowl. He thinks that's hysterical—I work in a bowling alley and I can't bowl?

"He sets his hands on my hips, like he's going to teach me. He untucks my shirt. And I know I should make him stop, but it feels nice, the way he's touching my skin, his fingers dipping down. And Cyndi Lauper is on the radio singing 'Girls Just Want to Have Fun.'" Melinda pulsed, as if she could hear the music. "And I am. Having a great time. I really am.

"Then, before I know what's happening, there's beer everywhere. All over me. All over the lounge lizard. And David's standing there with the others, doubled over laughing with their dripping beer bottles.

"David's friend grabs a fresh bottle, opens it, and gives it to me. He tells me, 'Go ahead. Let 'em have it.' And I think, why the hell not?

"I plug the opening with my thumb and shake the bottle. Hard. Then I let go." Melinda moved her hand, the knife aloft, in a wide arc. "David looks stunned, like he just swallowed a hamster." Melinda staggered sideways, hooting laughter. She dropped the knife but quickly picked it up again, then leaned against the wall, trying to catch her breath.

"After that it's all-out war. Beer's in my hair, dripping from my nose. Little pools of beer are in the molded orange plastic seats. And—"

Melinda stopped, emotion draining from her face. She took a deep inhale and folded her arms. "Then it gets really quiet. They're all staring at me. At my chest. That stupid yellow polyester bowling shirt that Mr. Cheesey makes me wear is soaking wet.

"I can feel David behind me. He whispers how sexy I am. He reaches around and unbuttons the top button of the shirt, and his breath is hot on my neck. He starts on the next button. *Stop!*" Melinda screamed. The word caromed off the attic walls. "He holds my arms behind my back, and buttons pop off.

"The boys are in a circle, all around me." The words came in a rush. "Their faces red. Looking at me. I know I should cover up. I should run home, and to hell with Mr. Kezey's stupid bowling alley."

Melinda pushed her tongue to the corner of her mouth, as if she were tasting beer. Sweet. Bitter.

"James Brown is on the radio now, and music is pulsing and throbbing, like it's inside me, and the boys are standing around me, all of them watching, all of them.

"Like I'm finally someone who rates a number." Melinda raised the knife, her fingers tightening around the handle as she stared directly at Ivy. "That's when David pulled me into the closet. He closed the door, and it's pitch black in there. He holds me. Touches me. He tastes of salt and beer, and I remember he's wearing a chain around his neck. And then . . . and then . . ." A momentary look of confusion crossed Melinda's face and quickly cleared. "He made love to me."

Made love? The unexpected words singed the air, even more shocking than if Melinda had said she was raped.

"Later I wake up, and I'm there on the floor of the closet, all alone. I open the door. The bowling alley's empty. My shirt's unbuttoned and my bra unhooked. My panties are gone. I rush to the girls' room and throw up. I look at myself in the mirror." Melinda ran her fingers through her hair. "My hair is stiff and grotesque. Vomit's caked all over me.

"I try to clean myself up. Then I mop with pine cleaner. But even after that, the place still stinks of beer and puke. And all the time I'm mopping and scrubbing, I'm crying and I can barely see, and I'm terrified that any minute Mr. Kezey's going to come back and find me, and he'll know what happened." Melinda's face contorted, and tears flowed down her cheeks. "And then everyone will know what I did." Melinda's look challenged Ivy to respond.

"I'm so sorry," Ivy said. It felt pathetically inadequate.

Melinda sniffed in derision. "Sure you

are. Now. Back then no one said 'Sorry.' No one called me after to see if I was all right." Melinda wiped her nose with the back of her hand. "Turned out I was pregnant. When I lost the baby, my mother said God was punishing me.

"Meanwhile you and David are dating, going to the senior prom, hearing from colleges, graduating. The perfect couple. The perfect home." Melinda pressed her lips together and narrowed her eyes at Ivy. "The perfect life."

"Why didn't you tell someone what happened?" Ivy asked. "Did you go to the police?"

"No one would have believed me," Melinda said. She shivered, her look turning dark and cold. "Just like you don't believe me now. Or they'd say it was nothing. And maybe to them that's what it was."

But Ivy did believe her. Theo had been there, she was sure of that. This had been the "ancient history," the "nothing happened" that he didn't want dredged up.

"You know," Ivy said, "teenagers can do incredibly stupid things, especially when they're drunk. Things that they come to regret later."

"It was no mistake. It was deliberate. Planned. They must have known that Mr. Kezey wouldn't be there, because otherwise they wouldn't have brought in beer. And where were all the other customers? It was never that empty on a Tuesday afternoon. When I left, the sign on the door had been turned to 'Closed.' I know David did that the minute they got there." Her look challenged Ivy to come up with another explanation.

But raising objections and rational observations wasn't going to dissuade Melinda from what she believed.

"I'll go with you to the police," Ivy said. "It's not too late to tell them what David did to you. It wasn't your fault. No one will blame you."

Melinda looked amused. "You think I care anymore what people think? I'm long past that. What I want is my baby."

"Please, please don't. After that there'll be no turning back. You'll be on the run. Always looking over your shoulder."

"Who's going to come after me? David? He'll be in prison for my murder. You? Sorry." Melinda gave a fake, pouty frown. "The police? If anything, they'll be coming after you. Because it's going to look like you ran off with your baby because you couldn't face the truth, that your husband is a murderer."

31

The door slammed shut behind Melinda. Moments later Ivy flew across the room. She grasped the doorknob, twisted it, and pulled. The door gave barely a hairsbreadth. It was bolted shut.

Ivy pulled harder. Braced a foot against the doorjamb and tugged, straining as hard as she could. Then, suddenly, she found herself staggering back, the brass doorknob still in hand. She just managed to catch herself from falling.

"Mrs. Rose?" Ivy jerked around at the woman's voice. It was coming from the dumbwaiter and being broadcast through the shaft. "This is Phyllis Stone from the Norfolk County Crime Lab. . . ." Melinda was in the kitchen replaying the message on the answering machine.

Ivy crossed to the dumbwaiter and quietly slid open the lower panel so she could hear more clearly. The message continued through to the end, with the woman giving her phone number and an address that was just across into the neighboring town.

A short time later, Ivy heard Melinda's voice. "Hello? I'm calling about coming in and giving a DNA sample? Phyllis Stone called me a little while ago from there. . . . Yes, this is Ivy Rose."

Ivy listened, too stunned to move.

"Mm-hmm. Sure. Thanks so much." There was a long pause. "Yes, I can come over this afternoon." Another pause. "Sounds fine. Yes, I'll remember. See you before five."

Then just the sound of rain, falling steadily on the roof and rushing through the metal gutters. Ivy stared into the dark shaft.

It made no sense. The police didn't need Melinda's DNA. They already had it. Detective Blanchard had said they'd collected it from a toothbrush they picked up in Melinda's apartment.

A toothbrush . . . In a moment of cold clarity, Ivy realized what had happened— the switch Melinda had made. The toothbrush they'd collected from Melinda's apartment was Ivy's lost toothbrush—the one that had mysteriously disappeared weeks earlier. Melinda had somehow managed to break in and steal it, then leave it in her own bathroom as if it were hers.

The DNA that the police now had labeled "Melinda White" was really Ivy's. And the DNA sample Melinda was about to give at the crime lab would be labeled "Ivy Rose," completing the swap.

The photo ID was the only possible glitch. Melinda had to hope that the lab technician would give the picture on Ivy's driver's license no more than a cursory glance.

But why go to all the trouble of swapping her own DNA for Ivy's?

The answer crashed into Ivy. *The fetal tissue.* The results of a DNA analysis hadn't yet come back, but soon they would. David would be identified as the father. The

mother's DNA would match the DNA off
that toothbrush from Melinda's apartment. The police would think they had
proof that David was the father of Melinda's unborn child. A murder indictment
would be on its way.

But how . . . ? Ivy knew the answer to
that, too.

July 14. A year and a half ago. Ivy remembered that hot, humid summer morning she'd spent lying on the table in the
emergency room at Neponset Hospital
and watching a nurse carry away the pla-
centa and the tiny corpse that would have
been Ivy and David's firstborn child. It had
gone to the hospital lab for analysis—a
lab where Melinda worked.

Anger unfurled in the pit of Ivy's stomach. Melinda hadn't disposed of those
remains. She'd somehow preserved them.
She'd taken their kitchen knife and run it
through the flesh and blood of Ivy's still-
born child. Then planted that knife and the
canvas bag and stashed them in the back
of David's truck. Perhaps even called the
police with an anonymous tip.

Element after element of Melinda's elaborately laid plan had fallen neatly into

place. David was in jail. DNA evidence would implicate him in a relationship with Melinda. Now Ivy would disappear, and it would look to the world as if she'd run off with her baby, unable to face the terrible consequences of her husband's guilt.

And the baby, her little girl? Ivy rested her palms on her belly. She'd be stolen away, raised by a crazy woman. Brought up in a home steeped in paranoia, nurtured by obsessive love and hatred the way Melinda had been, daughter to a woman who had sacrificed everything, including her own identity, to become her mother.

Unless Ivy stopped her.

There would be no time to wait for Jody or Theo to save her. The police were not about to ride in on white steeds. One of Grandma Fay's favorite sayings came back to her: *If you want your eggs to hatch, sit on them yourself.*

But how to escape? She could hear cars driving by, but there were no windows from which to signal for help. The bathroom window was too tiny to crawl through, and the view was blocked by the roof and the chimney.

If you don't go over, you must go under.

That was another of Grandma Fay's truisms.

Ivy stared into the dumbwaiter shaft. Within easy reach was the cable that had once controlled the dumbwaiter, still intact, descending into a dark abyss like the one Ivy was about to be plunged into.

She leaned into the shaft. For a moment she felt as if someone were rushing her from behind, pushing her forward. She saw herself hurtling through the inky darkness and landing thirty feet down, neck broken, body mangled.

She bumped her head, the sound echoing in the shaft as she reared back, then steadied herself against the sill, frozen, hoping Melinda hadn't heard. Sound traveled down as well as up.

Ignoring her churning stomach—fear, not labor pain, Ivy assured herself—she grasped the cable that ran through the middle of the shaft and slowly pulled. There was a creak overhead as the cable slipped about six inches, then caught. She increased the pressure until her arm was trembling. When she brought her hand back, the insides of her fingers were coated with flecks of rust, and there was a red line where the cable had cut into her.

Ivy considered the possibility. The cable. The shaft. If she could climb down, she could emerge from the shaft through the sliding panels that provided access to the second-floor landing. It was a way out—if she had the courage to try and the stamina and strength to succeed. She certainly had a full quota of desperation.

Wasn't it just another version of rope climbing—Coach Reiner's favorite drill and, according to him, the ultimate fitness exercise? No better way to build endurance and concentration.

Ivy would rather have done a hundred push-ups with a thirty-pound pack on her back than climb a rope. Climbing up, she'd been focused. Hand over hand she'd pulled herself up, the rope wound around one leg and anchored with the opposite foot. Descending should have been a cakewalk— just a brake and release, letting her legs and gravity do the work.

Yet no matter how many times Coach Reiner told her, "Don't look down," the minute she reversed gear, she did. Her mouth would go dry, she'd start to sweat, her hands would get slippery, and she'd have the sickening, stomach-roiling sensation that the ground was racing up to smash her in the face. It was humiliating when Coach had had to climb up after her, coax her into peeling her rigid fingers from around the rope and lowering her butt into a rescue sling.

But this cable was barely a quarter of the diameter of a climbing rope. It had sharp ridges. To shin down it, she'd need something to protect her hands and give her traction. And it wasn't flexible either— no way to wind the cable around her leg and use the friction to brake and release. She'd need a sling to bear her weight, like the one Coach Reiner had used to bring her down. And something to protect her hands.

But what?

Ivy scanned the room. The bedding had been stripped. Towels and shower curtain had been removed from the bathroom. Only a single item remained in the room— her gaze shifted to the straitjacket lying crumpled on the floor.

She walked over to it, picked it up by the sleeves. The thick fabric seemed sturdy enough. She held it out in front of her like an empty scarecrow. Yanked on one of the leather straps and examined the buckles. They were solidly attached.

She heard sounds from the kitchen. A cabinet being slammed shut. Then another. A drawer sliding open, then shut. Another drawer, and another. Melinda was looking for something.

Visualize. That's what Coach Reiner repeatedly told them. She saw how it could be done. It could work. It had to.

Ivy rolled up the body of the straitjacket, creating a thick sausage of canvas that could be wrapped around the cable to provide a better handhold. The sleeves and long straps sewn to the ends, hanging out on either side, had the makings of a sturdy sling.

She returned to the shaft. She leaned forward and reached in. It was just over an arm's length from front to back and side to side. She ran her hands across the plaster-and-lath walls and the rough, splintery two-by-fours that lined it. She could use those, plus the wooden sills around the dumbwaiter's windowlike openings on each floor, as footholds.

From below, Ivy heard what sounded like the refrigerator being opened. Closed. Footsteps growing faint and then vanishing.

Melinda could be coming back.

Ivy lowered the dumbwaiter panel until it was completely closed. She placed the straitjacket back on the floor where Melinda had dropped it. Jammed the doorknob back in place. On the floor she found the bent screw that had come loose. She picked it up and twisted it into the screw hole, enough to temporarily anchor the knob.

Heavy footsteps came from beyond the door, up the attic stairs. Ivy made it back to the bed as the bolt was slid back and the door opened.

Ivy gasped. Melinda had on a wig of long, straight dark hair with bangs. She'd changed into one of Ivy's maternity tops, and she'd stuffed something in it to make her look pregnant. She also wore Ivy's old green Doc Martens.

It was a weak attempt to pass for Ivy,

and anyone who knew Ivy would see through it. But the getup might fool a stranger, someone just seeing the photo ID on Ivy's driver's license and expecting a pregnant woman. After all, Mrs. Bindel had mistaken Melinda for Ivy when she'd seen her Sunday night, in the dark, wearing that wig and sunglasses as she planted the bloody clothing in the wicker trunk. Even Ivy, looking out her kitchen window, had been jolted by the resemblance.

"I need you to drink this," Melinda said. She held out a tall glass, filled with orange juice. In her other hand, she held the knife. "Don't worry. It won't hurt you or the baby. Just tansy."

Ivy had seen tansy in a wildflower catalog. Little yellow chrysanthemums—like the scraggly yellow flowers she'd seen growing in the ragged herb garden by the kitchen door of Melinda's mother's house.

"Nature's pitocin," Melinda added.

Ivy's stomach clenched and she drew back. Pitocin was what doctors used to induce labor.

Melinda crossed the room. "There are other ways I can take this baby." She let the implication linger. "But, believe me, this is far more pleasant and a whole lot healthier."

She put the straw to Ivy's lips. "Drink."

Ivy's sinuses filled with the citrus sweetness of orange over an acrid bitterness. The glint of the knife was the only thing keeping her from knocking away the glass.

Melinda poked Ivy's lips with the straw. "I said drink."

Ivy drew some juice into her mouth. She swallowed and gagged. There was that medicinal taste she'd noticed before.

"Of course, acupuncture is the healthiest way to induce labor," Melinda went on, like a chirpy TV ad for a natural food supplement. "Next to waiting for it to start on its own, that is. But it's too late for that now." She prodded Ivy with the straw again.

Ivy heard the clicking of Phoebe's claws on the kitchen floor, rising through the dumbwaiter shaft. The dog's wheezy breathing. She forced herself to drink, slurping to distract Melinda from the sounds traveling up from the kitchen.

"Won't hurt the baby. That's the important thing."

Ivy swallowed the last of the wretched stuff.

"Excellent. Now we wait." Melinda glanced at her watch. "Three to five hours. That's what the experts say."

Yesterday's labor pains—false labor, as it had turned out—had kicked in about four hours after Ivy drank orange juice from the carton in her refrigerator, orange juice that had the same bitter edge to it. What Melinda didn't know was that Ivy had drunk another half glass when she got home from the hospital, at least three hours ago. She could start getting new contractions any minute.

"Tansy's natural but strong," Melinda said. "Tricky. Too little? All you get is raging diarrhea," she said, her thoughts coming in bursts. "Too much? Well, that can kill you."

Ivy couldn't tell if it was nausea or dread that engulfed her. How much was too much? There was no way for her to know if she'd exceeded that threshold. She lay down and turned over on her side, hoping that Melinda would take the hint and go. The instant that Melinda left for the crime lab, she'd make her escape. Ivy could feel her narrow margin of safety slipping away.

"Tired?" Melinda said. "You can't go to sleep yet."

Through half-closed eyes, Ivy saw Melinda take a cassette recorder from her pocket.

"That message you've got on your answering machine? Downright hostile. We need to have something that sounds a bit more . . . reassuring. Sit up."

Ivy pushed herself up. She felt queasy, uncomfortably full. A taste like strong tea and iron filings lingered in her mouth.

Melinda unfolded some sheets of yellow lined paper and handed them to her. The handwriting on the top sheet was childlike, fat and loopy with little circles instead of dots over the *i*'s.

Hi. Sorry I can't take your call right now, and yes, I'm still waiting, if that's what you're calling to find out.

Melinda held the recorder close to Ivy's face. In the other hand, she held the knife, the blade cool against the back of Ivy's bare neck. Ivy shivered.

"Relax. Make it sound natural," Melinda said.

Feigning reluctance, Ivy began to read. In fact, she wanted to get through this as quickly as possible so Melinda would leave.

She finished reading the first block of text and went on to the next.

Sorry I missed your call. Thanks for the offer. You don't mind, do you? I just don't want company right now. I'll e-mail.

She kept reading. Each passage was a variation on how fine she was and how she didn't want to be bothered. It gave Ivy some satisfaction knowing that none of it would hold Jody off—not for long at any rate.

When at last Ivy finished, Melinda clicked off the recorder and tucked it away.

"Don't worry about your e-mail," Melinda said. "I've taken care of that, too. You're answering all your messages. Telling everyone how just fine you are. In fact, while you were napping, I e-mailed Kamala at Nextgen. That's your friend Jody, right? I told her we're still waiting for the 'water buffalo' to drop." Melinda drew quote marks in the air. "Cute. Amazing how easy it is to sound like someone when you have all their old messages to work with. She e-mailed right back, not in the least bit concerned."

"For now," Ivy said.

"That's right. We can't go on like this too long." For a moment Melinda locked eyes with her, and Ivy was terrified by the cold determination she saw.

Melinda looked at her watch. "Less than three to five hours." She ran her finger inside the neck of her top and hooked a silver chain that was around her neck. She pulled it out. Hanging from it was a silver hand. She rubbed the cobalt blue stone set in the palm.

Ivy's amulet.

32

Melinda grabbed the empty glass from the floor and slammed out of the room. The bolt shot into place, and her booted footsteps sounded on the stairs.

Ivy flew across the room to the dumbwaiter. From downstairs she heard Phoebe barking. Then sharp, frantic howls.

How long would it take Melinda to get to the lab? Ten minutes? She'd have to park, check in. Undoubtedly there would be papers to fill out and sign. The swab and then the drive back.

Worst case, Melinda would be gone for

twenty-five minutes. Best case, forty-five. Would the tansy take effect before then?

Focus on what you can control, let go of what you can't. Grandma Fay's voice in Ivy's head calmed her.

Ivy had to wait for Melinda to leave. She couldn't risk making noise that would alert Melinda to what she was up to. Seconds ticked by, then minutes as Ivy listened for Melinda's departure. What the hell was she waiting for?

Then Ivy heard her own voice, floating up to her through the dumbwaiter shaft: "Hi. Sorry I can't take your call right now. . . ." It was one of the messages Melinda had made Ivy record. Melinda was putting it on the answering machine.

At last Ivy felt a vibration as the front door to the house closed. A little later the car door slammed. The engine turned over.

Now was her chance—her only chance. She had to get moving.

She scooped the straitjacket off the floor, held it out in front of her, and rolled up the body, leaving the arms and dangling straps sticking out at either end. Then she raised the panel to the dumbwaiter.

Draped the rolled-up straitjacket over the edge of the opening.

She sat on the dumbwaiter sill and swung her legs over, inside the shaft. Staring straight ahead, she braced her sneakers against the side walls.

Was she insane? She was thirty-three years old and massively pregnant. Still, her arms and legs were strong. And her other options were nil.

The baby shifted inside her, and Ivy felt a rippling arc across her belly like a shooting star. It could work. It had to. She would do whatever it took to keep this baby safe.

Don't think. Just do!

Ivy grabbed the rolled-up straitjacket and leaned forward, fighting off a wave of dizziness and anchoring her senses on the steady patter of rain.

Don't look down.

She wrapped the center of the thick canvas roll like a candy cane's stripe around the cable—once, twice, three times—then pulled the spiral taut. Last, she buckled the straps at the ends of the sleeves together.

There would be no coach or teammates at the ready to climb up and rescue her, no mattresses piled up at the bottom if she fell—just a thirty-foot drop through pitch black to the packed-earth floor of the basement.

Visualize. She took hold of the canvas-wrapped cable with both hands and slowly transferred her weight to her feet, resting them on the edges of two-by-fours on either side of the shaft.

It's nothing more than a high curb, she told herself as she hooked one leg and then the other inside the strap sling and set her feet back on the ledges. She lowered her behind slowly into the buckled straps, bending at the knees, pushing down and feeling the spiral of canvas gradually tighten.

So far, so good. She ignored the fear that licked like flames at her insides.

She shifted more of her weight into the sling, feeling for two-by-fours farther down, just in case the spiral of canvas failed to generate enough friction to grip the cable. The cable rasped and groaned, but it held fast as the spiral of canvas kinked.

It was working. Now to descend.

Ivy transferred weight to her feet, easing up on the strap sling. The canvas spiral loosened. She tugged it down.

Would Melinda be arriving at the police lab already? Parking the car? How many more feet before Ivy reached the second-floor opening? Nine? Eight? In three-inch increments, that was going to take . . . The math was discouraging. She hoped she had that long.

Ivy felt for a lower foothold, then inched the canvas spiral down. She could barely see her hands in front of her face. Above her, growing dimmer, was the rectangle of light where the panel to the attic remained open.

She repeated the sequence again, and again, and again—bracing her feet against the shaft to loosen the canvas spiral and shift downward, then lowering herself into the sling, tightening the canvas roll, lowering her feet to the next foothold. She tried not to think about the darkness closing around her. Her every move echoed in the shaft.

Peristalsis. Eleven letters. She said the word, then spelled it as she continued inching her way down the cable, proceeding entirely by feel, imagining that the dumb-waiter was a snake and she was prey, slowly working her way through its digestive tract.

Arms and legs trembling with fatigue, Ivy kept going. Just as she was lowering her behind into the sling for what felt like the hundredth time, the phone started ringing. The sound reverberated in the shaft.

Ivy tried to ignore it. She felt for a lower foothold. Found it. The phone rang again.

She transferred her weight to her feet.

The answering machine clicked on.

The canvas spiral loosened, and she tugged it down a few more inches. Found a fresh foothold. The new voice message played, assuring the world that yes, she was just fine and still waiting.

"Ivy, where the hell are you?" It was Jody, screaming at the answering machine. "You know this makes me completely crazy. Are you screening this call?" A long pause. "Damn you!"

In the background Ivy could hear Riker's shrill cry: "Da-oo!"

"If my son grows into a juvenile delinquent, it'll be your fault. Would you pick up the frickin' phone?"

I'm here! Ivy wanted to scream back.

"Honest to God, you can be such a pain," Jody said, and hung up.

Focus. Concentrate.

Ivy's clenched hands felt sweaty, slippery like they used to get during rope drills for Coach Reiner, especially when she reached the top of the rope and looked down.

She could imagine Melinda, chatting up the receptionist and flashing Ivy's driver's license. Banking on her disguise to fool the technician.

Soon Ivy had to reach the second-floor dumbwaiter opening. How much farther? She found herself staring down into inky blackness. She gasped and shuddered, panic rising inside her. One foot slipped off its perch. Then her other foot slipped. She fell with a lurch, and a moment later she was dangling from the straps by her arm-pits. Her legs bashed against the rough plaster wall, and her own screams echoed around her. The tough leather cut into her underarms.

But the canvas spiral had tightened and held fast. She flailed for another foot-hold, and at last she felt an exposed two-by-four on one side and a wider ledge on the opposite side to anchor her feet against. She rested for a moment, panting and catching her breath.

The wider ledge—Ivy looked down and saw a sliver of lighter gray, seeping through at just that spot.

She steadied herself, sweat trickling into her eyes, legs shaking. All she had to do now was raise the panel and climb out. She envisioned her fingers uncurling, her hand reaching out and pushing the panel up.

Three, two, one . . . let go! With a clean swipe, she reached out in the dark, felt for where she knew the lower panel had to be, and pushed. Then she grabbed back on to the canvas-wrapped cable.

The cable shimmied and creaked, but the panel hadn't budged. Or . . . Was it her imagination, or did the band of gray light seem just a bit wider?

A shadow moved across it, and for a moment Ivy froze. Then she recognized the sound of Phoebe's claws on the wood floor just beyond.

She reached out again and gave the panel a harder push. The band of light widened to a quarter inch. She wedged her toe in the opening, and it rose an inch more.

There was Phoebe, just on the other side. The dog put her paws up on the sill, sniffed at Ivy's sneaker, and woofed.

"Shoo," Ivy said, as she pressed with her foot, raising the panel halfway. The dog rested her white-whiskered muzzle on the sill. "Go away!" Phoebe's back end wiggled in ecstasy. "Phoebe, sit!"

The dog obeyed.

"Stay!"

She lowered her head onto her paws. Amazing.

Little by little, Ivy managed to raise the panel the rest of the way. When it was open as wide as it would go, she planted her feet on exposed two-by-fours on either side of the shaft, grabbed on to both sides of the dumbwaiter opening, and shifted her weight.

The straitjacket loosened. Ivy held her breath as it slithered away into the darkness below.

Slowly, carefully, her legs trembling, Ivy lowered herself until one knee rested on the sill. Sideways, she pulled herself through the opening and just kept going.

With her hands out in front of her to break the fall, she tumbled out onto the floor beside Phoebe.

The dog licked Ivy's face as she lay there crying and laughing at the same time. Bruised but in one piece, she'd made it.

33

Ivy got to her feet and raced for the stairs. *Please let the side door still be unlocked.* She'd just reached the curve in the staircase when she heard a familiar squeak— the front storm door was being pulled open. She crouched, making herself as small as she could.

There was the sound of a key being inserted into the lock, turning. Ivy's mouth went dry. From between ornately carved wooden balusters, she watched the door open.

Melinda backed into the house. Ivy's

rain slicker barely covered her fake pregnant belly. She locked the door, dropped the key into her pocket, and let her purse—Ivy's purse—fall to the floor.

She took down the rain hood. She was wearing a pair of wraparound sunglasses and the wig of long dark hair. She was whistling. Apparently, things had gone well.

Ivy heard Phoebe chuffing and moving around above her on the second-floor landing. Melinda went still, then pivoted toward the stairs. She removed the sunglasses. Her gaze traveled up.

Ivy drew back, deeper into shadow.

Melinda tilted her head. She stepped to the base of the stairs. Wrapped her fingers around the feet of the bronze statue on the newel post and lifted it from its perch. Holding it upside down, the heavy base with its six-inch bolt raised like a club, she stepped on the first stair tread.

Grrr-ruff. Phoebe's warning came from behind Ivy.

Melinda took another step.

The dog gave four sharp barks and padded down the stairs, past the curve where Ivy was hidden. Phoebe dropped her head and gave a menacing growl.

Melinda lowered the statue. "Shut up, you stupid dog. I'll take care of you later." She set the bronze figure back on the newel post, then turned and walked off, into the living room.

Relief flooded through Ivy. She recognized the sound of the window seat being pulled open. A thump. Then what sounded like footsteps on creaky floorboards. What was going on? She raised her head. Waited for the familiar thud of the window seat dropping shut. Listened for the rustling of Melinda moving about in the living room. Waited for Melinda to turn the light on or to come back out.

But she heard nothing, no movement at all—just utter silence.

A wave of queasiness grew from a dull ache in her back. *Please, not now. Not yet.*

Ivy rose to her feet and moved down the staircase as quickly as she could, her belly heavy. As she started across the entryway, again she heard floorboards creaking, the sounds growing louder.

Through the doorway to the living room, she could see that the lid of the window seat was raised.

Too late to turn back. Ivy grabbed her purse from the floor where Melinda had dropped it and hurried through the dining room.

"Hey!" Melinda had seen her.

Through the kitchen Ivy raced. Into the mudroom. She reached the side door. Thank God, it was still unlocked. As she threw it open, the contraction, well into its relentless climb, ground her to a halt. She couldn't run. She could barely move.

She managed to push open the storm door and let it slam shut, then pressed herself in among the winter coats and parkas hanging from hooks on the wall adjacent to the door. She pulled the door fully open to mask her presence.

A moment later she heard Melinda. Felt the open door press harder up against the coats she was sheltered beneath.

The contraction grew, and sweat beaded on Ivy's forehead. She grabbed on to a jacket sleeve to steady herself. To keep from crying out.

Melinda had to be just on the other side

of the open door, looking outside, assuming that Ivy had run out into the night.

Ivy stopped breathing. The contraction was reaching its peak, and she couldn't have stirred even if she'd wanted to.

Scree. It was the storm door being pushed open. Ivy felt a cold, moist breeze on her legs. She could imagine Melinda standing there considering whether to go after her. *Get out! Go!*

The pressure of the open door against her eased. The storm door wheezed and snapped shut. Ivy counted to three and fell forward, slamming the wooden door. With shaking hands she rummaged inside her purse, turned it upside down, and dumped the contents on the floor. She found the keys and locked the door.

Then she leaned against the wall, panting for breath. The contraction had been longer than any she'd had before. She touched her belly and felt the muscles still softening.

It was only a matter of minutes before Melinda would realize the ruse. She could easily get back into the house—Ivy had seen her drop a house key into her pocket when she arrived.

Ivy had to barricade the doors and call the police. *Now!*

She ran into the kitchen, plugged in the phone, and dialed 911. Holding the handset to her ear, she grabbed a kitchen chair and dragged it to the side door. She wedged it firmly under the knob.

"This is 911, what is your emergency?" Ivy heard the dispatcher's calm voice.

"Please, please, send the police! She's trying to kill me!" Ivy screamed. She gave her name and address as she tore back to the kitchen and hauled another kitchen chair toward the front hall, jerking it free of the dining-room carpet that bunched up under it.

"Hello? Are you there?" the dispatcher said.

Ivy yelled the address again and had just managed to wedge the chair under the knob of the front door when she heard the screen door open. A key turned in the lock.

Ivy dropped the phone.

"Go away! I called the police!" she yelled through the door.

There was a heavy thud as Melinda pushed against the door.

"It's too late!" Ivy screamed. She backed

away. "They're on the line right now. They'll be here any—"

Melinda pushed again. And again. And again. The chair began to slide.

Ivy lifted Bessie off the newel post.

Another heavy thud as Melinda heaved all her weight against the door. The chair slid another inch. Another push and she'd be in the house.

Ivy ducked into the coat closet. She was just closing herself in when she heard the crash of the chair sliding away completely. She sat on the closet floor and scrabbled back as far as she could.

Footsteps. Melinda was in the house.

Ivy waited, peering out from among the pieces of luggage, through the barely open closet door, terrified that the door would pull open, sure that at any moment it would and that Melinda would haul her from the closet.

And then there were sirens.

For a moment Ivy caught a glimpse of Melinda moving across the entryway toward the living room. The sirens grew louder and louder until they seemed to come from inside Ivy's head. She heard a muffled thump.

Heavy footsteps, running, getting louder.
The closet door flew open. Ivy cowered.
The coats parted. There stood a police
officer, his gun pointed at Ivy. Flashes
from emergency vehicles, parked in front
of the house, lit the hall. The house behind him swarmed with uniforms.

"Thank God," Ivy whispered as she
crawled from the closet. Detective Blanchard
strode in through the front door, his gun
drawn. He rushed over to her.

Ivy's abdomen tightened. "She's here,"
she managed to say. "Melinda White."

Detective Blanchard offered Ivy his
hand and helped her to her feet.

Ivy stumbled. This time there was no
gentle preamble. In seconds it felt as if
she were in the grip of some beefy hand,
squeezing and squeezing, hardening her
body from the inside out. With a thud, Bessie hit the floor.

"Clear up here!" came a cry from upstairs.

"Okay down here," from below.

"Where is she?" Blanchard asked.

"I thought she went—" The contraction
choked off Ivy's words. With a weak wave,
she indicated the living room.

Gun raised, Blanchard approached the doorway and looked in.

Ivy hung back, leaning against the wall, counting and trying to keep from screaming. She crept forward into the doorway. Blanchard made a circuit of the room, checked behind the couch and the wing chair. Threw the window seat open and closed it.

He turned to face her, his gun down at his side. "There's no one in here."

Maybe she'd been wrong. Maybe Melinda had managed to get away in all the confusion when the police arrived.

Ivy pushed herself past him, the contraction nearly over. On the coffee table was a section of newspaper, folded in quarters. There was David's half-finished crossword puzzle, the one he'd been working on his last night home. She picked it up, remembering how she'd tossed it into the window seat. Twice. And not taken it out again.

That thump she'd heard when Blanchard had dropped the window seat shut—it was the sound she'd heard moments after Melinda had crossed in front of the closet on her way to the living room.

Ivy approached the window seat. Drops of water beaded on the painted surface of its closed lid. Her heart pounding, she raised it. It was empty—just four side walls and a floor. But there were dark spots on the bottom where the raw wood was stained with moisture.

Ivy reached in and felt along the inside edges. There was a half-moon cutout in the bottom panel. She anchored a finger there and started to pull.

Blanchard grabbed her wrist. He motioned for her to step aside and raised his gun. He reached in and pulled up. Like a trapdoor, hinged on the opposite side, the floor of the window seat swung open.

Ivy shivered, and it felt as if a sudden gust of cold filled the room. Beneath were narrow, steep, descending steps, more ladder than staircase. Light glowed from below.

"Police!" Blanchard shouted. "We know you're in there! Come out now!"

He jerked his head toward a uniformed officer who came up alongside him, his gun out.

Blanchard didn't wait long for an answer. "I'm coming in," he announced, and stepped over the front wall of the window seat and onto the top step. Ivy recognized the creaking sounds as he descended.

From below she heard muffled voices, scuffling sounds. Then nothing. Moments later Melinda emerged, hands cuffed behind her. The wig and the pregnant belly were gone. Detective Blanchard followed close behind, supporting her elbow.

Ivy backed away until she was in the corner of the living room and couldn't go any farther, her heart clanging in her chest.

Melinda stepped into the room. The strobes from outside lit her pale face. She seemed flat, emotionless as she looked around. Her gaze came to rest on Ivy.

"Her husband raped me," Melinda said, her voice calm.

Detective Blanchard stepped between Melinda and Ivy and nudged Melinda forward.

Melinda took a few more steps and turned again to look at Ivy. "Know what your precious husband said to me while we were doing it? He told me I was something else. He said I was special."

34

Ivy sat at the base of the stairs waiting for the ambulance to get there and take her to the hospital. Phoebe's furry coat was warm against her side. One of the police officers had called Dr. Shapiro and Jody.

Another contraction had just ended, and Ivy knew that it wouldn't be long before a new one began. She wiped the sheen of sweat from her forehead with the back of her hand.

Detective Blanchard emerged from the dining room holding Ivy's purse. "I imagine you'll be needing this," he said, and dropped it beside her on the step.

"Thanks," Ivy said, realizing that he'd gathered up everything she'd dumped onto the floor in the mudroom and put it all back into her purse for her.

"You okay?" he asked.

"I will be."

"I found these on the floor," he said. He showed her three driver's licenses, fanned out like a hand of cards. He gave them to her, one at a time.

Melinda White. Ruth White. Elaine Gallagher. The photo on each one was Melinda.

Ivy heard a siren approaching.

She handed the IDs back to Detective Blanchard. "I guess she thought she looked enough like me with that wig that she didn't have to fake my driver's license, too. She went to your crime lab today as me. Gave them a DNA sample. It won't match the DNA you have from the toothbrush you collected from her apartment, because that was *my* toothbrush. She stole it weeks ago."

Blanchard blinked, and the crease in his brow deepened. "You mean the DNA we collected from her apartment is yours?"

"That's right. And the DNA from the fetal remains you recovered from the knife that David tried to hide? That'll match the DNA from that same toothbrush. Because it's my DNA." Ivy started to cry. "David's and mine. Melinda was there working in the hospital when I had my last miscarriage."

The siren abruptly stopped. Blanchard helped Ivy to her feet and guided her out the door and down the front steps.

Ivy leaned forward. "My husband?"

"We'll get him there as fast as we can," Blanchard said.

A waiting EMT helped her into the back of the ambulance and strapped her in.

Detective Blanchard started to close one of the ambulance doors.

"Melinda's wearing a necklace that's mine," Ivy called out to him. "It belonged to my grandmother."

Ivy barely heard his reply, because a new contraction grabbed hold and felt as if it were wringing her inside out.

Push!

The pain that assembled in Ivy's lower back enveloped her entire body, and pres-

sure built inside her like steam, threatening to blow the top off a pressure cooker.
Harsh light glaring over her in the hospital delivery room seemed to pulse as,
with more urgency than she had thought
possible, Ivy knew it was time.

David was there with her, holding her
hand as she bore down and focused on
this single task, recruiting strength from
every part of her body. He'd come flying in
moments earlier, tying on his surgical
mask and replacing Jody at Ivy's side.

"I brought you this," he whispered, slipping Ivy's grandmother's amulet into her
hand.

This time labor had been fast and in-
tensely efficient. No leisurely stroll
through admitting. She'd been rocketed
directly to the delivery room and immediately hooked up to a fetal monitor and an
IV drip.

It was all that tansy, Dr. Shapiro had
said, and they were taking its effects very
seriously.

"Good. That's good," David said, the
surgical mask over his mouth puffing and
puckering.

It burned and stung as pressure built.

David's eyes crinkled with strain, as if he were pushing, too.

"That's right. That's great. You're a champ," he said.

Finally the contraction loosened. Ivy barely had time to recover before a new one began and rapidly roared to full strength. Dripping sweat, she pushed and pushed again, until it felt as if a locomotive were hurtling along at top speed in her head.

"The baby's crowning," Dr. Shapiro said, her voice calm and reassuring. "Push once more."

Ivy bore down again, and again, and again, each time Dr. Shapiro encouraging her to hang in there, that the next one would be the last.

"Stop!" Dr. Shapiro said. "Wait."

Ivy strained to comply. The urge to push was nearly irresistible.

"Blow, blow, blow," David said, his arm around her.

The room turned silent as Ivy blew, sweat dripping into her ears and down her neck.

"That's good, that's good, that's good," Dr. Shapiro said. "Now, one last time.

Push!" Her command reverberated off the walls.

Ivy pushed with every bit of strength she had left, then gasped as the pressure released itself, as though a cork had popped. There was a long moment of dead silence. Then a thin cry.

"It's a girl," David whispered in her ear. "Just like you said." He squeezed her hand.

Ivy strained to see the nurse tending the baby. Wiping her down. Washing her. Her little girl was rigid and red-faced, her eyes squinched shut and her mouth stretched open, tiny fists clenched and trembling. Watching, Ivy felt as if her heart would burst in her chest.

The newborn cry wasn't at all what Ivy had expected—rapid gusts of piglet squeals rather than full-throated yelps.

"I was so afraid I wouldn't make it here in time," David said.

"I was afraid that you wouldn't make it here at all," Ivy said.

The nurse brought the baby over to them. She was swaddled in a pink blanket, her hair already drying into wispy curls.

Ivy took the sturdy little bundle in her

arms. She brushed the baby's head with her lips. So soft. Liquidy gray eyes opened, and the baby gazed up at her like some wise old soul, and Ivy felt a surge of tenderness so intense that she could barely breathe.

"Hey, Sprout," she whispered. "My precious baby girl." This little one had killer eyelashes.

David touched the baby's cheek gently with the back of his index finger. "She's amazing."

Ivy probed the blanket and found a foot. The flesh, wrinkled at the ankle, reminded Ivy of a scrawny chicken wearing baggy, flesh-colored tights. Tiny toes were splayed—all five of them.

A tear trickled down his cheek as David kissed the bottom of the baby's foot.

This was what she'd almost lost. David, their baby, their life together, all their hopes and dreams for the future.

The room went fuzzy, and before Ivy knew what was happening, she was crying—completely out of control, heaving up great sobs as if deep inside her a dam had been breached.

She grabbed David's sleeve and sobbed.

A nurse rushed over and took the baby. David put his arms around Ivy and held her to him, rocking her.

"It's over, it's over," he said. He held her tighter. "I'm so sorry."

Ivy shuddered and burrowed into David's chest, her tears soaking the top of his hospital scrubs.

"You have every right to be angry with me. To be furious. I—" His voice caught. He stroked her head. Kissed her neck. "I didn't know. And then I thought I'd never be with you again. Never see the baby." She felt his chest heave. "Can you ever forgive me?"

Ivy couldn't answer. She looked up at him.

"Ivy . . ." His face was twisted in agony, his eyes filled with tears.

"So many lies," she said.

"I thought I was protecting—"

"Who?"

"You. The baby. Me." He hung his head. "I thought I was doing the right thing."

During the night Ivy was moved to a hospital room. David went home to clean up and get some sleep.

Early the next morning, she took a long, hot shower, letting the water beat on her aching back and sides. A magnificent red and purple bruise on her right hip and sore right shoulder were reminders of her narrow escape. A nick in her side from the knifepoint burned as she soaped it.

Ivy changed into a soft silk nightgown, a luxurious gift Jody had brought her, and got back into bed. Then she slept—her first truly restful sleep in more than a week.

When she woke up, sunlight was streaming into the room. David sat in the armchair and beamed at the baby he held in his arms.

Alert and wide-eyed, the baby stared up at him, her mouth a perfect oval.

Ivy yawned. Every muscle ached. She turned over onto her side and reached out to touch David's arm.

David smiled over at her. "She's a beaut, Ivy—she really is." He slipped his pinkie finger into the baby's grasp. "Think it's time we gave her a name?"

"Something strong. Maybe starting with *F* for Grandma Fay?" Ivy said.

"Fanny?" David said.

"I kind of like that. It's old-fashioned but sweet," Ivy said.

"Flora?"

"Flora Rose?" Ivy pulled a face.

"I forgot. Rule Four-dot-One-dot-Three." He kissed the baby's tiny fist. "Sorry, only one beautiful flower to a customer."

Ivy rubbed the stone in the palm of her grandmother's amulet, which was back where it belonged, hanging around her neck.

"Oh, I don't know. Flora is a very nice name." The voice came from the doorway. Ivy looked up to see Mrs. Bindel, sitting there in a wheelchair with Detective Blanchard behind her. "I once had a friend named Flora."

"Mrs. Bindel!" Ivy said. She pushed the button to raise the head of her hospital bed. "You're up and around."

"Around anyway. Up remains to be seen," Mrs. Bindel said. "May we come in? Just for a moment."

"Sure," Ivy said.

Blanchard pushed Mrs. Bindel over the threshold and into the room.

"I didn't want to wait," Mrs. Bindel said.

"I needed to apologize to you now. Al came this morning and set me straight, and I made him bring me straight over."

Al? Detective Blanchard actually blushed.

"I thought you were the one who conked me in the head," Mrs. Bindel said. "But it wasn't you. It was that other woman, the one who disappeared. Only I gather she's been hiding. Causing such a fuss. Horrid woman." She looked at Detective Blanchard, her eyebrows raised.

"Right," he said. "Melinda White was crossing through Mrs. Bindel's backyard on her way back to your house from her mother's when Mrs. Bindel caught her by surprise. She was afraid Mrs. Bindel would realize that she wasn't you. Says she just wanted to knock Mrs. Bindel out."

"She told you that?" Ivy asked.

Blanchard nodded. "She's being charged with assault, burglary, kidnapping—"

"Murder?" Ivy asked.

"Her mother?" Blanchard said. "No. She died of natural causes. Cancer. Melinda didn't bury her so she could keep receiving Social Security and pension checks.

So there will be fraud charges, too. And identity theft. Her sister, Ruth, is married and lives in Toronto. Hasn't been in contact with Melinda or their mother for years. Melinda rented a Florida apartment in Ruth's name and hired someone to forward her mother's mail to the house on Belcher Street."

"To Elaine Gallagher?" Ivy asked.

Blanchard's brow creased. "How do you . . . ?" Ivy could almost see the cylinders in his brain tumbling into place. She gave him an innocent look—she had no intention of offering up the fact that she'd broken in to the house and discovered Mrs. White's body.

"Elaine Gallagher died five years ago," Blanchard said. "Right here, in fact, at Neponset Hospital. Melinda was working here then. She must have used information in the poor woman's hospital records to set up phony bank and credit-card accounts. Applied for a new driver's license and posed for the photo. Then she put through paperwork to make it look as if Elaine Gallagher had bought the Belcher Street house. She'd taken a job with a real estate agency by then. We'd just about gotten it all figured out when . . . I'm sorry we were almost too late."

"She had keys," Ivy said. "Even after I had new locks installed." Ivy remembered the hardware store clerk's confusion when she came to have her own copy made—Melinda, with her wig and pregnant belly, had probably been in earlier to have a copy made from the spare set Ivy had left hanging by the back door.

"Yes, it looks as if she could get in and out whenever," Blanchard said. "And she'd watched you and your husband, knew your habits."

"She wanted our baby," Ivy said.

"I know. Now." The abashed look he gave her was probably the closest she was going to get to an apology.

Mrs. Bindel rolled herself closer to David's chair. "Oh," she said as she peered at the baby, now fast asleep in David's arms. "Isn't she cunning?" With her knuckle Mrs. Bindel caught a tear that had formed at the corner of her eye. "That house of yours, what it really needs is young people.

"But do me a favor. No more yard sales."

"When Melinda came to the yard sale, did you recognize her?" Ivy asked David after Detective Blanchard and Mrs. Bindel left.

David got up and set the baby gently into the hospital bassinet. He came over and sat on the bed next to Ivy. "I didn't. Not at first."

Unanswered questions tainted the air between them. Ivy remembered Mr. Vlaskovic's words: *Secrets can be toxic. The truth is rarely as dreadful or as terrifying as what one imagines.*

"Melinda told me that you raped her," Ivy said.

Anger flared in David's eyes. "You believe her?"

"Should I?"

"I didn't. I told her that, and she went nuts. We were up in the attic. She threw the glass swan, and after that it was almost as if she went into a trance. She remembered what happened at Kezey's, right down to the smallest detail. Listening to her was painful, and she seemed so sure of herself. It really shook me when she said I took her into the closet and did . . . what she said I did."

David gave Ivy a calm, steady look. "Not that it would surprise me if something like that *had* happened. A dozen guys and a girl. Seventeen years old. Smashed. Alone down there."

"She told me she got pregnant and then miscarried," Ivy said. "Stealing our baby was going to make up for the one she lost."

"I didn't rape her." David gave Ivy an anguished look. "Don't you think that if I'd done that, I'd remember?"

"I want to believe you," Ivy said. "She told me that she felt a chain hanging from your neck when you were with her."

"See? Have you ever seen me wearing anything like a chain around my neck? That wasn't me. That was . . ." David's mouth hung open as the implication sank in.

"Theo," Ivy said, remembering the Greek cross that hung from a chain on the rearview mirror in Theo's car. "Theo says you passed out. He says nothing happened. Nothing at all."

"He would." David held her gaze. "Theo

told me he's dropping out of the senate race. He says it's because once Melinda starts telling the police her version of what happened at Kezey's, it'll be a mess for everyone who was there. It won't matter what really happened. And besides, after all these years there's no way that anyone can prove it one way or another."

He took her hand. "Ivy, *if* I did what she said I did, would you ever be able to forgive me?"

"I . . ."

"Could you?" David asked. "Because whatever happened, I was part of it. Even if I didn't rape her, I was there. I did nothing to protect her. I could have. The guys listened to me. And at school afterward, I just went along when the rumors started going around. And after a while I just forgot about it. It was as if it had never happened."

Ivy gazed into the haggard face of the man who'd been her best friend and lover for half her life. She remembered the first moment when he'd entered her consciousness, his concerned face hovering over her on the track field. She remembered exchanging marriage vows on a hillside on Peaks Island in Casco Bay up in Maine. The first time she and David had stepped over the threshold of the house as home-owners and she'd run from room to room feeling delight mixed with abject terror at what they'd gotten themselves into, then returning to hug David and feeling once again grounded. She'd never for an instant doubted his essential goodness as a human being.

She had no doubt that Theo was lying, minimizing what had happened. She had no trouble believing that he'd have taken advantage of Melinda. She even had serious doubts about whether Melinda had been pregnant—had she seen a doctor? And how could she have known that the baby she lost was David's?

But Ivy couldn't stop herself from hearing Melinda's words: *He told me I was something else. He said I was special.*

That didn't sound like Theo.

What if David *had* gotten drunk at seventeen and had sex with a needy girl who had a crush on him, a girl who'd have done anything to get David to notice her?

Ivy couldn't turn back the clock and be a fly on the wall. She couldn't crawl inside

Melinda's head and untangle wishes and nightmare from reality. Even Melinda had come close to admitting that she didn't know for sure exactly what had happened.

All Ivy could do was cling to uncertainty and to what she knew in her heart about the man she loved. It was what she had.